One Sma

One Small Step

Michael Flavin

PRESS

Published by Vulpine Press in the United Kingdom in 2022

ISBN: 978-1-83919-468-9

www.vulpine-press.com

To my wife and children

The troubles are almost as old as Irish history itself. They wax and wane with different historical epochs but they have never ceased in eight hundred years. In Tudor times the Catholic Gaelic *tadagh* (natives) resisted the Anglo-Norman conqueror. In the seventeenth century the Protestant Planters fought the dispossessed Catholic kernes (rebels). In the eighteenth century the Protestant Peep O'Day Boys attacked at dawn, murdering the enemy in their beds, whilst the Catholic Defenders came upon the enemy on the road and smashed their heads into the dust. It was colonialist Protestant Planter against Catholic Irish native. It was Prod against Papist. It was Protestant Royal Ulster Constabulary policeman against Catholic Irish Republican Army guerrilla. It was the British Crown versus the Irish. It was a creeping war of submerged hatreds that ran back into history and was explosively fuelled by contemporary political events. The objective was always the same – to remove the British Crown presence from Irish soil.

K. Toolis, *Rebel Hearts: Journey's within the IRA's Soul* (2000).

Everyone uses the buses in Birmingham. It's not like London where they have the underground. Everything's overground here and better. You're not going to miss your stop because you can see it coming. You're not stuck in a dark place beneath the street.

You can wave from a bus, or just mind your own business. You can sit on the top deck and look down on the city. Next to the Odeon on New Street is a pub, The Tavern In The Town. The sign has the name of the pub and M&B written on it. Nearly all the pubs have M&B written outside them, or Ansells. Some, like The Mulberry Bush, have Brew XI on them, too.

On a busy day it looks like there's nothing on the roads in Birmingham apart from buses. Hordes of them nudging along New Street and Corporation Street.

You're always moving. From home to school. Visiting people. Shopping.

You keep moving in a city, or anywhere I suppose. It's only at the end of the day you go back home and if you've done nothing apart from move around, you might begin to wonder where you are at all, or where you belong.

21 November 1974

Four shadows huddle over a snarl of wires.

'Take your wedding ring off.'

'Why?'

'Because if two wires both touch the ring at the same time it will complete the circuit and we'll all be blown to smithereens.'

'Shite.'

'I'm sure that's what did for Jamesie.'

'Poor bastard.'

'What's a man doing wearing a wedding ring in the first place?'

'Come on now boys. Quiet. Concentrate.'

A hacksaw whines as it shaves off the end of a Phillips screw. The screw gets jammed into a Westclox clock face. A trembling hand wires the Ever Ready HP7 battery to the clock.

The hand coats the gelignite in ground down nitrogen fertiliser laced with sugar, diesel oil and a drop of nitro-glycerine. The hand packs metal shards and bolts around the explosive core.

No one breathes as the bomb is lifted delicately into the suitcase, cradled like a newborn baby laid down in its crib.

'How's that looking?'

'Dead-on.'

'Are you sure we've got the go-ahead for this?'

'Away with your shite-talk. You can forget all about go-ahead. We're paying the Brits back for Jamesie.'

A cold night and a clear, starlit sky. The warm glow of Christmas lights in the City; orange, green and red twinkling over the Bull Ring shopping centre. An illuminated scene of the stable at Bethlehem in a shop window, the wise men bearing gifts, the shepherds watching their flock. The Virgin Mary craning over her baby boy.

Eamonn hums 'The Broad Black Brimmer.' A voice tells him to shut the fuck up.

'It's alright for you,' says Eamonn. 'You're not carrying the thing. It's fucking heavy. More than two stone.'

'Shut up, you old woman. And be careful with it.'

Summer 1974

Our Christmas tree lives under my mum and dad's bed. It's not a real tree but that's a good thing because all the needles fall off the real ones. I like the silver trees best, the ones you see in shop windows and in the Green Shield Stamps catalogue, but we don't have one of those. Ours is green. I wish it was silver and I wish it was bigger.

The tree is wrapped tightly in black polythene and stays under Mum and Dad's bed from the sixth of January to the last week of Advent. There is a suitcase under the bed, too, and my parents' old record player. Snaky strands of black hair trail behind it whenever I drag it out. Curls and swirls of dust come out with it too, like broken spider's webs. I love the toasted dust smell each time I undo the shiny clips and lift up the lid. It's nearly my favourite smell. My favourite is hot tar. You get it when they're repairing roads and a steamroller flattens the tar, all shiny black, glinting in the sun.

Mum and Dad's record player has four speeds: 16, 33, 45 and 78. If you play a record at a slower speed than you're meant to it sounds like a drunk man, like one of the men at the Irish Centre at the end of the night. If you play it at a faster speed than you're meant to it sounds like someone in a cartoon, like Speedy Gonzales.

The records perch on a clip at the top of a spindle. You go to play a record, the clip clicks in and the record slides down. There's a lever at the side that you pull and the needle leaves its cradle and hovers over the black vinyl for a couple of seconds, like a kestrel. Sometimes the needle goes wrong and slides off the edge. It makes a noise like trousers splitting. When that happens, you take the pad of your forefinger and gently lift the needle on to the shear black band at the edge. There's a few crackles, like a fire on Bonfire Night, and the music starts. A big rumble and roll of the drums maybe, if it's The Gallowglass Ceilidh Band.

My sister, Maria, has her own record player in her bedroom. Hers only plays 33s and 45s, so it's not as good. She walks around the house singing Donny Osmond songs: 'Puppy Love,' 'Young Love.' The two of us only seem to meet on the stairs, where she barges past me. She tells everyone her hair is flame red and that sums her up, because she's always angry about something. She also keeps reminding me and the world how close she is to being an adult and she spends half the day standing in front of the bathroom mirror. This morning she was going round the house singing about being a teenager in love. It's alright if you're a teenage girl but no one writes songs about being a boy and being ten. My hair is black and I'm glad because if you have red hair everyone at school calls you ginger nut.

Girls either love Donny Osmond or Marc Bolan. I asked Maria why she loved Donny. She told me the nuns at St Agnes's said girls who listen to Marc Bolan are the ones who get themselves into trouble.

One time the two of us were arguing and she said 'bloody' to me.

I said, 'I'm going to tell Mum.'

She said, 'You'd make a bloody saint swear, you would.'

When Mum came back, I told her straight away. Mum shouted up the stairs, 'Maria, get down here!' Maria ran down and Mum said, 'Did you swear at Danny?' Maria said, 'I said blooming. I didn't swear.' But I just nodded and said quietly, 'She did, she did.' My sister was trying to smile but you could tell from her eyes she was scared. I think Mum believed me but she couldn't prove it.

Maria is leaving us at the end of the year. She's going to Birmingham General Hospital to do nursing. She'll live in the nurses' home. Her long red hair will get pinned up and trapped in a tight nurse's cap.

I know my mum is proud of her. I hear the way she talks about it to the neighbours. My mum went along to the interview. They told Maria at the end they would send a letter to tell her if she had got in. But when my mum talked about it to the neighbours she whispered and said she knew Maria had got it because the woman told her at the end of the interview, when Maria went to use the toilet.

Mum says I've got brains to burn because I notice things and am the best reader she's ever seen, which means I'll go to the boys' grammar school for Catholics, St Thomas's. All I have to do is pass the eleven-plus next spring.

You can see St Thomas's from the bus on the way into town. I pointed to it once when we went past it and said, 'That's my school.'

Maria was sitting next to me and said, 'No it isn't.'

I said, 'It will be.'

'Then why was your last report rubbish?'

Mum was sitting behind us. She poked Maria's shoulder, hard. 'It was not. It just said he could be a little bit more confident. Didn't you see that big piece of writing he did? You remember, the one the teacher read out to the class? They put it in the envelope along with the report.'

Mum sat back her in her seat. I looked out the window. I couldn't see St Thomas's anymore. Maria leant over to me and whispered in a posh voice, 'A very nervous child. Needs more confidence.' She looked the other way and put her hand over her mouth, like she was stopping herself from laughing. The bus rumbled, like it was laughing too. Mum patted her own hair.

Daniel Cronin, class Junior 3

When I grow up I would like to be an astronaut because it would be interesting to visit the Moon and the planets. The first man to walk on the Moon was Neil Armstrong. He said, 'One small step for man, one giant leap for mankind.' He had two friends with him, Buzz Aldrin and Michael Collins. All three of them were Americans. The Russians have astronauts as well. The first man in space was a Russian. His name was Yuri.

If Neil Armstrong called at my house and asked me to go on a mission with him, I would say yes. I might have to bring a friend with me so I would have some company if things got lonely or dangerous. Maybe Neil, who sits on the same table as me.

There's nothing on the Moon but there might be aliens on the other planets. The one I would like to go to most is Saturn because of all the rings around it. That is where I would go if I was an alien from another galaxy. Perhaps they have Daleks there, on Saturn.

If there were Daleks on Saturn you would have to get out of there quickly, so you would need to leave someone back in the rocket with the engine running.

In space, you float. Your feet are not stuck to the ground like they are down here, and you can be free. Spaceships have round windows and when you look out of them you can see the stars and the planets close up. Planet Earth is below you and you can wave to the people even though they cannot see you.

You wear a space suit in space. They might give you special pyjamas for sleeping, but maybe not.

A good piece of work, Danny, in paragraphs and with good spelling. See if you can write a bit more next time. Add it to the bottom of this page.

There are no astronauts in Birmingham. There are no astronauts in England or in Ireland. If I want to be an astronaut I will have to go to America. I don't know if you get there by boat or by aeroplane, but I do know it will be a sad day when I leave. People in my family do not cry but they can still look sad as I wave goodbye to them, and maybe my mum will rush forward and give me a kiss, but they will all have to watch me go. There will be a big bang and lots of fire and rumbling as the rocket moves slowly at first but then gets faster and faster until it is just a cone of light in the sky, getting further and further away.

My sister is going to leave home too because she is going to be a nurse. It will just be my mum and dad left at home together. I hope they will be happy and not lonely.

Very good, Danny. Can you keep it going for just a little bit longer?

17

It must be hard for astronauts when they are leaving home because they might not see their families for a year. Their Mums must be sad but proud at the same time. Their Mums want to kiss them but the astronauts are wearing the big space suits. Maybe the astronauts like it that way, so they do not have to be kissed in front of their friends.

Their families are left behind to watch the rocket take off into space. A big bang and lots of fire and rumbling as the rocket moves slowly at first but then gets faster, looking like a shooting star. The families wait until the rocket has gone out of sight and then they are alone.

Maria's records look different to Mum and Dad's. Hers are light blue in the centre with MGM written at the top of the blue bit and a picture of a lion roaring. I like the picture but the music never sounds like it's right for a lion. You see the MGM lion at the beginning of films, too. There's writing underneath it; one of the words is 'ars.' That's really funny but I can't say so because there's no swearing at home.

Mum and Dad have strange records. Where Maria has MGM they have Parlophone and Pye. If I spelled pie like that at school I'd get told off. Mum and Dad have got a record of a lady called Doris Day singing 'Que Sera Sera.' She looks like Mum except her hair is light and Mum's is jet black.

My dad sometimes sings 'Que Sera Sera' around the house. I don't like Dad's voice when he sings. It wobbles and it's too high for a man. When we're allowed to watch *Top of the Pops* he starts acting like the singers, rocking from side to side and singing out the corner of his mouth. I pretend he's funny but he looks like an eejit. My mum and Maria laugh. I don't know if they think he's funny or if they're just pretending and they really think he's an eejit, like I do. Mum and Dad have got records by Ruby Murray as well, and Shirley Bassey. I played one of Shirley Bassey's once. It was called 'I who have nothing.' It was rubbish. There was no guitar or drums, and it was slow all the way through.

When I'm looking at Mum and Dad's records, I get a funny feeling in my belly. The records mean they did something before I was born. I can't imagine what the world was like back then, though you see old things on television. Mum and Dad don't buy records anymore.

There's another record. It's by a man called Hughie Maguire. The cover has a green border going all the way around it. It has a picture of Padraig Pearce on the front. I know who he is. He's a man who fought and died for Ireland to be free. He's a hero. There's something written underneath his picture on the front cover: 'Ireland unfree shall never be at peace.' He must have said that.

On the back there's a picture of Hughie Maguire. He's a fat man. He wears a green soldier's coat and hat. It looks like one of the hats the Thunderbirds pilots wear, or the hats the Boy's Brigade wear. They meet at Feldon Street school on Friday nights. I see them walk past our house in their uniforms. I wonder what uniform Hughie Maguire is wearing? Maybe it's the IRA's one.

I've played the Hughie Maguire record a couple of times when I've been on my own in the house. He has a weedy voice like my dad's and it sounds like he's singing out of his nose. It's only him and an accordion and one drum. He sings 'The Boys of the Old

Brigade.' It's mainly in English but there's one line in the chorus that's in Irish. It sounds like, 'Ah gra ma kree.'

This time the brigade is not the Boy's Brigade. It's the IRA. I know that because the men at the Irish Centre in town sing it, especially when they're drunk. I asked my mum what 'ah gra ma kree' meant. She told me it was Irish for 'love of my heart.' That sounded like the kind of thing you'd hear in those songs my sister likes.

One of the men who works with Dad came round once. It was strange to hear someone with a Birmingham accent in our house. My mum and dad make fun of the Birmingham accent. They say, 'It's pouring, says the Brummie.' Mum and Dad never use words like pouring for rain. It's either raining or it isn't. The man who came round saw the Hughie Maguire record and said to my dad, 'Are you one of them?'

The front cover of one of Mum and Dad's records shows a large group of men and boys, all lined up in three rows like they're a big football team or a school. They wear uniforms of green jackets and hats. They have drums on the ground in front of them. That's them: The Gallowglass Ceilidh Band. Not many of them are smiling in the photograph. They don't look very friendly.

Inside our front door we have a tiny well for holding Holy Water. It's a picture of the Virgin Mary above a little plastic bowl with the water in it, and the whole thing is screwed into the wall. I'm not tall enough to reach the top of it but I will be soon. The Virgin Mary wears a blue shawl in the picture and there's a glowing halo on top of her. She wears a big hood. All you can see of her face is her mouth. Her lips are raised a little like she's smiling.

Each time I leave for school my mum dips her fingers in the water and flicks it on me. She says it keeps me safe. She tells a story about when we first came to England. One of our neighbours called round to say hello and as the woman was leaving my mum flicked Holy Water over her. The woman didn't know what my mum was doing. She just thought a mad Irish woman was chucking water around. She didn't come again.

There's a plastic Virgin Mary in the pantry. The top is her crown. You unscrew it and the water is inside. I drank some once, hoping it would make me more holy.

We have a glass case in our front room. It's set-up against the wall in the corner. It's the first thing people see when they come in. There's plates in it and cups and saucers and glasses for whiskey and beer. It's got a full tea set all the same colour but we never use it. There is a little doll in the glass case, too, a plastic dancer. One of her arms reaches out, like she has a partner that only she can see. You can wind her up by twisting a key in her back.

Our glass case would be called a press in Ireland, but glass case sounds better than press, which is something you do to a thing if you squash it. You open the door of the glass case and there's a smell from it. It's like old wood, or a bit like a church, like the smell of polish and old age mixed together. You get the same kind of smell at Long Lane library, but there it's mainly of all the books. I'm only allowed a ticket for the kids' section but when I'm fourteen I'll get one for the whole library and I'll be able to read what I want. I'll read all the science-fiction books they've got.

I don't know how the plastic dancer came into the house. Like a lot of things in the glass case it's just there and I can't remember a time before it. The dancer was probably Maria's though I suppose it might have been Mum's from when she was a girl. It's only little, about four inches high. She has black hair and bright blue eyes and a wide white toothy grin and she wears a little crown. Her dress flares out from her waist to the ground. If you wind the key to set her off you have to put her on a flat surface like a table or the fireplace. She's no good on a carpet or a rug because her wheels get stuck. She has to be free to move. She glides back and forwards and spins with her pretend partner. You can hear her whirring and you can look at the smile that never moves. Maria says I was scared of the doll when I was a baby, that I used to run and jump on Mum's lap if anyone wound it up.

There's a framed photo on top of the glass case. It's black and white. It shows Mum holding Maria when she was a baby. Mum is smiling and she looks a lot younger. She's holding Maria in her arms like the way the Virgin Mary holds the Baby Jesus in pictures. You can see Maria's face but she's fast asleep, her mouth hanging open and her two little fists screwed up under her chin. The photo was taken in our garden and you can see the back of the house. A bit of my dad's face is peeking around the back door. It's in shadow so you can't see what he's thinking.

I wonder what would have to happen for us to use the cups, saucers and plates in our glass case? Maybe someone would have to get married or die.

My dad found me playing in the front room one night and told me off. It was a game I'd made up where I was an astronaut, but when he asked me what I was doing I just said, 'Nothing,' because it was easier than telling the truth and I didn't want him laughing at me. I still play at being an astronaut in there when he's at work. Mum doesn't mind.

We have a fireplace in our living room. It used to be a real fire before the central heating was put in. The house used to be freezing in the mornings in winter. Mum scrunched pages of *The Sun* into balls and put little hunks and shards of wood on top of the paper. She lit it and put coal on top of it all. You'd see smoke rising from the coal lumps when they started to catch fire and you'd know it would start to get warm soon. Mum and Dad said everyone burned peat back at home, but in England they burned the hard, black lumps of coal, all rough and dusty. Holding a block of peat in your hand was like holding a part of the earth, but coal felt like a big stone. Something that didn't belong to you.

The coalmen came a couple of times a year. They were loud in the street and lots of people came out to look. Our shed got filled up. It looked like we would never get through all the coal but we always did, and in the summer there was just a small pyramid of the stuff at the back of the shed and a carpet of black chunky dust. My mum tried to keep me out of the coal shed because of my asthma.

I've had asthma for as long as I can remember. I have a foam pillow because of it. Mum, Dad and Maria have feather pillows. Foam pillows are like a new sponge, all springy. Feather pillows are heavier; your head falls into them. My asthma means I have a lot of time off school and that's the only good thing about it. I haven't had a bad attack for a long while. You can't breathe at all. You can suck the air in but when you try to push it out it won't go, like there's a wall and the air can't push through. You really want to breathe quicker but you have to slow right down to make the attack go away. Dr Burnett told me to count to seven when I breathe in, eleven when I breathe out, any time I feel an attack coming on. I can't always count that high when I've got asthma but it helps to think about something else until it's gone away.

When it won't go away Mum takes me to Dr Burnett's surgery. It's about a mile from our house. I like it when me and Mum walk there in the autumn at night-time. The sky is clear but it's not cold. I can see all the stars and try to count them. It looks like there will only be twenty or thirty, but the more you look the more stars appear, squeezing and popping out of the blackness like sugar icing from a bag. I like the streetlights, too, and what they do to my shadow. It disappears under the light then starts to lengthen as I walk away. It vanishes as I come underneath the next light. Mum's shadow does the same. Your shadow always comes to meet you in the end.

You can see the light shining from Dr Burnett's surgery when you're at the top of his road. It makes it seem like it's closer, like there's not so far to walk and you're not going to feel worn out when you get there. You open the door and the waiting room is on the right. The floor has white tiles with little coloured lines on them. The chairs are all against the back of the wall. There are no comics in his waiting room, just a magazine called *National Geographic*.

When Dr Burnett is ready to see the next person, a large buzzer sounds in the waiting room. The sound is deep and gravelly, like someone is cross with you. There's a couch in Dr Burnett's room but he never asks me to lie on it. Mum always tells him it's my chest again. He writes a prescription for Spincaps. They're medicine for asthma and come in two parts. There's an inhaler that looks like a small rocket. When you unscrew it into the two pieces there's a propeller and, on top of it, something that looks like a tiny eggcup. That's where you put the other part, the capsule.

Half of the capsule is yellow and half is clear. You put the yellow half into the egg cup and you screw the rocket back together. You suck on the inhaler and whatever's inside it gets breathed down into your chest. It feels like tiny specks of dust in your mouth.

When I first got the inhaler, I thought it was great that it looked like a rocket. Opening it up to put the capsule in was like seeing the inside of a spaceship. I liked playing with Spincaps, too. If you held them in your hand long enough they started to go all soft. I opened one up and poured the dust in my mouth. It was dry, like plaster off a wall. I drank a lot of water to wash it away.

Mum found one of the Spincaps I'd pulled apart and got mad. She put one hand on her hip and held the broken Spincap up with the other hand. 'A shilling each, that's what these cost!' she shouted. 'A shilling each!' But there aren't shillings any more. She means five pence. I didn't say it though. When she's mad I just agree. It doesn't matter. And if you don't argue they shut up quicker.

Maria told me no one pays for medicines and Spincaps anyway but I wouldn't say that to Mum because she'd just start going on about it again. I sometimes think what it would be like to live without her and Dad.

21 November 1974

The walk into town with two bombs in two cases takes ten minutes. They split into pairs.

Through the door of The Tavern In The Town and down the narrow stairs, step by step. The handle on the suitcase creaks. The jukebox plays a love song.

He slides the case under their table and splays his hand, feeing the circulation return. The D handle on the case has dug deep into his palm. He pulls on his ring finger and it cracks. He shuffles in his seat. The carpet is sticky.

His beer is flat and there's no head on it. Typical bloody English. He thinks about complaining.

Someone lights a cigarette at the next table. The match hisses gleefully. A woman chuckles. The man next to her says, 'And you'll never guess what. The fucking battery was flat.' The woman breaks into an explosion of laughter.

Summer 1974

When I was little, I asked my mum where I came from. She pointed to the picture of Jesus. We have a small clock on our fireplace and a big, framed picture of Jesus above it. He wears a cloak. There are neat folds in it, the same number on each side of his body. His heart is on the outside, right over his chest. The heart has his crown of thorns wrapped around it, looking like barbed wire. His hands are turned towards you and you can see the bloody marks of the nails on his palms. There's blood running down his wrists. He looks straight at you with his head a little to one side and he looks sad, like somehow you've done this to him. My mum said that's where I came from, that Holy God gave me to her. I wondered if he called her over, reached back into the picture and took hold of a baby and handed it over and it was me.

My mum uses the picture a lot. When I've done something wrong she points at it and says, 'Holy God is looking at you.' But it's not Holy God, it's Jesus. They're different but Mum talks about them like they're the same. Holy God seems nicer. It's like he'd never tell you off. Jesus always looks like he's going to blame you for something. Mum told me Jesus died for our sins. I asked her if people were better behaved after he died. She said they probably were for a bit, but now they were as bad as ever. If I ask her something difficult, like why God, Jesus and the Holy Ghost are all one person, she says it's a divine mystery.

Each night before they go to sleep, my mum and dad kneel down and pray in their bedroom. If I go to the toilet I can peep through the door and see them, one on either side of the bed, facing each other, their hands clasped and their eyes shut.

My mum wears a long white nightdress and presses her forehead against her clenched hands. Her lips move and I try to work out what prayer she's saying. Once, as I walked by, I caught her whispering, 'And lead us not into temptation.' I could also see the statue of the Virgin Mary on top of her dressing table. Mary wore a white robe with a long blue cape on top of it. Her hair was covered with a white scarf. She held her hands out from her waist like she was flying, or maybe dancing, or waiting for someone to give her a hug. Her skin was pale. There was a red smile painted onto her face. Not a big grin, but just enough for you to know she was happy.

I suppose Mum and Dad have prayed together like that ever since the day they got married. It must have been strange the first time, saying your prayers with someone doing the same across the mattress from you, knowing they'd be in the same bed as you from now on.

Before they were married they must have said their prayers alone, or maybe they did it next to their brothers and sisters when they were younger, a row of children all praying, their words overlapping, a hum from them. My dad told me he slept in the same bed as all his brothers and sisters, bundled together like baby mice. All those little prayers whispering around the room, bouncing off the walls of a tiny house in a row of tiny houses.

Mum and Dad tell me and Maria that we must say our prayers. I don't know if Maria does it. I do say them most of the time but sometimes I do it in bed because it's too cold and sometimes I don't do it at all but say I have. My prayers are Our Father and Hail Mary, followed by Matthew, Mark, Luke and John:

Matthew, Mark, Luke and John,
Bless the bed that I lie on.
There are four corners to my bed,
There are four angels at my head,
One to watch and one to pray,
And two to take my soul away.

My dad says, 'Stick your tongue out,' when he thinks I'm lying. I stick it out. He says, 'There's a black mark on it. That means you're lying. Tell the truth and shame the Devil.' I think he's lying. I've looked at my tongue in the mirror and told a lie and there's no mark on it. It's the same when I pull a face and he says, 'If the wind changes direction now, your face will stay like that.' Lying is a sin. I try not to lie but sometimes I do because I don't want to get told off.

My dad is a bus driver. Other people's Dads have different jobs. Pat Stapleton's Dad has a pub in Digbeth, near the Irish Centre. David Hennessy's Dad works at British Leyland in Longbridge. Neil Gordon's Dad works in an office. I've seen him at their house when he gets in. He wears a white shirt with a light blue, silky tie. His car keys are on a key ring and he twirls them round his finger. His shoes are always shiny.

My dad's bus stops at the Town Hall when he gets into the city centre. Not many people get off there. The bus turns round the bend and heads into New Street. That's where everything gets busy. There's shops on each side. Hudson's bookshop is there and lots of shoe shops and a place where they sell thirty-two different flavours of ice cream. They'll serve it to you in a tall glass if you want and you can watch the ice cream melt and the different colours run into each other. I'd rather have my ice cream in a cornet because you can eat it, but you can't eat glass.

My mum buys books in Hudson's. My dad has never been there. He says books are a waste of time and money. Mum reads a lot. She gets her books from the library as well as Hudson's. I've seen them piled up on her side of the bed: *The Princess Bride*; *Rubyfruit Jungle*; *Time Enough For Love*; *Fear of Flying*.

Mum buys a book for me when she goes to Hudson's. I ask for one about space. She's bought me loads, like *Journey to Jupiter*; *Destination Mars*; *Spaceship to Saturn*. There's a series of them all about space missions and written by the same man, Hugh Walters. There's the same four astronauts in each one. They work for UNEXA, The Universal Exploration Agency. All the countries work together in UNEXA and there's no falling out. Two of the astronauts are English, one's American and one's Russian. The captain is Chris, one of the English ones. The other English astronaut is young. He's called Tony. He's the one I pretend to be when I'm reading. You don't get Irish astronauts. The American one is called Morrey and the Russian is Serge. I suppose they're names they have in America and Russia but nowhere else. Loads of people in Ireland are called Patrick or Michael, like my Uncle Pat. The English have a lot of different names but you don't get Irish people called Trevor, Wayne, or Darren. If a kid at school has that name you know he has an English Mum or Dad.

One night, Mum was sitting on a chair in the living room, watching *Coronation Street*. It was a rubbish programme but I sat on the floor next to her, because I had a question.

'What are your books about, Mum?'

'They're mostly about ladies, Danny. Women, you know.'

'What do the women do in them?'

'They're searching for something.'

'Do they find it?'

'Sometimes.'

'And the other times?'

'They make mistakes, Danny. They make big mistakes.'

It sounded even more boring than *Coronation Street* to me but I didn't say so.

'Mum, if I wrote a book for you, would you read it?'

'I would.'

I rested my head against her leg. She didn't move. They played the music that told you Coronation Street was over. It was slow, like someone was sad, or maybe just bored.

Searching Beyond The Stars, by Danny Cronin

The heat from the rocket was deadly. It roared underneath Danny, like there was a huge fire and he was right in the middle of it. The heat made him want to cry out but he was pinned down into his seat as the rocket tore free of Earth's gravity. The pain will soon be over, he thought, and I'll be able to float free as a bird in the cabin.

Nobody at Mission Control had told him exactly what his voyage was about. They just told him he would be going beyond the solar system to never-before-explored regions of space.

'Who knows what might be there, Danny,' said the Brigadier, stroking his moustache thoughtfully. 'Maybe there's aliens, maybe the dinosaurs survived on other planets, or maybe there's nothing at all.'

'I won't let you down, Sir,' said Danny.

The Brigadier nodded, like Danny had said something really clever.

In the days before take-off Danny started to feel worried about the mission but everyone was so busy they never stopped to ask him. Now he was just going to have to go ahead. They had a party the night before the launch with music and dancing, but Danny just sat quietly.

Danny looked out of the porthole. If he met an alien he wouldn't know what to do. He wished he'd asked the Brigadier.

Space was as black as anything but he could see a wisp of white, too. He wondered if it was stardust, or the tail of a comet as it raced by, screeching through the air like God had thrown it.

I handed the piece of paper with my story on it to Mum. Her lips moved as she read it.

'That's very good, darling,' she said. 'What happens next?'

'I don't know. I can't think of anything. I might write the ending next, or just a later bit and then do something to join them up.'

'Whatever it is, write it under this bit and I'll look after it for you. I'll keep it with my own books because it's just as good as any of them.'

I said to Mum, 'I've written a letter too, about applying to be an astronaut. Will you post it for me?'

Dear NASA,

My name is Daniel Cronin but most people call me Danny. I live in Birmingham in England. I want to be an astronaut but don't know how to join. I am very interested in space and read about it all the time. I'm not all that brave yet but I could learn to be. Maybe you could put me with Neil Armstrong for my training, so I could learn more quickly?

If you let me know how to join I will get over there as soon as I finish school.

Yours sincerely
D. Cronin.

'But Danny, you need an envelope and you need to address it.'

I ran to the drawer and took out an envelope. I wrote 'NASA' on one line and 'The United States of America' below it.

Mum smiled. 'I don't think that's enough, Danny.'

'Will you post it for me?'

'I doubt that's enough on the envelope, Danny. You need to know the full address.'

'But every postman in America will have heard of NASA, won't they? Will you post it, Mum?' I tugged at her sleeve.

'I will.'

'Will it get the special stamp, the airmail one?'

'It will.'

I moved in closer to her.

My dad's bus goes down to the bottom of New Street, where there's the ramp leading up to the Bull Ring shopping centre and

New Street station. That's where my dad's bus turns left into Corporation Street. The Bull Ring has all kinds of shops. There's one where you can watch a machine in the window make doughnuts. They rumble along a conveyor belt like it's a factory. The doughnuts are still warm when they hand them over to you in a brown paper bag. The fat stains the paper. When you've finished eating them your lips are dotted with little grains of sugar.

Halfway along Corporation Street is Rackhams. It's the biggest shop in town. It looks all bright from the outside with its big windows but inside it's mostly boring. There's a floor of toys and games high up but the rest of it is just clothes and stuff.

New Street carries on after the bus turns left. There's a Lyons café just past the City Centre Hotel, and if I'm good while we're shopping and don't moan, my mum takes me there for a Pepsi and a bun. The bun has chocolate on the top and cream on the inside. It's better than a chocolate éclair because it's bigger. We sit by the huge window at the front, looking at the buses and the shops and all the people.

Opposite Lyons is The Tavern In The Town pub, the Hasty Tasty café, Radio Rentals and the Birmingham Odeon. The Odeon is the biggest pictures I've ever been to. My older cousin Seamus came over from Derry and took me and Maria there to see *Jason and the Argonauts.*

There was a huge, golden monster chasing Jason and his friends. It was a statue that came to life because the Argonauts arrived on the island and stole something from it. Jason got behind the monster and pulled this lid off its heels. The monster swung his sword down but Jason stayed underneath it. He was low to the ground so the monster couldn't get at him. A load of liquid poured out of the hole in the monster's heel and it fell over and died. That was all you had to do to beat a monster, find its weak spot.

Near the end of the film Jason fought a bunch of skeletons. That was the scariest bit. Every time he cut a skeleton down into a heap of bones on the floor it just put itself together again and carried on. Destroying the skeletons was no good because it just created more of them.

At the end of the film, Seamus and Maria got ready to leave straight away. I asked if we could stay for a bit because there was still music going on and they were showing who had played each part. When it was all done the huge curtains in front of the screen swished towards each other until they bumped. The folds rippled. Seamus stood up and said, 'That's it now. It's all over. Will you come on?'

Films are better than telly but there's good telly programmes in the summer during the school holidays. My favourite is the *Banana Splits*. The song for it is great and there's everything in the programme, like cartoons where one man says, 'Size of an elephant' and he turns into one for a while. The rest of the year isn't as good as the summer but there's *The Flintstones* on a Friday, about five o'clock. It's one of the things everyone talks about on Monday: 'Did you see *The Flintstones*?'

Doctor Who is good, too. It's on Saturdays. He has an old car and an assistant called Jo. I like her but I don't say that at home because Dad and Maria would tease me. Doctor Who gets help from the army; a man called Brigadier Lethbridge Stuart works with him. I like Brigadier Lethbridge Stewart. He always wears a soldier's uniform and a green beret. The Brigadier looks like

Hughie Maguire on the cover of Mum and Dad's record but the Brigadier isn't fat. Instead, he has a moustache and a stick. Whiskers Greatrex has a moustache, too. He's in the Hugh Walters books, part of the UNEXA team at mission control. He says things like, 'Good show,' and 'young feller-me-lad,' and 'Old Boy.' You never hear Irish people talk like that. Whiskers Greatrex used to be a Royal Air Force fighter pilot and he was in the Battle of Britain when England beat Germany. Being a pilot is a good job to have if you're going to work on space missions.

After my dad's bus has gone along Corporation Street it turns left and heads towards Colmore Row. It's quieter there. There's a lot of banks and a casino. Dad told me about two of his bus driver mates from work. They left the Irish Centre, bought a couple of pies, parked up and went in to the casino. They lost twenty pounds each and when they came out the pies were still warm. My dad told me I must never gamble when I'm older because I might lose everything I've got.

At the end of Colmore Row the bus turns right again, then left, then it's heading out of town. From the big roundabout you can see the Rotunda. That's a huge, round building with big, glass windows, like a giant drum sticking up into the sky. It has an advert on it for Double Diamond beer, the two Ds overlapping. At the bottom of the Rotunda there's offices and a pub, The Mulberry Bush. I suppose it's called that because of the nursery rhyme, 'Here we go round the mulberry bush.' I asked my dad if he ever drank in The Mulberry Bush. He said yes, but a long time ago.

Because my dad is a bus driver he gets a special pass which means he never has to pay when he gets on a bus. My mum has one, too. They have their photos on them and they use them a lot because we don't have a car. We don't have a phone, either. Maybe it's because my dad's a bus driver and doesn't have a lot of money. Pat Stapleton has a phone. I suppose he has more money because his Dad runs a pub.

Me and Maria don't get free bus passes like Mum and Dad. It isn't fair to leave us out. My mum's got her head tilted to one side in her photo and her mouth is open and she's smiling. She looks like someone's just asked her a question and she's happy even though she doesn't know the answer and is waiting for you to tell her. She shows the photo to people if anyone comes to visit.

We have a big box of photos in our front room, stowed away in a cupboard. Mum gets it out when Dad's at work. I'm only interested when I'm in them. There's one of me on my First Communion. I'm outside St Michael's, smartly dressed in shirt and tie and short trousers. I'm holding my hands together like I'm saying prayers and I'm smiling, though you're supposed to look serious when you've had Holy Communion. I was worried it would be dry and dusty but it tasted good, like ice cream wafer. Father Duggan held it up to me at the altar, like it was a special biscuit. 'Body of Christ,' he said, like he was whispering something secret. 'Amen,' I replied, lifting the wafer into the roof of my mouth with my tongue and feeling it stick there and dissolve slowly.

Mum likes looking at all our photos, especially ones of herself when she was younger, before she met my dad. There's one of her on Brighton Beach, taken when she was eighteen. Her hair was much longer and the wind was pulling it towards the sea. It made me think of Rapunzel, a story we were told in the Infants, where a girl's hair grows long enough for a knight to climb up on it, and she escapes from the tower where she's kept prisoner and marries the knight. Mum lived in Brighton for a bit, long before she met my dad. The beach was all stones in the photo and it was on a slope. I asked her if it was uncomfortable. She said it was. I didn't understand how a beach could be any fun if it was stones instead of sand. I asked my mum why she left Brighton and went back to Derry. She said she couldn't remember. I asked her who took the photo. She said she'd forgotten that, too. She held onto the photo and put it to one side.

There was another one showing my mum kissing the Blarney Stone. It's in Ireland and it's supposed to make you good at talking. Mum told me the photo was from her honeymoon. She and my dad came down from the North, crossed the border and got as far South as Killarney in the end, travelling by train. I can't imagine what they would have looked like. Maybe my dad wore a suit and tie, like Neil Gordon's Dad. Maybe his hair was black, like Mum's. He's gone grey now.

My dad gets sweets on his bus. Some of the passengers give them to him. It's mainly old people, especially old ladies. My favourites are toffees covered in chocolate, but a lot of the time he gets mints. Some give Trebors and some give Polos. Maria likes Trebor but I like the Polos because of the hole in the middle.

We're not supposed to take sweets from Dad's pocket. We're supposed to wait until he gives them to us. Dad will give me a sweet at home if I've been good. When he's got none and if he's not around I run my fingers along the bottom of the pocket. There's always a thread or two of a cigarette there. You feel it under your finger like you'd feel a little worm. It sticks to your hand and you have to pick it off.

38

A couple of times I've ridden with my dad on the bus, just to pass the time in the summer holidays. I run upstairs to see if one of the two seats at the front is free. They're the best ones because there's big windows in front of you and to the side. You can look out over everything. If there's lads smoking and swearing at the back you ignore them.

If you're heading home, you catch the number nine. It's an important bus because it stops in New Street, Corporation Street and Colmore Row. At Five Ways it goes straight and you're on the Hagley Road.

You get strips of shops near to a pub. The Ivy Bush. The Holly Bush. Maybe there used to be a lot of bushes in Birmingham before they built the factories, shops and houses, because of the pub in town called The Mulberry Bush.

A bus going up a hill grumbles and groans, like it's finding it hard, like it has asthma. When it stops it lets out a hiss as the doors open, like it's getting its breath again.

If it's the number ten bus you head left at Five Ways and into Edgbaston, where the houses are bigger and there's more trees. I don't know who lives there. Maybe teachers and bishops. The number ten is the one my dad drives, so if I caught a bus out of town to go home, and my dad was driving his own bus at the same time, we'd be going the same way along Broad Street but we'd head in different directions at Five Ways and maybe he'd see the back of my bus going its own way, with a puff of smoke.

The journey ends at the terminus. My dad switches the engine off and it judders to a halt. He takes a break before starting again. He climbs out of his seat, stretches his legs and has a cigarette or two. He smokes Woodbines. I don't know why because there's no adverts for them. Instead, there's adverts for Silk Cut or Marlboro. They're the best ones because they have a cowboy. I'll smoke when I'm old enough, unless my asthma means I can't.

When my dad's driving his bus everyone relies on him to get to work or school or mass, or to get home. There's bus drivers all over Birmingham doing the same thing, an army of them.

There is a pantry leading off from our living room and a wooden chair next to the pantry door. My dad hangs his bus driver's jacket on the back of the chair. The sweets are in his right-hand pocket. I put my hand in the pocket to feel if there's any there. That way I know whether to ask for one from him.

Sometimes I've taken a sweet without asking. I've bundled up the wrapper really small and put it at the bottom of the bin. I haven't told the priest about it in confession.

My cousin Seamus, who took me to see *Jason and the Argonauts*, didn't go back to Northern Ireland after his holiday. Instead, he went to London to find work. I asked him what Derry was like. He said the Prods in the Waterside painted their kerbstones red, white and blue and hung Union Jacks from their telegraph poles. He also said that as you go into the Bogside there's a big sign painted on the side of a house where Rossville Street meets Lecky Road. It's got black letters on a whitewashed wall and says, 'You are now entering Free Derry.'

The IRA patrol the streets. Seamus said you can have great times in Derry because you're running your own town. It began a few years back when people fought against the Prods and the RUC. The lads who ran the barricades became heroes, blocking the roads with hijacked milk floats, bread vans, cars and lorries and buses tipped over onto their sides. I thought about the noise a bus would make if it was tipped over, the huge crash of all the windows smashing at once. Falling over like an elephant shot in the jungle by a hunter.

Seamus said a burnt out bus looks like a skeleton because all you can see is the metal bits between the windows, like ribs. I thought of people burning a bus like my dad's bus, and about Jason and his Argonauts. They were heroes because of the brave things they did, never giving up even though they were fighting against bigger enemies.

I asked him why the people needed barricades. 'To protect theirselves,' he said. 'To stop the RUC and the Brits getting in. The barricades are ten feet high with ramps along the top so people can walk across them.' Standing at the top of a barricade would be great, with the wind in your hair, looking at the city underneath you. You'd feel like a knight, all you'd need would be a sword and a shield.

Seamus said the little kids march up the road singing, 'If you hate the British Army clap your hands.' He said the Brits hate Free Derry, that the Brits and Prods call the city Londonderry but its real name is Derry and all the best bits are Catholic: the Bogside, Creggan and Shantallow, places where they fly the Irish flag. He said you know someone is really from Derry if they've been baptised at St Eugene's Cathedral.

Seamus was silent for a bit, smoking, before he told me how the Parachute Regiment, the Paras, ran up Rossville Street to Free Derry corner on Bloody Sunday. The people were on a peaceful march. It was cold but sunny and there were twenty thousand of

41

them from Creggan and Shantallow and all over, with a big banner saying 'Civil Rights For All.' I didn't know what civil rights were but didn't want to stop him telling his story.

Seamus

'You could hear the revving of the soldiers' armoured cars. I saw the Paras' red berets bobbing up and down and heard the crack of their rifles. Then I heard the screams. Women and children howling and crying, scrambling behind walls or dustbins. The shots echoing round the streets so you couldn't tell where they were coming from. A helicopter buzzing overhead like it had gone mad.

'Father Daly, our priest, waving a white handkerchief as he ran to help the dying. There was blood on it, dripping from the bottom corner.

'I saw a Para kick a dead body from the pavement into the gutter. A set of false teeth fell from the dead man's mouth. The man's hand was still holding a cigarette. One of his slip-on shoes was left behind on the pavement, pointing up the road, out of town. Everyone was either screaming or praying, and there was Father Daly in the middle of them all, waving his white handkerchief covered in blood.

'It snowed that night. You could hear the murmur of prayers from all the flats, that and the crying.

'It rained during the funerals, Danny, the rainwater and the tears running down everyone's faces. People nailed bits of wood together in their houses and sheds so they looked like coffins and wrote 13 on the side. They carried their homemade coffins at the funerals, so it looked like there were hundreds of us being buried that day.

'Later that year we had Operation Motorman. The Brits invaded the Bogside, thirty thousand charging in at four in the morning, all to destroy Free Derry. Royal Navy battleships in Lough Foyle, tanks on the street and helicopters dropping soldiers onto the ground. Operation Murderman we called it, Danny, Operation Murderman.'

I thought about living in Derry. You'd be scared to death. You could just be watching telly and the door might burst in and you'd be dragged away. Or maybe the Paras would run up your street firing guns. There'd be nothing you could do unless you had a gun of your own and even then you'd be outnumbered. I was glad we'd come away from all of that to a house in Birmingham where we were safe.

I asked Seamus what he thought about the British army. He said he wouldn't give a soldier the steam off his piss, and he wouldn't give a drop of his blood if a soldier was bleeding to death in front of him.

Seamus told me that any time the army raids the Bogside all the women blow whistles or bang dustbin lids against the ground so people in the next street know the Brits are coming. They hammer the lids down, louder than the armoured cars. The Brits pour out and start breaking in the doors, shouting and swearing. Seamus said the Brits used tear gas but its real name was CS gas and the Yanks used it in Vietnam.

At first it felt like a burn, then it got into your eyes, nose and lungs and you felt like you were on fire. He said the gas came through the cracks in doors and windows of the people's homes, so you'd be breathing it in and it would be choking you even if you thought you were safe at home, so if you were an old person or a child and you just stayed in and did nothing at all, it made no difference. The gas still got you, and sometimes the Brits fired it straight into houses. He said you knew the gas was coming when you saw the soldiers put on masks. After they'd fired it, they moved forward, and even though you couldn't see them you'd know where they were because you heard them on their walkie-talkies, one of them carrying a big radio set on his back, their voices crackling.

I'd be no good in Derry because of the CS gas. It would give me an asthma attack. I'd be better as an astronaut looking down from space, hoping the fighting would stop.

Seamus said everyone was mad after Bloody Sunday, raving mad, even outside the North. The British Embassy in Dublin was burned to the ground. There were bombs, too, in Belfast and Derry.

Seamus said the soldiers stuck torch batteries or metal nuts and bolts or broken razor blades in their rubber bullets. Little kids picked the used ones off the ground and sold them to reporters or kept them as souvenirs. The bullets were big; they could be as big as a boy's hand. You'd know if the army were using rubber bullets because they made a dull thump when they were fired. Rifles made a crack and that was how the first people knew something was wrong on Bloody Sunday, because the guns were cracking not thumping.

Seamus asked me what the City's real name was. I said Derry. He patted me on the head and said, 'Good boy.' Seamus also told me that the lads in Derry threw stones and petrol bombs at the police and the Brits. You got good stones by breaking up paving slabs. For a petrol bomb you just got a glass bottle, used a rolled-up bit of carpet for a fuse, lit it and hurled it. You could gather the petrol bombs up in milk crates and keep them at the top of tower blocks, so they'd be ready when you needed them.

He asked me if I could keep a secret. I nodded. He told me you could make a real bomb by packing a beer can with six-inch nails, leaving just enough space for a stick of gelignite. If you put cardboard around the can and taped it up it would do the job every time, but once you lit the fuse you had no more than ten seconds to get rid of it.

Seamus said gelignite was a funny thing. It sweated, little beads of liquid forming on its surface. It gave you fierce headaches and it smelled like marzipan. The smell made me think of Christmas cake. Mum made one each December, putting a thick layer of marzipan over the fruit cake before smothering the whole thing in white icing, wrapping the cake up like you'd wrap a bomb. Mum had two little plastic figures moulded together. A boy and a girl, ice skating and grinning. They always stood in the centre of our cake.

I thought Derry must be a really dangerous place, with all the shooting, bombing and stones. I'd read a book called *Passage To Pluto* where they said Pluto was all scarred and full of craters. Derry was like Pluto. If snow fell on the night of Bloody Sunday it might have covered some of the blood stains, the way icing covers marzipan, making everything look clean again. Watching the snow fall would give them something else to think about, something to take their minds off all the bad things. The little snow-flakes tumbling down gracefully, not being kicked into the gutter like the man shot by the Paras.

I thought about holding a petrol bomb. The second you lit the fire you'd have all that power just raring to go and it would be hissing like a sparkler on Bonfire Night.

Seamus told me another thing. He said there was a girl. She'd been at the same school as him but she was younger. She went out with British soldiers, meeting them at the Services Club in Bond Street. People found out.

The girl was paraded through the streets and tied to a lamp-post. Her hair was cut, hot tar was poured over her head and a load of feathers got dumped on top of her. I couldn't believe people would do that. They were just people from Derry, people like us. How could they tie someone up, a girl they knew? In *Destination Mars* the other three astronauts tied Chris up, but that was because Martians had taken over their minds. Maybe it was like that in Derry and something had taken over the people's minds. The hot tar gave the girl scars for life.

Seamus saw her tied-up. Her head was bowed down. She was nearly naked from the waist up, just a torn vest to cover her. I asked Seamus why the people did it. He shrugged and said, 'She shouldn't have gone out with Brits. It was a warning to others, and anyway it's not as though they could shoot her. It's wrong to shoot a girl. What they did was letting her off lightly, really.' I asked him how old the girl was. 'Dunno. Maybe fifteen, sixteen, seventeen. It's all the same.'

I thought of Seamus and the other people, watching. Did they cheer, like the girl was a guy on Bonfire Night, or did they boo like she was a villain in a film or pantomime? Or maybe they were just silent because they didn't know the right noise to make for something like that. If they were silent, they might have heard her crying.

There must have been a stain on the ground afterwards because tar is black and it's hard to get rid of even if you just get a little blob of it on your shoe. The smell of the hot tar and a tied-up girl the same age as Maria, or younger, feathers floating around her like snowflakes. The girl crying cold sobs. The burns. Stains all over Derry's streets, from tar, or blood from a handkerchief.

The last thing Seamus said was he'd seen a lad he knew firing a gun. It was a Lee Enfield rifle and the muzzle flashed fire when it was shot. I thought that sounded great but didn't tell anyone at home. I told the lads at school but they said they'd all seen people firing guns, too, and it was no big deal.

Francis Byrne said he'd fired one himself. He set the pretend rifle against his shoulder, squinted one eye to show us how he had taken sight, and pulled the trigger.

'What did you hit?' I asked.

'A pile of bullshit,' said David Hennessey.

I didn't tell the lads about how to make a bomb and I didn't tell them about the girl covered in tar and feathers.

Pat Stapleton said they shot people's kneecaps off in Northern Ireland. They put the gun to the back of the man's knee and pulled the trigger and Abracadabra the kneecap came flying off. 'The pain is unbelievable,' he said. I asked him why they did it. He said, 'I don't know, they just do.' Neil Gordon asked who they were. Pat shrugged. He showed us how it was done by bending down, making a pistol shape at the back of his knee and making a 'ka-pow' sound. I felt sick but didn't say anything to the others.

The Brigadier stood stiff as an ironing board.

'Look chaps, we're going to have to go into battle sooner than we wanted.'

'Why's that, Brigadier?' said Danny. The other young astronauts looked at him. He was the brave one for asking the question.

'You must have seen the news, all of you. The situation has got really bad. We have to take action now, even if we don't have a plan yet. We have to do something and do it now. The thinking can wait.'

But Danny thought. He thought of his family, how he would have to leave them behind. He thought about the Earth's future and he realised the Brigadier was right. There were times when you had to act to stop a really bad thing happening, even if it meant doing a thing yourself that was a little bit bad.

All the young astronauts looked out of the window of the space training headquarters because it had started to snow. People were scurrying and hurrying home with their coats wrapped round their faces so you could not see who they were. Some of them were waiting at the bus stop. Some were carrying big bags of shopping. All those people would rely on the astronauts to defend them.

21 November 1974

'Christ, Eamonn, I'm scared.'

'No time for shite-talk. You're to obey orders. Just drink up and don't draw attention to us.'

'I can't even swallow. HolyMaryMotherofGod –'

'You'll be getting a belt in the gob if you don't get a hold of yourself. Listen, the timer's set. There's no stopping it now. The sooner you drink up the sooner we can get out of here.'

'But look around you, Eamonn. They're just boys and girls, like people you'd see at a dance back at home. Look at those two boys just coming in, they're not out of their teens.'

Eamonn glances over. Two young lads in office clothes, ties pulled down like schoolboys at home time. Scuffed shoes.

A girl with long red hair steps towards the bar. Her skirt flows. Eamonn fixes his gaze on her. He shivers. Grips his glass. Drums it on the table.

'If we bombed somewhere that mattered, Eamonn, somewhere like the Bank of England in London, we'd hit them where it hurts, in their pockets. Brits are obsessed with money.'

'We're soldiers, Boy, this is what we do. And anyway, I'll phone a warning like we're told to. These kids will all be out safely, back with their mothers, all in good time. Sure, I wouldn't harm them. There won't be a drop of blood spilt, just another blown up building and another reason for the Brits to pull out. The Inland Revenue have an office above this pub, and we'll put it out of action for a while. Now, and for the last time.' He holds the glass to his comrade's face.

They drain their beers, walk quickly up the stairs, their footsteps thudding like quickening heartbeats, out into the cold darkness of New Street, leaving the suitcase behind, snug under a table.

A voice pipes up, 'Two pints of Harp please.'

Summer 1974

Pat Stapleton has long trousers. So does Neil Gordon. Me and David Hennessey have short trousers. I want long ones but Mum won't let me. Neil and Pat are allowed to have their hair long, too, over their ears. My mum takes me to the barber's and just says one word, 'Short.'

I asked my mum and dad when Seamus was coming back. They said they didn't know. I wanted to tell them the stories about the gun and the kneecaps and the girl with the tar and feathers, but I knew they'd go mad, so I stayed quiet. Sometimes it's best to hold back what you know. That's not the same as lying, so it's not a sin.

My dad doesn't drink anymore. He's joined the Pioneers. They're a Catholic group who don't drink at all. He has a Pioneer badge he wears on his jacket when we go to mass on Sundays. It looks like a little shield. It has a small red heart in the middle of it and a cross on top of the heart. My mum says Dad used to drink too much, used to get steaming drunk, but now he's a bus driver he has to watch himself because he has responsibilities.

The only other time I went to the Odeon was to see *Peter Pan* with Mum, but it wasn't as good. There were girls in it, Tinkerbell and Wendy. There's another film called *The Battle of Britain*. That's the one I really want to see because it's all about planes fighting in the sky in the war. There's another film, *The Island At The Top Of The World*, where they find a secret island of Vikings at the North Pole. Maybe I'll get to see those films if Seamus comes back.

When my dad isn't working at the weekend he watches Gaelic football and hurling at Glebe Farm, or he does things in the garden and in the house. He always has sandpaper in his hand. It's rough to touch and after he's been using it there are tiny specks of wood in the air. I try not to breathe them in.

He has a pair of overalls. They're brown. Not a dark brown but lighter, like tan, almost like the colour of an animal's skin. I asked him where he got them from. He told me he had a factory job when we first came over, before he got the buses. I asked him what the factory was like. He said it was in Longbridge and made Austin cars and it was OK, but everyone called him Paddy except for one man who called him Spud. The other men asked him if he kept a pig in the kitchen back at home. I didn't understand why they would say that. No one would have a pig in the house.

I asked what the buses were like. He said there were lots of Irish working on them because the hours were long, with early starts and late finishes, and the Brummies didn't like working. Right from the start he could make fifteen pounds a week if he did overtime. He also said Brummies were cold and didn't know how to enjoy themselves and all they thought about was watching the clock and listening out for bells and buzzers and hooters in factories, wanting to be told what to do all the time.

I asked him if all the Irish people in Birmingham worked on the buses. He said no, a lot of them worked on the lump. I didn't understand what that meant. He told me it was working on a building site for cash in hand, no tax. I'd seen men working on building sites. The rasp of the shovel scooping up the cement. The big concrete mixer and a man stripped down to his vest and trousers pouring sloppy stuff into it, the big drum turning around and around, grumbling like it was being made to work too hard.

I asked Dad how men got those jobs. He said they stood in pub car parks in the early morning at places like the Coventry Road, or The Highgate Hotel, or The Mermaid pub in Sparkhill, and waited for vans to pull up and offer them work for a day or a week. I asked him why he wasn't on the lump if it meant you didn't pay tax. He told me he wasn't cut out for that kind of work, digging trenches in the rain and the snow, and anyway it was dangerous because you worked for a gangerman who could be rough, and you didn't know from one week to the next if you had a job, and if you got ill there'd be no sick pay. You'd do your day's work and they'd pay you in the pub and you'd have to buy the gangerman's drinks if you wanted more work.

'It's the country men, Danny. They're used to slaving on farms all day and all night. They come over on the boat every day of the week.'

'And is the gangerman Irish as well?'

'He is.'

'Why would he treat other Irish people like that?'

'There's no knowing what some people will do. They'll stop at nothing.'

'Dad?'

'Yeh.'

'Were you married at St Eugene's?'

'How do you know about St Eugene's?'

'Seamus said you know someone is from Derry if they've been baptised at St Eugene's. I thought you and Mum might have got married there.'

'Seamus should mind his own business. We were married at St Mary's, in Creggan. What else did Seamus tell you?'

'Nothing.'

'Sure?'

'Yeh.'

Our garden is only small but it's still a garden. My dad grows potatoes and beans. The beans grow up bamboo poles. They have rough green leaves and a bright little red flower. Potatoes are different; the plants are green but the potatoes grow under the ground. My dad also grows rhubarb at the bottom of the garden. When autumn ends, he cuts everything right back so there's just bare earth and little stubs of plants. I asked him if he was killing everything. He said no, a plant would always grow back if it had strong roots.

We have the rhubarb as pudding on Sundays. It's stringy and you have to put a lot of custard or cream on it to make it taste good. The cream is called Carnation and comes in a tin. My mum puts two holes in it and pours it into a creamer before putting it on the table. The creamer looks like a cow. You tip it forward and the Carnation comes out of the cow's mouth. If we have tinned fruit instead of rhubarb the Carnation mixes with the syrup. When you've finished you tip your head back and drink the syrup mixed with cream.

Our house was given to us by Birmingham council and we pay rent for it each week. My mum says when we first got it, she couldn't tell the difference between our house and the other houses on the street. They looked the same to her, like they were stone dead, no character in them at all. She had to put something of hers on the windowsill in the front room so she'd know which house was our one when she came back from the shops. A pair of gloves or a brightly coloured headscarf.

My mum tells a lot of stories about us. If anyone comes to visit, they always get told one. There was one about when my sister started at St Agnes's school. Loads of new things came into the house, hats and blazers and satchels and things like that. There was a special purse with the St Agnes crest on it, a cross above a lamb. The purse was on a long strap so it could go over Maria's shoulder. She got a new alarm clock, too, in a cardboard box. It had two big shiny bells on top of it and a little hammer that banged between the bells and made a noise.

I played with the new things without asking. I put the purse inside the alarm clock box. I couldn't say alarm clock back then, so I said 'lary.'

The next morning, I woke up early because of all the noise. I went to the top of the stairs. Maria was panicking. She shouted, 'Danny, have you seen my purse?'

'It's in the lary box,' I told her. She ran downstairs, grabbed it and ran out.

Mum loved that story. I heard people say she spoiled me. I once heard my Aunty Kate say, 'Never was a child so spoilt.' I didn't really know what that meant but I knew it wasn't good and wanted to say it wasn't true.

One Sunday morning I was sick with asthma and couldn't go to mass. I was pleased but pretended not to be. They left me by myself. I was alright at first, but I started to hear things. I thought the stairs were creaking, like there was someone else in the house. I was scared I might hear a door open.

I hid at the back of the pantry. It was dark and cold, but it meant if anyone was inside the house, they wouldn't see me. I sat cross-legged on the pantry floor. The darkness was different to the darkness at night. Because it was only a small pocket of the dark it felt safe, like I knew there was a light just beyond it. I could stretch out my arms and touch a wall at each side, like I was in my own cell.

After a while I could see the outlines of the tins. I could reach my hand back and touch the cold shelf behind me. It made me feel safer still, to know where everything was. I pretended I was on a space mission, searching for a new planet.

The year I started school I went into prep class. At half three each day the Mums came to collect the kids. There was one day my mum was late. I said to the teacher, 'My mum hasn't come for me,' just before she walked in the room. The teacher repeated what I had just said. It became another story: 'My mum hasn't come for me.'

In the Infants we had a play at Christmas. I was one of the readers because I was good at it. It was an important part but everyone had something to do. It was the story of Jesus and Bethlehem and the wise men and the shepherds and angels. Francis Byrne was Joseph and never stopped going on about it, even though he didn't have to say a load of lines, not like me.

Mum went back to Northern Ireland a couple of years ago because her oldest sister died. That was my Aunt Nora, but I don't remember her and don't know what she died of. We had mass cards for her in our house, narrow little things like bookmarks with Aunt Nora's photo on them and some words: Nora Mary O'Brien, and her date of birth and death and a prayer.

I asked my mum about mass cards, and she told me it's just what we do to pay our respects. We also say 'Sorry for your trouble' to anyone who's had a death in the family. A lot of the mass cards get signed by the priest. I suppose it shows the priest said a mass for the dead person. I've seen my dad sign a cheque. It must be the same thing as the priest signing the mass card.

The other thing my mum did when Aunt Nora died was say the rosary at home. That was the second time I'd heard her doing it. The first was the night before Maria's eleven plus exam results arrived in the post, when Mum did it on her own in her bedroom and I could her hear her mumbling the prayers as I stood on the landing. She knelt down on her side of the bed but Dad was on a night shift so there was just a gap where he should have been. When the results came the next day Mum went out and bought Maria a game she wanted called Frustration. We spent the rest of the day playing it, pressing on an upside down plastic bowl to make the dice bounce around.

Mum has her own rosary beads. They're on a necklace and you get a row of beads and a gap; a row of beads and a gap; all the way round. Each bead marks a prayer. Women don't wear rosary beads as necklaces. Instead, they grip them, like they're clinging on to something.

People speak fast when they say the rosary. The words flow into each other. There's nine Hail Marys in a row. One person will say: 'HailMaryfullofgracetheLordiswiththeeblessedartthoua-mongstwomenandblessedisthefruitofthywombJesus.' Someone else will answer, 'HolyMaryMotherofGodprayforussinnersno-wandatthehourofourdeathamen.' It goes on and on. They move their fingers along the beads as they count through the prayers. Me, Dad and Maria all had to say the rosary the night Aunt Nora died, along with Mum. She was strange all the way through it, her head bowing and coming back up again.

Maybe the dead look down from heaven on the mass cards and they listen to the rosary and it makes them happy to be remembered. Only Irish families have mass cards. Maybe the English aren't bothered about their dead, like they're not interested in hard work.

Maria told me people get buried with their rosary beads. Maybe their cold hands still worry along the thread and their dry lips mouth the words. A row of dead people in a line in a ceme-tery, all praying at once, the soft murmuring underground, coffins rumbling and trembling in the soil.

I asked Mum to bring me a present back from Derry when she went to the funeral. I asked her for a gun. Lots of boys at school have guns. They have Lugers, which is a German gun, or Bren guns. I think they're English. I didn't mind what I had but I wanted a gun you could put caps into. Caps make a bang and they smell like proper gunpowder. David Hennessy put a lit match in-side a full box of England's Glory matches one playtime at school and it flared up in a bright yellow light. A sharp hiss and a bang.

A small cloud of grey mist drifted up into the air. The smell afterwards was like the smell of caps, all smoky and heavy. Someone told the nuns and he got the cane. Mother Assumpta had a school assembly. She was at her maddest. We all sang a hymn: 'Keep me my God from stain of sin, just for today.'

Mum was gone for days. I woke up one morning and Maria told me she was back. I said, 'Did she remember my gun?'

It was a silver gun with the letters P.I. on it and the hammer at the back moved which meant there was a place for the caps. That same day I went up the alley to Barker's and bought a roll of caps for my gun. I felt a little bit scared when I pulled the trigger the first time, like it was going to explode or something like that. The bang was loud but it didn't hurt, and after that I was firing caps the rest of the day, out in the back garden taking aim at the runner beans and potato plants and at the birds in the sky. The smell hanging in the air. Maybe that was what Derry smelled like.

The next time Maria was angry at me she told me she bought the gun from Rackhams and they only pretended Mum brought it back from Derry. I didn't know and I didn't care.

Barker's is our nearest shop. They have a bit of everything there. They've got sweets. My favourite are flying saucers. They're like two bits of communion wafer with sherbet in between them. They stick to your tongue. Pat Stapleton brought a bag of them into school one time. He held each one in the air and said, 'Body of Christ' as he gave them out to us. Most of us said 'Amen,' but I didn't because I knew it was a bad thing to do. He could go to hell for it.

Barker's have the newspapers in the window. There's always lots of copies of the *Daily Mirror* and *The Sun*. If you walk out the back door of our house and down to the bottom of the garden, you can go out through the back gate and walk up the alley to the shop. You can look at the papers before going in to get what you want. I've seen *The Times* in there and wondered if we'd be allowed to buy it, or whether you have to be different to us.

There's nettles growing in the alley and there's bindweed which makes big white flowers in summer that no one likes though I think they're pretty, and the bees disappear into the middle of them and never come out, like they're time travellers. Or maybe you could wrap a bee up in the flower and take it home. There's also blackberry bushes, the tight branches all tangled up in each other. If you wade into them they leave you with scratches. The bushes make bunches and clumps of berries, like raspberries only darker and sweeter. I like to pick them straight off the bush and eat them in the alley. Maria says I shouldn't because the dogs piss on the berries and I should bring them home and wash them, but I like having them on my own, not sharing with anyone, the juice running down my hands leaving a dark red stain on my fingers and all over my palms.

Mum took hold of my wrists once after I got back. She looked at my hands. She tutted and walked off. My hands stayed where they were, stained deep red, my fingers sticking together. I looked at my hands and they looked back.

The astronauts had an assembly. The Brigadier said that one of them had been misbehaving and had fired a laser gun without permission. He asked who had done it. No one said anything. The Brigadier said

they would all just stay there until the person who did it owned up.
They would stay all night if necessary. Danny knew he had not done
it but still felt bad. Finally, a young astronaut that Danny did not
know put this hand up slowly. The Brigadier said, 'Thank you for
your honesty. Now come here.'

The astronaut hesitated, then walked forward. Two older astro-
nauts took him away. Danny did not know what was going to happen
to the boy but there was a lamppost outside and Danny thought the
young astronaut might get tied up to it and have tar and feathers
poured over him, or maybe they would shoot him with a laser gun.
Maybe behind the knee.

21 November 1974

They all meet up again. Nod.

'Done?'

'Done.'

'You lads get off home. Keep your heads down for a bit. Just go to work and do everything you'd normally do. I'm away to give the Brits a ring. Let them know what's coming their way.'

The other three slope off, their shoulders sagging like they're bearing something heavy, carrying the weight of the world on their shoulders. They do not speak. They disappear into the dark.

He walks up the street, alone. He whistles and rubs his hands.

Summer 1974

I was only two when we left Derry and came to Birmingham. Up until then we lived with my grandparents, my dad's Mum and Dad, but I don't remember it and they're dead now. Dad told me he'd left school at thirteen and got a job on a golf course carrying the players' bags. He made a shilling a day but a lot of it went in bus fares to and from work. He didn't know any of the men playing because it was a members' club for Protestants.

We used to live in the Bogside, but I don't like to tell anyone that here, because in Birmingham bog means toilet. The other part of Derry is the Waterside, which sounds nicer. The people who live in the Waterside are the ones who call it Londonderry. They're Protestants but we call them The Prods. Between the two sides is the River Foyle which flows into Lough Foyle. Dad said the Foyle is the fastest-flowing river he's ever seen, so it's like there's a barrier between the two sides of Derry and it's hard to cross, like having a sea or ocean between you. It's like that Bible story where Moses parts the sea so they can walk across.

Mum says we came to England by boat in the middle of the night and we had a rough crossing – the cold, stiff breeze from England blowing in our faces. There were so many people coming over from Ireland at that time for work and there were hardly any seats, so we were all sitting on top of our bags. Mum said from where she was, she could see up to the first-class deck, where people had lots of seats and miles and miles of space to walk around, as free as birds and never looking down. A lot of the people on the boat were men travelling alone, coming over to work on the buildings, on the lump. Mum said there were some girls by themselves, coming over to work as nurses. They sat close to families and held their bags tightly, staring at the ground or out at the sea, not talking to anyone, little white handkerchiefs in their hands. A girl biting her lower lip, looking back at the place she came from, that she might never see again. A lot of people prayed during the crossing, the Hail Marys mingling with the sound of the wind and the waves. Someone started a song but no one joined in.

Mum said we had to wait an hour and a half in the rain at Heysham for the train. We travelled down the country, changed at Crewe and arrived in Birmingham. All the buildings had a fine coating of black coal dust. She said we had trouble finding anywhere to live over here until the council housed us. We stayed at my Uncle Pat's at first, the four of us sleeping in one room.

I knew things were bad in Northern Ireland because of The Troubles. I remember being here in England and seeing a family on the telly, running down the middle of the road, carrying a sofa between them, one of the children not wearing any shoes. My mum said they were Catholics in Belfast and they were running away from Prods. Hundreds of them had been burnt out of their homes, with the RUC and the B Specials just standing by and laughing or, even worse, hitting the Catholics. I imagined a truncheon whistling through the air and cracking a skull, a splurge of blood like a bottle of ink or milk knocked over.

I couldn't see why the people running away needed a sofa. I asked Mum if we brought a sofa with us from Derry, because we had one in our front room. She laughed and said no.

I still didn't understand why we left, so I asked my dad. He didn't lift his eyes up from *The Sun* while he answered me.

'Did we leave because of the Troubles?'

'We left before that.'

'Why?'

'Sure, we had our own troubles.'

'And what's the RUC?'

'The Royal Ulster Constabulary, the police.'

'And the B Specials?'

'Police, too, same as the RUC, only worse. Dressed in black from head to foot they are.'

'The police are meant to be good, aren't they?'

'Not those ones.'

He turned the page. He didn't look at me. Benny Hill was on the television and said, 'I'd kick my wife in the teeth, but why should I improve her looks?' The people laughed. My dad kept looking at his newspaper like I wasn't there.

I wondered about our troubles. I would have been a baby and too young to get into trouble, so maybe it was Maria who was in trouble, or Dad, or Mum.

Maria told me that when the Catholics ran from their homes the Prods just came in, smashed the crucifixes and holy statues and stole all their stuff, and the police didn't do anything to stop it. The Prods set fire to houses and everything. That was the meanest thing I had ever heard, especially as the Prods didn't get into any trouble for it. A row of houses all on fire and no one trying to put the fire out.

It wasn't right to use one word, trouble, for two things when they were so different. I also thought about marching. We marched at the Irish Parade every year. Did that mean the Paras might start firing at us? I imagined the red berets bobbing up and down as they ran up the street, getting closer. I thought of the smell and sound, like thousands of caps all being fired together, people falling to the ground as they were shot, or screaming as they ran away, blood running down their faces and hands and staining the streets, the smoke from the guns like a fog spreading everywhere, smothering and suffocating the people. Maybe the Paras would fire CS gas and I wouldn't be able to breathe, even if I could escape the bullets. It would be like the worst asthma attack ever. I could feel my breathing getting harder just thinking about it. I was glad our house was safe and there were no Paras, or marching in our street, or CS gas.

Most of my aunts and uncles are still in Northern Ireland but one of my dad's sisters, my Aunt Bridie, lives in New York. We get a card from her at Christmas. It arrives in a blue envelope with wavy lines across it and the words 'air mail.' My mum told me Aunt Bridie's family put her on a boat to New York when she was fourteen and that was that. They knew they would never see her again. I wondered what it would be like. On the one hand you'd have the adventure, but on the other you'd be arriving in a big city knowing no one and nothing.

Everyone in New York lives in big houses and drives big cars, so maybe we could go and visit. Francis Byrne brought a Superman comic into school one time and it looked like there was always something amazing happening over there, huge buildings and huge cars and the cops tearing around at a hundred miles an hour. I know Superman is like Father Christmas but America must look like that, all big and busy. Our old comics in the box in our classroom are things like *Victor* and *Hotspur*. They're stories about the war, with brave British soldiers called Tommies killing Germans and Japanese. The heroes in comics are always soldiers or the police, or people with special powers.

Our class has a hamster. It's called Whiskers. We had a vote on what to call it. Whiskers came first and Katy came second. Bridget Rafferty chose Whiskers. I don't like her, she pushes people, but it's a good name for a hamster. Before the hamster we had goldfish in a bowl but they weren't so good, just little orange clouds in the water. One morning I came in and one of the goldfish had died, floating on top of the water with mould growing on it, its little mouth hanging open.

Sometimes I get a lift to school with Mrs Cochrane. I walk to her house and she drives us from there. She's got a boy, Anthony, who's in the Infants, and another one, Andrew, at Moat Hill, the comprehensive. I like Andrew but he doesn't talk to me. I suppose it's because he's older than me. Noel and Rory Lambert come round to Mrs Cochrane's house for a lift, too. I don't like Rory Lambert. He's one of the tough lads at school.

Mrs Cochrane has a cat. The cat only likes me, because I'm gentle with him. I'm not loud and I don't chase him. I stroke him. He bends his head down and licks my hand. His little head bobs up and down. His tongue is rough, like he's stroking me with a Brillo pad. But I let him do it because he likes me and not the others. One time he climbed into my lap and started digging his claws into my school jumper, first with the right paw then with the left. He was staring ahead and his eyes were glassy, like he was somewhere else. I'd rather stay and stroke the cat and have him lick my hand than go to school.

I was with Neil Gordon, playing in the street by his house. Andrew Cochrane came along and asked if we wanted to see something in his Adidas bag. It was a magazine, the sort they sell on newsagent's top shelves. It was all naked girls. In the first photos the girl was wearing something and by the last one she was wearing nothing at all. There was another picture of a girl who was naked and tied up. She was in a normal room with a chair and a carpet, like our living room. Myself and Neil both looked at the picture. Andrew pointed to one of the girls and said, 'Her tits are massive.' I'd already seen her but had looked at all the black hair between her legs.

The first thing I could ever remember was being in the bath with my mum. She had the same tuft of black hair too. Maria had red hair on her head, so the hair between her legs might be red. Andrew pointed at the girl again and said, 'Phwoar.' I thought that was what you were supposed to say when you saw a naked girl so I repeated it, and Neil said it, too.

I asked Neil later where girls like that came from. He said his big brother Hugh told him there were whores in Moseley. I didn't know what a whore was. He said whores were girls who swore and were cheeky to their boyfriends. I still didn't really get it but I knew the magazine had to be kept a secret. I didn't say anything about it at home. Maybe that was a sin, and looking at the magazine was a sin, but I wasn't going to tell the priest about it in confession. There were some things you stayed quiet about.

Neil is my best friend at school. The first time he came to my house we found a spot in my garden where there was an ants' nest. The little black creatures were busy motoring in and out of a gap between two slabs. We boiled a kettle and poured it down the gap. We stamped on the ants as they dashed out. They seemed to be getting bigger and there were more of them. When the flying ants came out we ran back inside and watched them through the window. It had got hard to keep track of the ants as they darted left and right. The flying ones were impossible to kill, a scurrying little black cloud like a tornado over the paving slabs.

My other friend is David Hennessy. We decided we were both going to like football, to be like the older lads. I said so at home. I wanted to support Derby because they'd been the league champions but Dad said I had to support a local team. Maria supported Aston Villa so I couldn't like them.

I saw Birmingham City on television. They had Trevor Francis. He was young and had long hair. He wasn't rough like some of the others. I had seen *Star Soccer* on television where they said Ajax were the best team in Europe. They showed Johann Cruyff doing tricks with the ball, keeping it up in the air and balancing it on the back of his neck. He had long hair, too. I liked the name Ajax. Mum used Ajax for cleaning. I asked her to buy it instead of Harpic. The football team Ajax had a white shirt with a big red stripe down the middle. Birmingham had blue shirts with a big white stripe down the middle. I decided to be a Birmingham supporter, which meant I hated Villa. Dad said more Irish supported Villa. I didn't care.

Each Monday my mum gives me dinner money to pay the teacher. There's a few of the kids who don't pay for their dinners.

I don't know why. Another couple of kids have sandwiches instead of school dinners. The sandwiches look a lot better. You see the plastic tubs the sandwich kids keep their lunch in and you see the red flash of a Kit-Kat wrapper or something like that. Sandwiches are loads better than school dinners. The food is terrible and the dinner ladies shout at everyone and say they won't dish the food out until everyone's quiet. At the end of dinner we all stand up and you can hear the scraping of hundreds of chairs across the wooden floor. We all sing, 'God is great and God is good, and we thank him for our food.' No one teaches you how to sing it. You just learn it as an infant by listening to the bigger kids sing it, and as you go up the school it's the infants who listen to you. It's the same at the end of the day when we all stand up, say a prayer out loud and put our chairs on top of our desks, and the next morning we come in and take the chairs down and the whole thing starts again.

I go to St Michael's school. There are lots of Catholic schools in Birmingham. There's St Gregory's in Bearwood. We've also got St Agnes's and St Thomas's, both in Edgbaston. Then there's St John's in Balsall Heath and St Gerard's in Castle Vale. There's loads more. I suppose it's because there's so many Irish over here. Men on the lump or on the buses. Women who work as nurses, like Maria will, or looking after their children like Mum. There's Irish all over the city.

We watch *ATV Today* at home. Some people watch *Nationwide* instead, like Neil Gordon's family. A few nights back, the main story on *ATV Today* was about a boy. He was in hospital with his arm all bandaged up. He looked sad. He was my age. He was on *ATV Today* because he'd been out in the park and some

71

older boys got him and poured acid on his arm. His Mum was on it, too. She looked angry. She said she would go out looking for the boys that did it. The interviewer asked what would happen if she found them. She said, 'God help them.' She didn't say anything else, just looked straight down into the camera.

The next day there was a party on *ATV Today*. It was their birthday or something like that. They had a special cake in the shape of the ATV thing, like two ovals on top of each other. They said they would give it to the boy with acid on his arm.

The day after that, at the end of *ATV Today*, they said the boy made it up, that he poured the acid on himself. I wondered what happened to the cake. We talked about him in Mrs Cochrane's car. She said, 'Look what happens when you tell lies.'

When I was small, back in the Infants, someone hit me at school. It didn't hurt but I told my mum when I got home. She said, 'If someone hits you, hit them back.' A couple of days later there was a moon landing and we were allowed to watch it. While we were in the hall, waiting for the television to be wheeled in, David Hennessy hit me. Not hard, just messing, but I remembered what my mum told me and hit him back. The teacher came in. She shouted, 'Daniel Cronin, what are you doing?' I said, 'He hit me so I hit him back.' And that was that, I was sent to the classroom and wasn't allowed to watch the moon landing. I wanted to cry but held the tears back, because if you're a boy and you cry everyone makes fun of you.

I love space and rockets to the moon and all those things. That's why I read so many books about it. PG Tips tea used to have a card inside each packet with a spaceship on it and you could collect the cards and stick them in an album. I tried to fill it all in, opening the packets of tea as soon as they came into the house.

There's a television programme called *Tomorrow's World* where they say we'll all be able to travel into space soon, that we'll be able to live on different planets. That's what I want to do. There's another programme called *The Tomorrow People*, but it's made up while *Tomorrow's World* is real science.

The Tomorrow People can talk to each other just by thinking, and they can move anywhere just by thinking really hard. I'd like to do that but I know it's not possible, but living in space in the future will be. We'll be able to float and no one will shout and we'll all work together like the astronauts and scientists in UNEXA.

One time at school, last year, we had to write about what we wanted to be when we grew up and I wrote that I wanted to be an astronaut, so I would have to go and live in America to do the training. I described being weightless in space as you just float around the capsule. You can look out the windows and see all the stars close up. You can look down on Earth and wave to your family and friends, even though they can't see you. The teacher read it out to the class. Everyone kept quiet and listened.

The teacher called me up to her desk and asked me what else I knew about space. I told her the Americans had a Skylab, a place where they did experiments and sent information back to Earth. It used to have astronauts in it but not anymore. It was rolling around the solar system with no one in it to mind the instruments or do repairs. She told me to go on, asked me what I thought of

Skylab. I said an empty house didn't make sense. It needed someone in it, a family with the parents looking after the children and Skylab was the same, it should have someone in it so it wasn't just a lonely thing, slowly orbiting the Earth, getting misty and cold. She smiled.

I pretended to be an astronaut at home, playing in the front room. I spoke from the back of my throat so that my voice crackled.

'Danny to Mission Control.'

'Yes, Danny?'

'I'm going to land the capsule on the surface of the planet.'

'OK, Danny, you be careful now. Make sure you can breathe inside your spacesuit.'

'I will.'

As I land the capsule its spindly legs bend but they don't break. There's a cloud of brown dust on impact, rising up from the surface. I have a co-pilot, Neil Gordon, and we move into the airlock and wait for the door to slide open so we can step down onto the planet. We're wearing space helmets. They make our breathing sound really loud. Wearing a space helmet makes everyone sound like they have asthma, so if someone does have asthma it makes no difference.

I want to be the first one to set foot on the new world. Neil will have to go after me because I'm in charge of the mission. I have big space boots but I'm being really careful because the surface might not be firm enough.

As I step down from the last rung of the ladder I realise it's OK. It's just like a dry and dusty path, firm beneath my feet. I can walk on the new planet, take small and big steps, leap from one spot to another, much further than I could on Earth. I can see if they've got anything growing on the planet's surface, like bushes with strange green berries or other signs of life. There might be writing or drawing on a rock, or maybe a page from a book. A message from one world to another in a language I can't read.

'Danny to Mission Control.'

'Yes, Danny?'

'Everything's OK. Repeat, everything's OK.'

21 November 1974

He picks up the telephone, stabs his index finger into the round dial. He knows the number by heart.

The phone is answered by a woman's voice. '*Birmingham Post and Mail*, news desk.'

The pips interrupt like an alarm. The coin won't go in. The fecking coin won't go in. Someone's battered the phone. They've bent the coin slot. Nothing will go in.

'Hello? Hello?' The woman's voice is cautious but cheerful, like this might be a joke.

'The code word is Double X –'

The line goes dead. Dead as all the dead ever.

He looks back at the phone like it has insulted him. 'Vandals,' he says, aloud. He shakes his head.

He looks up the road. There is no other phone box in sight, just a large poster for Double Diamond beer on the wall in front of him, the two Ds overlapping.

He strokes his tongue along his top lip.

Summer 1974

I like the spaceship cards in PG Tips but I can't stand tea. Mum told me to try coffee. We had a jar of Maxwell House so I gave it a go. It was a little bit better but I still didn't really like it, so Mum bought Camp Coffee. It came in a bottle instead of a jar. The bottle had a picture of a soldier sitting down, while a brown man with a turban stood next to him, like he was the soldier's servant.

Camp Coffee was a thick, black liquid with a warm, sugary smell. It tasted good but the milk changed its colour from shiny black to dirty brown. I tried it without milk and liked that more. I put three spoons of sugar in as well. It's one of the things my family talk about. All the things they like that I don't, and the things I like that they don't.

We still buy a lot of tea because Mum, Dad and Maria all like it. Dad says he likes his tea so strong you can balance the spoon on top of it. When the kettle boils Mum warms the silver teapot with a splash of the boiling water. She scoops the tea into the pot. She has a spoon like half a little hollowed out ball, made of silver. The tea is little bits and strands of leaves. Some of them look like scratches and splinters from a dead matchstick. She covers the teapot with a woollen tea cosy. It looks old and the wool is all crusty. Mum told me her Mum, my Nana, knitted it, but she died before I was born.

You can get Ty-Phoo tea or PG Tips. I like PG Tips because of the cards in it and because of the adverts on the telly with the monkeys. They do funny things. The people who do the adverts, the PG Tips people, make it look like the monkeys are talking. One monkey, dressed as an old lady says, 'Tea, Mr Shifter?' to a monkey dressed as a removals man. It's one of those things everyone says. 'Tea, Mr Shifter?' For a while the PG Tips cards were all about spaceships and that was the best time. Now it's all about dinosaurs. I read the back of one of the cards and it said a Tyrannosaurus Rex was sixteen feet high. I told that to Neil at school and he laughed at me. He told Miss Blake but she said I was right. So now he looks stupid.

Mum and Dad tell other Irish people that I've got a Brummie accent. They also tell them I don't like bacon and cabbage. They think it's an amazing thing, but bacon and cabbage is disgusting. 'Imagine,' they say, 'doesn't like bacon and cabbage. Imagine.' They get a big lump of bacon and cook it in boiling water in the biggest saucepan. When a joint of bacon simmers you can smell the salt in the steam. If my mum lifts the lid a cloud rises to the ceiling. I hate cabbage, too. It's all slimy and bitter. The bacon gets plonked onto a plate and it's in a lump. There's a big block of white fat on the end. That's the bit I can't eat at all. I pick at the stringy meat but it's still salty.

Mum and Dad are pleased when I like something that's Irish not English, but I don't like anything Irish. Not the food, not the music, not mass. Mum and Dad asked me if I wanted to go to Irish dancing lessons because Maria went when she was younger. I shook my head. Dad tutted.

Our parish priest, Father Duggan, comes in to school. We like it because it means no lessons but he doesn't say anything very interesting. The nuns say Father Duggan fought in the Spanish

Civil War. I don't know what the Spanish Civil War was but it's hard to imagine the priest fighting. He's bald on top and the hair at the side of his head is grey. He wears glasses. I asked my dad about the Spanish Civil War. He told me communists murdered priests and nuns but it was OK because General Franco won in the end. I told him Father Duggan fought in it. Dad said, 'Good man,' and asked me what I thought of Father Duggan. I said he seemed alright. Dad told me when he was a little boy back home the priest would punch you in the head if you said or did anything he didn't like, or if he didn't think much of the look of you.

Father Duggan told our class the soul is like a room and we have to keep the room tidy in case God comes to visit. He said we will all die and when we do, we will have to spend some time in purgatory to pay off our sins before we get into heaven. He also told us we must honour our father and mother and always obey them.

Father Duggan tells us stories from the Bible. He told us about a woman who was going to be stoned to death. Jesus said, 'Let he who is without sin cast the first stone,' and everyone stopped what they were doing and dropped their stones. No one ever asks Father Duggan any questions because he's a priest so what he says must be true, but I wondered why they would do it to the woman in the first place. She was like the girl Seamus told me about, the one who got tarred and feathered. Maybe the woman in the Bible had gone out with the wrong person.

Father Duggan also told us the story of Judas. We knew it anyway but it sounded better when he said it. Judas betrayed Jesus for thirty pieces of silver. He handed Jesus over to the Romans and they crucified him. Father Duggan said we must never betray

Jesus in our thoughts or in our deeds. He said being like Judas was the worst thing you could be. I thought about it. Money was good to have but you wouldn't crucify someone for it. I didn't understand why Judas would do it. You couldn't just swap someone for money. Maybe he felt bad on the inside, maybe someone had done something bad to him and so he did something back. Father Duggan said the money didn't do Judas any good because he hanged himself, and because he committed suicide he could never get to heaven even if he was sorry for what he did. So that was Judas: just a lonely, dead body with no one to mind it, hanging from a tree, twirling in the air. And maybe the people just stood around, booing.

Danny's life was in the hands of the people back at mission control, but could he trust all of them? It would only take one of them to secretly be on the side of the Space Paras to ruin everything. He had to trust the people around him while knowing that one of them might let him down. One of them might be like Judas.

If the others at mission control found out and caught a hold of the traitor they might pour acid on his arm. That would teach him and it would stop others doing the same thing.

It made Danny feel lonelier than ever, just him alone in space, at the front end of the spaceship where it went down and down until it reached a sharp point, like the tip of a spear. That's what Danny was, the tip of the spear, and there might be a handful of other astronauts out there in their own capsules, all thinking the same way, all driving their spaceships. A space army on the opposite side to the space paras. Danny stepped back from the instruments on his control panel and floated for a while so he would not have to think about it.

Some of the lads at school are altar boys at mass. They get to do good things like putting the candles out after mass is over. They have a pointed cup on the end of a pole and they use it to put the flame out. If you're sitting near the front you catch the smell of the smoke, something warm and familiar settling down in your head like a cat on a cushion. There's a boy, Callum Conway, and he puts the candles out with his finger and thumb. I wish I was that brave but I'd be frightened of getting burnt.

I would like to be an altar boy, it would make mass less boring but they have to be there on Sunday for early mass. Sometimes our class has masses of its own and that's when I might get chosen to be an altar boy. Only the boys do it, not the girls. Girls get to do other things, like bring the bread and wine to the altar while everyone sings a hymn.

The school sends some of us up to the church for funerals, too. I was chosen for one, along with David Hennessy and Brendan Sutton. At the end of it, as they were carrying the coffin out, there was a big cross to carry, a giant crucifix at the end of a pole. I said I would hold it. It was too heavy for me. It waved around in the air, swinging from left to right. I was worried it was going to topple over and hit the lid of the coffin. Father Duggan took it back off me. He shook his head.

The three of us didn't go to the graveyard, we just stayed in the church after the big black cars drove away. The coffin had a big wreath of flowers on top of it like a noose. There wasn't a point to being in the church anymore. It was just an empty building with high windows and dust in the air and an echo if you spoke. Brendan Sutton said, 'Shit' and it ran around the church like a whispered secret.

There was a huge crucifix behind the altar showing Jesus nailed to the cross and bleeding. He had a tidy beard. All he was wearing was a small piece of cloth hanging down from his waist. You could see his ribs. The three of us walked slowly back to school. Brendan swung off the railings and sang 'Kung Fu Fighting.'

It's two miles from my house to St Michael's church. We walk there and back every Sunday. I hate mass but I can't say that. If I ever say anything Mum and Dad say, 'We won't take you to mass then,' and I know they mean it as a punishment but I can't think of anything better. But I also know how mad they'd be if I admitted it, so I pretend not going to mass would be a punishment.

We walk there, no matter what the weather's like. As we head up Hurst Green Road there's a big golf course to our left with only a line of railings between the course and the pavement. When it rains there's no protection and we get soaked. My mum tries to pretend it's all part of the fun. I hate it. I hate the hour of listening to hymns and the same prayers week after week. I hate it most of all when Father Duggan gives his sermon and it goes on for ever. There is a mass at nine without so much singing but we're never ready for that so we go to the eleven o'clock mass which is the longest one of all. It has a choir and everything. It can go on for an hour and a quarter. I try to make the time go faster by finding things to look at, but all they have on the walls is the Stations of the Cross, the story of the crucifixion from the Last Supper onwards. There's one picture of Jesus on his knees. All he wears is a small blanket and his crown of thorns. The blood drips down, the cross lies on top of him, much bigger than he is, and the caption underneath says, 'Jesus Falls For The Third Time.'

At school, the teachers and nuns say, 'That's all Holy God asks of you, just one hour a week,' but it feels longer. And some kids don't go to mass. They're the ones that have one Irish parent and one English one. But I've got two Irish parents so I'm dragged up there every week.

On our way we see men playing golf. It's always men. After we've passed the golf course we walk under a motorway bridge where someone has sprayed 'Moat Hill Boot Boys' and 'Daz Woz Ere' in big red letters on the wall, and after that we walk through the Green Hall estate. It's a bit like ours but it's blocks of flats instead of houses. You see children outside. There's a boy in his vest and pants who's out there all the time. He was playing with a bicycle tyre one morning, rolling it and chasing it. No one in my family ever says anything about him or about the other children playing outside. Maybe it's because they're English and we're Irish.

There's a pub on the estate, too, with a flat roof. It's called The Full Moon. It has a sour smell as you walk past, like it needs a wash. It has a sign high above the door and sticking out, a silvery-white full moon against a black and starless night. It swings and creaks in the breeze.

The confessional box is on the left-hand side of St Michael's. Our class troops up there a couple of times each term. We all say the same things: 'I was naughty, I was disobedient.' Some kids say, 'I swore.' I don't say that one. I don't swear much anyway but I don't want the priest to get mad at me.

You can't see the priest in the confessional box. There's a screen between him and whoever is in there. You kneel down on the bare wooden bench. You start by saying, 'Bless me father for I have sinned. It has been one month since my last confession.' It's usually longer than that but I always shorten it a bit so I don't get told off. After you've told the priest the things you've done, you say The Act of Contrition, and at the same time the priest says something but you can't make out the words because he mumbles and it's probably in Latin anyway. We always finish saying our things at the same time. The priest gives out prayers to say, some Our Fathers and Hail Marys. On the way back to school we say to each other, 'What did you get?' We all get the same prayers.

One of the only times mass isn't boring is Ash Wednesday. We go up to the church from school and kneel on the altar while Father Duggan dips his thumb in ashes and smears it on our foreheads, making a sign of the cross there. I don't know why. We all want to be the one with the biggest smear, and if you're lucky the mark of the ash is still there at home time, so your Mum gets to see it.

Dad buys the *Sunday People* and the *News of the World* on the way back from mass. He'll spend the rest of the day reading them. Some days me and Maria get sweets to share, a packet of Rolos or Munchies. It's OK if there's an equal number but there's always an argument if one's left over.

During the week my dad buys *The Sun*. They always have a big headline on the front page and a naked lady on page three. It's always a lady, never a man. On page four they have a cartoon. In

The Sun's cartoons the ladies all have long hair and big grins showing all their teeth. They have their hands on their hips and they
aren't wearing anything on top. Dad licks his thumb and turns
the page when Mum comes into the room.

Some Sundays my dad isn't with us because he's driving his
bus. One time, a priest at St Chad's Cathedral in town told him
he shouldn't work on a Sunday. My mum said he should have
said to the priest that if he didn't drive his bus people wouldn't
get to mass. My dad nodded. He didn't say anything.

One of the hymns we sing, in church and in school, is Faith
Of Our Fathers. Like the other hymns it's boring but it must be
important, too, because you hear people's singing get louder in
church when they stand up to do it: 'Faith of our fathers, holy
faith, We will be true to thee till death.' That last bit about being
true until death gets repeated at the end, like it's the important
part. I suppose it's a hymn about being a Catholic but most of the
hymns are about God, Jesus and Mary. At Christmas and Easter
they're more about Jesus. I don't know who decides what hymns
to sing. I suppose it's the priest, or maybe the priest gets told by
the bishop, and the bishop gets told by the Pope.

We only go to St Chad's when it's something special, like the
Irish Parade. That's when all the Irish people march through the
streets of Birmingham. They have it on the Sunday closest to St
Patrick's Day. We dress up in our best clothes and Dad wears his
suit. Our aunts and uncles send us St Patrick's Day badges. They
come in the post, attached to cards. It's usually a bit of a shamrock
set in a thing that looks like a harp. I don't like wearing it on the
way to school because none of the Feldon Street lads wear one,
even though Mum and Dad say I should wear it. It's different

when I get to school because lots of us wear the St Patrick's Day badge there. If a kid has two Irish parents you know they'll have a St Patrick's Day badge.

There's music at the Irish Parade, played by the Birmingham Irish Pipe Band. They have big drums that go through your belly with a rumble when they bang. They're always played by men, or the older lads. The younger ones have a small drum they hold in one hand while they beat at it with a club in the other hand. I asked my mum what the drum was called but couldn't hear her answer properly above the noise. Maria wrote it out later for me at home, *bodhran*. That didn't sound like what my mum had said, because I hadn't heard a 'd' sound.

Being at the Irish Parade is like you're in the middle of an explosion. You can feel it juddering your ribs, shaking them about. The Parade always starts with massive rolls of drums and you know something is about to happen. People raise Irish flags high on poles. The breeze laps at the material like it's licking them. The air crackles with the sound. There's one flag for each of the thirty-two counties. The Derry one is red on the left half and white on the right half, with the name of the county in Irish, *Doire*. At the head of the Parade stands the Irish flag, the green, white and gold tricolour, carried by a girl. When the flags catch a big breeze they stretch out like they're taking a huge breath.

There's thousands of us all marching through the streets at once. The big drums boom, the little drums bang. The pipes squeal. Some people sing along with the songs. The thud of thousands of feet echoes all around us. Some groups march together and have banners if they're from outside Birmingham. You see one for Nottingham, another one for Wolverhampton and another for Coventry. The Parade ends with the Irish national anthem, followed by mass at St Chad's. It's packed. They put loudspeakers up so the people standing outside can still be part of it.

The last time we went to the Irish Parade I was marching behind a big man and I tried taking the same length steps as him as we strode down the middle of the road. There were no cars or buses, just thousands of Irish people marching, our feet pounding the streets.

There were two men standing outside the Rotunda taking photographs of us. They weren't smiling or joining in. They just stood there with their cameras going click click click as we marched along. I waved at them but they didn't wave back. I thought we might end up in the *Birmingham Evening Mail*. There was a visiting band, too, over from Ireland, the Killishall Accordion Band. Maria told me they were from Tyrone, just below Derry. Their accordions moaned and wheezed, the sound rolling out over the crowd with the breeze, people singing along: 'No, nay, never.'

I asked my mum if we were the only people who marched. She told me the Orangemen marched in Derry and all over Northern Ireland on the twelfth of July. They started with a big bonfire on the night of the eleventh, with the Pope on top of it instead of a guy, and then the sound of drums and flutes and shouting went on all day on the twelfth. She said Catholics kept their heads down, that it wasn't safe because the Orangemen threw stones and sang songs about burning Catholics and being up to their knees in blood. She said you could feel the windows of your house shake as they marched past because they had a huge thing called a

Lambeg drum and the deep sound of it would go right through you. Mum said the Orangemen beat the Lambeg drum until their knuckles bled. It made no sense to me. No one would want to sing about being up to their knees in blood. The thought of doing that and having blood sloshing about and coating my legs made me feel sick. I might open my mouth and the blood would rush in, choking me. Thank God there were no Orangemen or anything like that in Birmingham.

You get people outside St Chad's selling *Republican News*, a newspaper about Ireland. I've seen my dad buy it but he never lets me read it and it isn't left lying around the house the way the *Sunday People* and the *News Of The World* and *The Sun* are. He reads it in his chair and passes it to Mum. When she's finished she folds it up and leaves it on top of the telly. Dad picks it up later and takes it somewhere.

I asked Maria about *Republican News*. She told me it was about all the bad things the British Army do and all the good things the IRA do. That made no sense at all because it's on the telly all the time that the IRA are bad. They shoot guns and set off bombs. The people on the news say, 'The IRA has admitted responsibility for the attack.' That's stupid. If you've done something bad you try to keep it a secret, not tell everyone about it. It's not like confession.

Dad has his chair in front of the television and on Sundays he puts the *News of the World* down to watch *Star Soccer* on ATV at two o'clock. If Birmingham are on I watch it with him to see Trevor Francis. My dad calls him 'Fransheen.' I've heard 'een' before. It's an Irish word for little. I suppose my dad thinks Trevor Francis is only a boy, but I'm a boy too. My dad's quite little. He has a lot of brothers but they all seem bigger and older than him. When they come over to visit they call him, 'Billeen.' He doesn't seem to mind. I would if I was him.

There was one time after mass when Dad must have been in a good mood. He bought the papers as usual but he also got me the *News of the World Football Annual*. I had never seen it before. It was a small book, smaller than the ones on the bookshelf in the classroom at school, but it was thick, with hundreds of pages. The book had details of all the football clubs. It listed who played for them and how much the player cost and which club they came from. I looked up Birmingham straight away. There was a whole page on them, with their record win and their record loss and their major honours. I saw they had played in the F.A. Cup final twice and had won the League Cup once, against the Villa. I showed it to Maria. She took the book off me and pointed to where it said Villa had won the F.A. Cup seven times, more than anyone else. I took the book back.

On BBC they have *Match of the Day* but it's on after ten on Saturday so I'm never up for it. But there are some Saturdays when Dad works late, not getting in until after eleven. I ask Mum if I can stay up for *Match of the Day* and she lets me. While the programme's still on we hear Dad open the door. I disappear and hide. I hear Dad ask Mum, 'Is Danny up?' She says no but I think she must be nodding her head or something because Dad will say something like, 'Shame, because I've got a sweet for him,' and he'll start rustling a sweet paper. That's when I come out from where I've been hiding.

One night I made her promise she wouldn't tell him. I pointed and looked her right in the eyes and said 'Promise.' So when he asked if I'd gone to bed and she said yes, he didn't say anything. Then I came out and said 'Surprise!' I could see by the way Dad looked at Mum that he was cross with her.

I took the *News of the World Football Annual* with me when we went to see my Uncle Pat and Aunty Kate in Balsall Heath to show it to my cousin Gerard, but he wasn't there. He's hardly ever there. He's eighteen. I heard the grown-ups say he's got a girl-friend.

The crater erupted. Danny was thrown back. He saw a red liquid gush out of it. Danny stood up quickly because the red liquid was already up to his knees. He heard a chuckling sound, like someone was glad to see him in trouble.

Back in his capsule, Danny read his space manual to see if there was anything about craters erupting and what might come out of them. There wasn't, but he remembered there was an extra part of the manual that the Brigadier kept to himself. Danny saw him reading it but the Brigadier had stuffed it in his pocket as soon as he realised Danny was there. Danny wiped the last of the red liquid off his spacesuit and stared at the rumbling crater.

I was in the house by myself. Dad was working, Mum was shopping and Maria was out with her friends. I was watching telly but the picture was rubbish. I moved the aerial around and saw something had fallen down behind it – a copy of *Republican News*. One of the headlines on the front page was, 'Are You A Deserter?' I'd heard of deserters before. They were people who ran away instead of joining the army. It said, 'There are organisations within the Republican Movement to suit all – young or old. There is a place for each of you.' I didn't know about that. Maybe it was something like the Boy's Brigade. Maybe you could join and have the uniform.

I opened up the paper. On the second page there was a letter to a cardinal. I wasn't sure what a cardinal was but I knew it was a kind of priest and was higher than a bishop. We had Bishop Casey come into our school once. We all had to stand up and say at the same time, 'Good morning, Your Grace.'

The letter in *Republican News* was being rude to the cardinal, saying he didn't do his job. I didn't get it, and didn't understand how they could get away with being rude to a cardinal.

I kept turning the pages. There was a prayer:

O, Sacred Heart of Jesus,
Look down on us today,
Make us strong, fearless soldiers,
Ever ready for the fray,
'Gainst Thine and Ireland's enemies,
Wherever they may be,
O, Sacred Heart of Jesus!
We put our trust in Thee.

Republican News was like a prayer book as well as a newspaper, and on the next page they were asking people to sell it. There was a coupon to fill in, like the ones in *The Sun* for joining the Army or the Air Force. It said, 'I would like to become a *Republican News* seller and help to spread the gospel of Irish Republicanism.' It was like they were talking about their own religion with their own priests. Maybe they had their own church, too, and a place like the Irish Centre.

The biggest thing in the paper was stories on two different pages about Michael Gaughan. I'd never heard of him. The way they talked about him made me think he was a saint, or maybe he wasn't real and it was a made-up story like the ones I read about the four astronauts, or the superheroes you got in comics. The newspaper said Michael Gaughan died aged twenty-four on hunger strike. That couldn't be real. There couldn't be a thing like a hunger strike, no one could do it, though Jesus went into the wilderness for a bit because that was where the Devil tempted him.

I read the second story about Michael Gaughan. There was one bit that said, 'There are some things which, when looked at and defined carefully, the Church tells us may never in any circumstances be done, such things at blasphemy, contraception, lies, perjury.' All the teachers at school say I'm great at reading and they get me to help some of the ones who aren't so good, but I really couldn't understand this story because I didn't understand what contraception and perjury meant, though I did get the bit about lies always being wrong. It made me think that maybe you did get a black mark on your tongue when you lied, after all. Maybe contraception and perjury left a mark too, whatever they were. The name of the man who had written the story about Michael Gaughan was at the top of the page. He was a priest.

At the back of *Republican News* they had letters people had sent in. One was by the men held in Long Kesh prison. They wrote, 'Go to Mother England if you must, and there discover, not equality but that you are just another stupid Paddy.'

I folded the paper up and put it back where I found it. I wiped my hands on my trousers. The Hugh Walters stories were more interesting. Newspapers were boring. Space adventures were better. There was no such thing as a hunger strike.

21 November 1974

He hears a sound he knows too well. The unholy rip of a bomb going off.

He blesses himself, murmurs, 'Sweet mother of Jesus.'

He catches the bus home. It is almost deserted, just him and the driver on the bottom deck.

Alone in his room. He plugs in his fire. The two, ash-grey bars redden slowly. He draws the curtains closed, kneels down by his bed, blesses himself, says a prayer for his parents. He sidles under the sheets. Whimpers in his dreams.

Summer 1974

The Irish Centre is in Digbeth, not far from the Bull Ring. As you walk in you're hit by the warm, sour smell of cigarettes and Guinness, wrapping around you.

I like the thought of going to the Irish Centre but when we're there I get bored. The singing and dancing don't end until at least midnight and I just want to go to sleep. We always meet up with the McAnespies. They're from the Bogside, too. They have a girl, Ailish, but no boys. Ailish and my sister go off together and I'm left behind.

Mum and Dad spend half the night saying hello to people they know from back home. There's one man who always comes over. He's small and looks more like a boy than a man, with rosy cheeks and a grin that goes right across his face. One of his teeth is missing. He sings some nights and there's shushing because people want to listen. He sings slowly like it's a hymn, but he doesn't sing about God. He sings about Ireland instead.

'Hello, Annie,' he calls to my mum as he comes over to our table.

'Bout ye, Jamesie?' says my mum.

I asked her about him. She told me he was from Belfast and she knew some of his family and friends. She'd met his wife a couple of times as well.

'Is his wife here?' I asked.

'No, she's at home with their children.'

95

'In Belfast?'

'No, here, in Birmingham.'

'He's a funny man. He's always smiling,' I said.

'He hasn't much to smile about.'

'Why, Mum?'

'His brother was shot dead back home.'

I took a gulp from my drink. The Coke fizzed, little sparkly bubbles on the surface, tingling my nose.

'Who shot him, Mum?'

'The Brits did, Danny, the Paras.' She took another large sip from her Campari and soda. It was bright strawberry red and looked like pop. The ice cubes twirled like they were dancing a reel.

I thought about what Seamus said about the Paras, how they ran into the Bogside shooting, and all the people were screaming and crying. I felt sorry for Jamesie, watching him make his way round the tables saying hello to everyone.

'Was his brother in the IRA, Mum?'

'Just listen to the music, Danny.'

The ceilidh moaned. The Paras shot all the Catholics on Bloody Sunday, Seamus said so. I was scared by the thought of them charging up the road. Shouting and swearing. Killing people. Kicking a dead body into the gutter. Probably laughing about what they were doing, about how much they were scaring the people and hurting them. I thought about a war film I'd seen where the soldiers dropped to one knee before they started shooting, like the way Mum and Dad and Maria and me knelt at mass, went down on one knee and blessed ourselves before we went home. I was sorry for everyone in Northern Ireland but glad the Paras didn't do it here. England was safe.

The Paras wore red berets. Maria told me the IRA wore black berets. Maybe that was how you told them apart. You'd know which one of them was coming up the road and you'd know whether to run or to cheer.

Mum took the last sip from her glass and put it down on the table. She looked around for my dad. A lot of the other women talked to each other around the tables but Mum didn't talk to other women. She sat upright in her chair with her legs crossed at the knee.

'There's always more men here than women, isn't that right, Mum?'

'Yes.'

'Are all the men like Jamesie, their wives at home with the children?'

'Not all of them. Some men come over to England and leave their wives and children behind in Ireland.'

'What does that mean?'

'A lot of lonely women is what it means, Danny.' She shifted in her seat.

The band started playing a slow tune. The lights dimmed. Couples swayed in the darkness.

'A man can come to the Irish Centre without a woman, but a woman can't come without a man. Have I got that right, Mum?'

'You get most things right, Danny.'

Jamesie smiled at everyone. I came out of the toilet one time as he was going in. He said, 'Hello, you young gurrier,' and rubbed the top of my head. I could feel the hardness of his wedding ring. A lot of men at the Irish Centre called me a gurrier, or a gossoon. One man called me a scut. I told Mum and she said, 'Well, you're not one, not often anyways.'

'What's a scut?'

'A very disobedient boy.'

'Jamesie called me a gurrier.'

'Well, he's a terror. Tell him that next time you see him.'

Jamesie had bright blue eyes. His tie was pulled down like he was late for school. Even as he was pissing in the toilet I could hear him singing, his clear voice echoing against the walls:

'But when ye come and all the flowers are dying, And I am dead, as dead I well may be, Go out and find the place where I am lying, And kneel and say an Ave there for me.'

I let the toilet door close. It sighed, sealing off Jamesie and his voice but I knew he was still smiling and singing in there without an audience, because smiling and singing was what he did.

Jamesie must have stopped smiling the time his brother got killed. Because Jamesie had a boy's face I could imagine tears rolling down it, and he'd go to sing but there'd be nothing there.

Every night the man on the stage at the Irish Centre says, 'And now it's time for The Siege of Ennis' and lots of people get up, even ones who haven't danced all night. They line up in fours. There's a lot of shifting about while they get it sorted so that men aren't facing other men. When the accordion starts playing people skip forwards then back, then move to one side, then the other. They grab the person opposite them and reel them around. A strong man can lift a lady's feet off the floor. I've seen men do it to Mum. My dad doesn't do The Siege of Ennis. At the end of the reel one line of four moves under another's arms, so they're facing a new set of four people and the whole thing starts again. The music is fast and it never pauses for breath. Everyone goes at it full speed from the first note to the last.

The Siege of Ennis is over when the accordion slows down and holds the one note for a long time. The dancers have red faces and they shake themselves down, like they've just stepped out of a shower. It must be how the Tomorrow People feel when they've jaunted to another part of the world or a new planet.

Some of the men at the Irish Centre play card games for money. You know there's been a big win when you hear a roar from one table. Through the night there'll be three or four roars, each one sounding like an explosion in one part of the room. My dad doesn't play. I asked him why. He said, 'Sure, it's not my thing. I'm not cut out for it. I just like listening to the music.' Maybe playing cards and dancing were like the drink, something he used to do but didn't do anymore. I asked him if you had to be clever to win. 'Not really,' he said. 'If you're dealt a bad hand there's not much you can do about it.' He lit another Woodbine and blew out his match. He drew hard on his cigarette.

We were at the Irish Centre one time when they had dancers. There was a sign up on the stage saying Conradh na Gaeilge School of Irish Dancing. I knew the first bit was Irish but didn't know how to say it. The dancers were mainly boys and girls of my age, with a small number of older ones. I counted and there was sixteen of them in all. The boys wore jackets, shirts and kilts, but the kilts were plain green instead of the tartan ones you see Scottish people wear on television. The girls had dresses with lots of stitches in patterns all over them, and all the girls had their hair done in tight curls.

When they walked onto the floor everyone walked off it to give them space. The dancers organised themselves into four lines. The music started and they all began doing the same dancing steps, looking straight ahead, their arms shot down by their sides. They skipped and kicked. The girls' hair bounced. Half the line stepped to the left and half to the right. They crossed each other and changed position. All the time this was happening the people watching were clapping or whooping. I edged along my seat and held Mum's hand. Her foot tapped.

At the end of the first piece the dancers all bowed and there was cheering and clapping. The band played another piece and it was even faster. Mum leaned over to me and said, 'It's 'The Rakes of Mallow.' This time the dancers jumped higher, kicking their legs out in front of them.

They got into circles and joined hands in groups of four. They got back into their lines, shot their arms down by their sides again and the music got even faster. The dancers were all clipping their shiny dancing shoes on the wooden floor at the same time until it sounded like running or drums. I thought the floor might collapse. One of the musicians on the stage picked up a bodhran and started hitting it fast with a little club. The bodhran had studs round the side. The man hit the studs with his club and it sounded like another pair of dancer's shoes. Everything in the room was a blur of drumming and dancers leaping and kilts and hair flying around and the bang-bang-bang of shoes on the floor.

The dancers all stopped at the same instant, along with the music, as though they'd all been killed stone dead. The dancers banged their shoes on the floor one more time and stood to attention. There was a second of silence before the room exploded in applause. Loads of people were cheering and whooping. Someone shouted, 'Good man yourself!' My mum leaned over to me and whispered, 'Wouldn't you like to do that? You could have lessons.' I shook my head. The dancers bowed again. She let go of my hand.

When the people are drunk at the end of the night they sing together, without any music from the stage. One man, maybe Jamesie, starts up with a song and the others join in, like they're replying to him. Someone might play a tin whistle, too, wailing along with the tune, running higher than it one minute, lower the next.

There's one they sing every night, 'Lough Sheelin's Side'. You can tell it's a sad song because it's slow. Mum told me Lough Sheelin is in the Republic and the song is about the Famine. I know that word because of what the teachers and nuns say about Africa. People over there are dying because they don't have anything to eat. They show famine on telly sometimes and you see flies on children's faces, even across their eyeballs, and the little children haven't the strength to wipe them off. I didn't know they had famine anywhere apart from Africa.

Maria told me the Famine killed loads of us and made more move to Britain or America. That was why there were so many Irish all over the world. It made me think of a book Mum bought me, *Destination Mars*, where Martians had escaped from a dying world. They wanted to come and live on Earth because they weren't safe anymore.

The singing at the Irish Centre was a bit like mass, where the priest called something out, 'Lord hear us,' and everyone replied, 'Lord graciously hear us.' At the Irish Centre it wasn't singing about God, it was singing about their home and sounding sad about it. It was different when it was a song about the IRA because it was usually louder and it sounded like a march or a jig, the words bouncing around the room, people tapping out the rhythm on the tables.

Danny got his tray and took it over to the serving hole. He pulled the lever but no food came out. He pulled again. He called mission control on his radio.

'There's no food,' he said.

'We'll look into it,' said the crackly voice, 'but you might have to go without this meal until the next one comes around.'

Danny felt his tummy rumble. There was no food. He would be hungry in his little space capsule, just looking at the wall and trying not to think about dinner.

He thought back to the astronauts' parade at the end of their training. There was music and they all marched, but even then Danny wished he was already on his mission. He wanted to do more than just march. Marching was boring. Other people liked singing and dancing but Danny didn't. He wanted to be in space.

Home is the house I live in, but when Mum and Dad say home they mean Northern Ireland. If someone at the Irish Centre asks, 'How are things at home?' it means they're asking how things are in Derry. My mum and dad do it, too. They'll say, 'How's things at home?' and home means Belfast or Cork or Galway or Dublin.

Wherever the person they're talking to is from. So, home means Ireland but it means a bit of Ireland and it can mean something different every time. My home is Birmingham but it feels like that's the wrong thing to say, that it shouldn't be my home.

The stage at the Irish Centre is big and very long. All along the wall at the back there is a painting of rolling green hills, a couple of lakes and a sun setting in the sky. The painting has one small cottage in it, in a valley, with smoke curling from the chimney. I asked Mum if it was Ireland. She said yes. I asked her what part. She said she didn't know and started looking around the room. I asked her to guess. She told me to leave it alone.

A man asked my mum to dance. My sister was with Ailish McAnespie. Mr and Mrs McAnespie were out on the floor, dancing together. There was just me and my dad sitting there, staring at the big silver ball hanging from the middle of the ceiling, right above the dancers.

The ball turned around slowly. The lights above the stage bounced off the little panels on the ball, casting small diamonds of light onto the dance floor below, the ball turning in a slow arc like the beam of a lighthouse, the dancers' shadows stretching out and swaying and falling away, like Peter Pan's shadow in Wendy's bedroom.

The band was playing 'The Galway Shawl'.
'She wore no jewels,
No costly diamonds,
No paint nor powder,
No, none at all.'

My dad wasn't saying anything. I went to the toilet and could feel a weight at the top of my nose, like I was going to sneeze. I'd had a nosebleed once before and the blood smeared my top lip like a moustache. I was worried there might be another nosebleed coming. I came out, walked up to my mum and the man and told her. My mum whispered at me to sit down. She turned her back, rested her hand on the man's shoulder and raised her neck. The song ended. There was clapping. Another song started straight away, 'The Black Velvet Band': 'She was both fair and handsome, her neck it was just like a swan.' The dancers swayed around me in the darkness, thin silver lights streaking across their faces. Their eyes reminded me of Mrs Cochrane's cat when it was digging into my jumper. A faraway look, like they were all somewhere else, somewhere they'd rather be. The floor sparkled. The smell of perfume like a forest in the jungle.

My dad was by himself. I went back to our table and sat next to him. Neither of us spoke. The band played the final song of the set. My mum swayed to the back of the floor, into the darkness where we couldn't see her.

The next day she shouted at me when Dad was out working, even though I hadn't done anything.

They play lots of different songs at the Irish Centre. They play 'The Men Behind the Wire' and everyone claps and cheers at the end of it. My mum doesn't sing along but a lot of people do. I asked Maria why people cheered after the song ended. She said it was because the song was about the internees in Northern Ireland, in Long Kesh, but that didn't help me at all. She also told me 'The Men Behind the Wire' had been banned and so had another song,

'Dance Up and Down with your Knickers in the Air'. I didn't know if the second one was a real song or not, but it sounded like it was more fun than 'The Men Behind the Wire.'

It's the same with 'The Broad Black Brimmer.' Mum told me a brimmer is a hat. I didn't know why anyone would sing a song about a hat, but everyone does sing it, and the singing is loudest when they do the final lines of the chorus. All the 'B' sounds make it feel like they're marching. When I asked Maria she said it was an IRA song and it was a bit about now and a bit about the Irish Civil War in the nineteen twenties. That was something else I knew nothing about. It made me wonder if Ireland had always been at war and it made me think I might be stupid because of all the things I didn't know.

When 'The Men Behind the Wire' ends the accordion holds the last note, the man up on the stage stretching out the instrument like a Spanish dancer's fan, people raising their hands above their heads to clap, or clenching their fists and cheering.

The people go back to their tables. The collection starts and everyone tosses coins in the bucket, the money clanking like a drum. Some people put notes in the bucket instead of coins. Maria leant over to me and said, 'That's for the families of the internees.'

The bucket had writing on it: An Cumman Cabhrach. I asked Mum what it meant in English. She said it was the Irish Prisoners' Dependants' Fund. That sounded like too many words to me. I told Mum the families were lucky to be getting all that money. 'It's not just for the families,' she said. I asked her what that meant. She shook her head.

There's another song about a man called James Connolly, with a line in it about the IRA and a place called Sackville Street. I asked Mum where Sackville Street was. She said it was in Dublin. I asked her who James Connolly was. She said, 'Just a man.' A few seconds later she said, 'The British shot him after the Easter 1916 rebellion. First, they shot him in the shoulder and the legs, then they shot him to death.' I asked her why all the songs were about men. She mumbled 'I don't know,' and looked around the room while the band played a waltz.

It's strange that the IRA get mentioned in songs my mum and Dad know because the IRA are bad, you see it on the news. I also still didn't understand why anyone would want to sing songs about things that happened so long ago. Maria's songs were all about being in love but at least they were about now, not about things that happened before I was born.

The Hughie Maguire record at home is also songs about Ireland and the IRA. There's one, 'The Merry Ploughboy,' where he sings about joining the IRA. It's also strange that the British Army shoot a lot of people in Ireland. I thought they were good. You can fill out a coupon in *The Sun* about how to join them. I didn't know why anyone would want to join the IRA, or sing about joining it.

At the end of the night the band plays the Irish national anthem and everyone stands up and sings it in Irish. Some of the men stand with their feet apart and their hands behind their back like they're soldiers. I don't know any Irish, to me it's all 'sh' and 'v' sounds, so I just make shapes with my mouth, pretending to sing along, and I'm all bleary eyed because I want to sleep. My mum and dad know all the words. I don't know if Maria knows the Irish national anthem or if she's just pretending, like me. She told me the English name for the Irish national anthem is The Soldier's Song. Everything's about war and soldiers in Ireland.

The British national anthem is different. There are hardly any words to learn, you just keep singing 'God Save The Queen' with other little words thrown in.

There was one line in 'God Save The Queen' I couldn't make out at all. I asked Miss Blake about it and she told me it was, 'Long to reign over us.'

All night at the Irish Centre you see pints of Guinness lined up along the bar. The barmen and barmaids never pour it right to the top. They pour it about two thirds of the way and let it settle before pouring the rest. Guinness is good to watch because it looks like a dark, cloudy milk at first until the white separates from the black and then it looks perfect, like someone has drawn a line with a ruler right under the head. It's like in *Journey To Jupiter*, when the astronauts look out of the window at a planet and describe it as a jewel on a black velvet cushion.

It's a shame when people drink the Guinness because it spoils the perfect shape. The Guinness settles back down but has a white smear on the inside of the glass, like the mark a foamy white wave might leave on a rock or the side of a boat.

Men stroke the glasses, rubbing along the glass with their thumbs. You watch them take a drink from their pint, smack their lips and say, 'It doesn't taste the same over here.' They drink it anyway. I asked my dad if he ever drank Guinness. He said he used to, back home. I asked him if the men were right that it tasted different over here. 'Oh God, yes,' he said, 'You've never had proper Guinness until you've had the stuff made in the Guinness yard on Grosvenor Road.'

'Where's that, Dad?'

'Belfast, son.'

'I thought Uncle Pat said one time that the Guinness brewery was in Dublin.'

'That's a different one, but the best Guinness comes from the North. The best of everything comes from the North. Wait til you catch the smell of peat fires on an autumn evening. It makes you blink and clears your head at the same time. You can't beat it.'

'Will we go back to live there?'

'One day, I hope. Maybe. I don't know. When you go across the water it's not always so easy to go back.'

Women don't drink pints of Guinness. They might drink wine, or they might drink pop, like me. The glass for my mum's Campari and soda looks bigger than the other Mums' glasses. She lifts it up by its long stem. She takes a sip from it. Sometimes she dabs her lips softly with a tissue after she's done it. All night she drinks Campari, except when she's dancing with men.

One time there were some boys at the Irish Centre of about my age but they all had long trousers and mine were short. They were standing by the fruit machine pretending to be big. The machine was hiccupping high-pitched noises. I asked Mum if I could play with them. I went over but they laughed at my short trousers and told me to go away. Later, I was sitting at a table with my dad. My mum was dancing with a man. One of the boys walked towards us, pointed and laughed before running off. Dad raised his eyebrows at me. I looked at the floor.

My dad drinks lemonade at the Irish Centre. I like Coke but sometimes they just get me orange. And it's not proper orange. It's not the stuff we have at home, orange squash, and it's not the stuff we have at Christmas, Corona orangeade. The orange at the Irish Centre has got little stringy bits of orange in it and the taste is too strong.

I spend all my time thinking about when we can go home and if we're going to get a taxi, which is warm and special, or whether we're going to get the night bus, which is cold and has people shouting on it because they're drunk. Dad told me people talk a lot when they're drunk and sometimes they talk too much.

My mum smokes a few of my dad's Woodbines when we're out. She gets him to go up to the bar each time her glass is empty. She holds it up to him and waggles it without saying anything. He carries it off and brings it back full, with a couple of fresh ice cubes dancing around the top. One time there was a slice of orange in it. Mum lifted it out with her fingernails, shook it, and passed it to me. I bit into it but it tasted all sour and bitter and I spat it out into the ashtray. I watched it get smothered under ash and matchsticks for the rest of the night.

My dad smokes a lot, not just at the Irish Centre but every day. He has one as soon as he wakes up. I saw a programme on telly, one of those boring programmes like *World in Action* or *Panorama*, and they talked about smoking. There were charts showing what happened if you had twenty cigarettes a day, or forty, and going right up to one hundred. I asked Dad how many he smoked. He said forty to sixty. I was disappointed. I wanted him to be higher up than that.

Nearly all the men at the Irish Centre smoke. You see them lighting up. Some shake the match as soon as they have lit their cigarettes, like they want to be rid of the flame. The dead match has a black head like a beret. Other men hold the match and watch the fire until it singes their fingertips. They leave the strands in the ashtrays, like little black wands. Some of the ashtrays are made of glass. Some are metal and have advertisements for beer on them, like Brew XI or Double Diamond. I once saw my Uncle Pat prod a cigarette in the bottom of a teacup. It hissed, like it didn't want to be put out.

There was one time when I recognised the man singing on the stage. It was Jim Hegarty. I knew him because he was on the buses, too. I think my mum was frightened of him because her voice always hardened whenever she mentioned his name. Jim was one of the ones who held the bucket and went around shaking it and collecting the money. Jamesie did it too. Jim Hegarty wrapped his arm around Jamesie's shoulder and said, 'Here's my boy.'

We had the police at our house once because of Jim Hegarty. He's an inspector on the buses and he had a row with two lads who didn't have the right tickets. They were going to beat him up. My dad pulled the fire extinguisher out of his cab and threatened to use it on the two lads. They ran off.

Mum told me the policeman who came to our house was taking a statement from my dad. He balanced a big pad of papers on his lap. It was a Sunday, just before mid-day. I could smell roast lamb. Lamb's my favourite. Mum gets it from Fred the butcher down the road. She buys it with the extra bit of bone at the end. She gives me that bit once the lamb's cooked and I pull the tight brown skin with my teeth. If we have lamb on Sunday I know we'll have shepherd's pie during the week, Mum turning the handle of the mincer, little strings of lamb squirming through the holes.

When we don't have lamb on Sunday we have chicken. I watch as my Mum draws the insides out of it. I look at the stuff that's come out of the chicken. The smell is bad, like something rotting, like a bin that hasn't been emptied in a hot week in summer. My mum points to part of the insides and says it's the chicken's eggs. They don't have shells. It's like the chickens aren't ready to be born yet.

Every Friday we have egg and chips. Mum heaves the big saucepan onto the stove, with the wire mesh basket inside it where the chips get plunged into the hot oil. There's a loud sizzle and crackle when the chips go in the wire thing, like they're angry about being cooked.

Fred the butcher has a daughter called Hazel. She's a teenager. My mum says that when I was born and she brought me home, everyone came to have a look. Fred and Hazel came. Hazel offered my mum threepence for me.

The policeman who took the statement was about the same age as my dad but he was taller. My dad is small. He doesn't have muscles on his arms. Fred calls Mum his darling. Mum laughs a lot when we're in Fred's shop.

Fred's window has plucked chickens with the necks flopping to one side. They look like they're sleeping, with the strange red bit across the top of their heads like wounds. They're stripped of all the feathers, little pin marks on their flesh. They might be better off dead, because they'd be freezing otherwise, on the cold shelves of Fred's shop, all stripped bare. People looking at them through the glass.

I don't know how they got killed. Maybe a bullet from a gun at the back of the neck, so all the meat wouldn't get ruined. Or maybe the chickens just died of old age like my grandparents did, too tired to carry on.

The policeman finished taking the statement. Dad had to sign a piece of paper that said it could be given in evidence. The policeman put his pen back in his top pocket. My dad walked him to the front door while Mum went back into the kitchen. The policeman whispered something to my dad. I couldn't hear it but the last words sounded like, 'I know.' He patted my dad on the shoulder like he was a grown up and my dad was a child.

Dad stood as still as stone by the front door. He whistled after the policeman had driven away, but it wasn't a tune, like 'Lough Sheelin's Side.' It was more like he was tired, or thinking about something. He rubbed his chin.

Over dinner, Mum said to Dad that Jim Hegarty would get him into trouble. Dad just carried on eating and didn't say anything. He didn't finish the food on his plate. He pushed it away and blessed himself. A piece of chicken lay across the middle of his plate. Mum saw me looking at it. She said, 'Do you want it?' I nodded. She speared the chicken with her fork, lifted it from his plate and onto mine.

Jim Hegarty sings 'The Men Behind the Wire' at the Irish Centre and he does raffles. Another man does them with him. He's called Walker. My dad always says hello to Walker and asks him what he's up to these days. My dad nods, listening, while Walker talks.

Dad doesn't have many friends but he goes around the Irish Centre with Jim Hegarty and even sells a few tickets. He chats with people as he makes his way round the tables. You see him lean in so he can hear them above the music, pressing his tie down if it leans too far away from his shirt. He lifts his eyebrows, like he's interested in what they're saying.

I was sitting next to Dad one night after the raffle. Our losing tickets were scrunched up on the table. My dad turned to Mr McAnespie.

'Do you know that man Walker?'

'I've seen him around and about. I know him to say hello to, you know.'

'Who does he mix with?'

Mr McAnespie shook his head and looked away.

The prizes are things like a bottle of whiskey, or a tin of biscuits, or an alarm clock, or a teddy bear. The money goes back to Northern Ireland to the families and things like that. I saw a little girl with the winning ticket. She took the teddy and held it tight.

One time Dad went to the pub with Jim Hegarty and drank again. He told my mum it was only shandy. Mum didn't talk to him that day.

I bought shandy once. Shandy Bass. I got it from Barker's. It was on the shelf along with the Coke and Fanta. My mum found the empty can in my school bag. Mum and Dad shouted at me.

I had a day off from school that week because of my asthma. My dad said it happened because of the shandy, that it made me ill. My sister joined in. I knew they were lying but I played along because I didn't have asthma at all. I just didn't want to go to school.

When I don't go, there's just me and Mum in the house. Dad's at work and Maria's at St Agnes's or out with her friends. My mum sings when my dad is not there. She lets me water the geraniums in the front room. They smell like the shops where they sell string and bamboo sticks and fertiliser.

I was also off from school one day in the week after the police came to take a statement from my dad. I asked my mum if she had ever been in trouble with the police. She told me about a thing that happened in Ireland when she was a teenager. There had been a bunch of them cycling to the dance but she didn't have a lamp on her bike. The policeman saw her and she got fined. 'The policeman called out my name and I had to stop.' My mum must have really wanted to go to the dance if she broke the law for it.

Danny saw a planet. It was a beautiful, green one, with hills and rivers. 'That's not where you're going Danny,' said the Brigadier over the radio, 'and anyway, it's not what it seems down there. It's a strange planet. It plays tricks with the brain.' Danny pressed down on the thruster, the engine got louder and the spaceship moved on, lumbering through the galaxy, leaving the green planet to turn in its slow orbit. Danny didn't mind the Brigadier's instructions. The green planet probably wasn't special and maybe he would get another chance to visit it after he had completed his mission, when he was an experienced astronaut.

~~The b~~

The other astronaut, the famous one, had been shot in the legs by the Space Paras. All the oxygen had rushed out of his spacesuit and he had died. You could hear the crackly laughs of the Space Paras as they ran off afterwards. Danny ran over to the hero but it was too late. Other astronauts would have to be the heroes now. Younger ones.

Danny wondered what they would do with the hero. Would they give him a funeral where a boy would have to carry a cross too heavy for him? Then he remembered. There was zero gravity on the planet. It would feel like it weighed nothing at all. Danny felt better.

My Uncle Pat and Aunty Kate live in Birmingham, too. They're in Balsall Heath, next to Moseley, the place where the whores are. When we go to Balsall Heath the adults spend the day sitting in the kitchen, talking about what Derry used to be like.

My aunt and uncle have the same picture we have of Jesus on the wall and they have another picture of a smiling man with big, perfect teeth. My mum told me it was John F. Kennedy and he was the first Irish Catholic to be President of the United States of America. I wondered if my aunt had met him. I asked if he was still the President. 'No,' said Mum. 'Someone shot him dead.' I looked again at his big, toothy grin and felt sorry he had died.

Maria doesn't go to Uncle Pat's anymore because she says she has lots of homework, but I still have to. We were there one Sunday and when they started talking I sat in the hall and bounced a red ball from one wall to the other. I could still hear them. Aunty Kate kept mentioning Sean O'Sullivan. My mum had worked in his house a few years before. Sean O'Sullivan was the biggest builder in Birmingham, even though he'd come here with only five pounds in his pocket. People said he built houses all over the country as well. There were vans and lorries with 'O'Sullivan' on the side of them, all over Birmingham.

Aunty Kate said, 'Why did you stop working for Sean O'Sullivan?' My mum didn't answer her. Aunty Kate asked the question again. I heard a chair scrape along the floor and the back door open and someone walk outside. I heard my dad say, 'Annie.' Another chair scraped back and there were more footsteps. It was quiet for a minute. Aunty Kate said, 'O'Sullivan's wife threw her out, and that's the long and the short of it.' Uncle Pat said, 'Why can't you leave it alone?' I picked up the ball and held it tightly to my chest.

The next day was quiet. I was at home and asked my mum what she did for Sean O'Sullivan. She said she just worked around the house. I asked her if she was a maid or a servant or something like that. She said she was. I knew what a maid was because I knew my mum came over to Brighton to be a maid when she was eighteen, long before she met my dad. She didn't marry him until she was twenty-four.

There was one time when we all went on a coach trip to the Malvern Hills. I walked up one of them with Uncle Pat and he pointed out kestrels hovering above their prey. They were holding their position in the sky, tilting their wings to keep still. They were like a helicopter as they stared at the little mice below, deciding which one they were going to swoop down on and eat.

I sat next to him on the coach on the way home. I was getting sleepy. He showed me a bundle of lights far away. They weren't strong beams like you'd get from a lighthouse, just a dim glow. 'That's Birmingham,' said Uncle Pat. I was surprised. It was just a place. It could have been anywhere.

Uncle Pat and Aunty Kate's house is right by the cricket ground. It's a big one. They play international matches there. You know when the West Indies are playing because there's tins of beer in the street. Red Stripe. I've only ever seen the empty cans all over the pavement when the West Indies play and you know something has happened because you hear a roar from the crowd, erupting and rushing out of the ground. The streets are empty because it's a Sunday but there's a noise of thousands of people all shouting at once and rattling tin cans, like a wave of shouts rolling over Balsall Heath and heading into town. It's like it's the West Indians' turn to be heard. We have the Irish Parade and they have the cricket.

Uncle Pat and Aunty Kate have Gerard, my cousin, but he's even older than Maria. I like Gerard but he doesn't speak to me much. I suppose it's because I'm a lot younger. We always go to their house because my mum and dad have bus passes, but there was one Sunday when I was little when they came to us instead. Gerard spent most of the day in our garden, throwing stones at birds.

One day at their house he was at the bottom of the stairs and called me over to him. He had a thing in his hand that looked like a periscope but it wasn't a long tube. Instead, it turned round towards the end. He was holding it against the wall. 'Look through this,' he said. 'It's magic. You'll be able to see through the wall.' I did what he said.

Suddenly, I was looking at my mum, my dad, Aunty Kate and Uncle Pat. They were caught in a circle, like they were inside a goldfish bowl, or one of the globes they have in the classrooms at school.

I watched the grown-ups locked in a small circle, talking about home.

October 1974

My mum sent me to Barker's on Saturday morning to get some shopping. She gave me her big white handbag to bring it home. I walked up the alley, the handbag smacking against my legs.

There were boys from Feldon Street school sitting on the ground outside Barker's. They laughed at my white handbag, my short trousers and because I was still wearing my school jumper out of school. I told Mum when I got home. She said they were jealous, that their Mums wouldn't trust them to go out for shopping, but I knew she was only saying that. They weren't jealous. They don't have to carry their Mum's handbag, they don't have to wear short trousers and they don't have to wear school clothes when they're not at school.

It's getting darker so I stay in more and watch television. People on the telly say kids should be interested in General Elections. They have programmes like *Newsround* that say it's important, so I try to pay attention. I know Harold Wilson is the Prime Minister.

The television people put party political broadcasts on before the news at six o'clock. Politics is an argument. There are two sides every time. I've started to look at the broadcasts. They all use the words 'since the war' at the end of sentences. I know they're talking about the Second World War but don't see the point because it was so long ago. Mr Dyer, the caretaker at our school, wears a green beret. Someone told me it means he was in the Royal Marines in the war but he's just a little old man.

I saw a party political broadcast yesterday for one party I hadn't heard of before. They're the National Front. There were loads of Union Jacks everywhere in their broadcast and a huge one at the end, rippling in the breeze.

It's fun to draw the Union Jack at school. The swastika is fun to draw, too. We show each other how it's done. There is a girl who is good at Art and she showed the rest of us how to do a star out of two triangles, one the right way up and the other upside down. I tried but couldn't do it on my own. I'm no good at Art. If I was English and liked the Union Jack the boys from Feldon Street wouldn't laugh at me.

It's not only the flag. England has St George as its patron saint and he killed a dragon. Ireland has St Patrick. My dad said St Patrick got rid of all the snakes in Ireland but that's not as good as killing a dragon.

There were a lot of strikes at the beginning of this year, people not turning up to work because they wanted something. We had to cook on a camping stove in the living room when there was no electricity. There was a blue canister at the bottom of the camping stove with the gas in it. There was a ring at the top. You turned a handle on the canister and you heard the gas hissing like a snake. Mum lit the gas with a match and there was a little roar, like when the wind's blowing outside but it's dark and it's night and all the windows and curtains are closed so it sounds like it's a long way away.

Neil Gordon told me about going camping with his Dad. I've never been camping. It's not the sort of thing my dad does. But cooking with the camping stove felt like we were camping for real. My dad was on nights, so it was just me, Mum and Maria sat around the stove, cooking in the dark, the only light coming from the flame.

My mum put beans in a saucepan and placed the pan over the flame. The sound changed. It got softer and lower, like the flames knew the fun was over and they'd have to get down to work. I looked at the flames and thought about the pan getting hotter and hotter. Mum gave us bread and butter. We had special little sausages too, cooked with the beans in the pan. We ate our dinner sitting around the stove, the only light the little orange and blue flames.

I looked over at my mum's face. It was in shadow. I could only see the line of her nose and the sharp whiteness of her teeth, her head bending down, the paleness of her skin, her forehead lit up by a blue flame. Strands of Maria's hair turned golden in the light. The only thing that scared me was the thought of the gas running out, of there being no light and me left in the dark.

After the strike was over, I heard my mum telling Mrs Gow across the road that it was the first time she had felt properly hungry since she was a young girl in Ireland. I didn't want to be left out so I said it was the same for me. Mum told me to be quiet, that I didn't know what I was talking about.

Neil's whole family went on a camping holiday last summer. We didn't go anywhere. Last Easter, Dad and Maria went back to Ireland. Me and Mum stayed here. I asked Mum why we didn't go, too. She said it was because of my asthma and because of money. She said she'd go back to work when I went up to St Thomas's. She'd maybe become a dinner lady or a cleaner. I didn't like the thought of her having a job like that. She might be cleaning toilets. She said that's what Dad thought, too, and he'd like to find a way to get more money so we could all go on holiday together, but it was hard to get extra money when you were only a bus driver. I asked if he could get another job. She said he didn't have the time, he worked all the hours God sent, and how could you get more money unless you had the time?

If we had stayed in Northern Ireland we might have had more money. There's a big shipyard in Belfast, I'd seen it on the telly, Harland and Wolff, and my dad might have got a good job. I mentioned my idea to Mum. She told me Harland and Wolff didn't give jobs to Catholic men, and if they did the Catholics wouldn't be safe there because they'd be badly outnumbered. She said a lot of job adverts in papers in the North said, 'Catholics need not apply.' I asked her if Catholic women could get a job at Harland and Wolff. She told me women didn't work in shipyards but there was a shirt factory in Derry where some of the women worked. That didn't sound so bad to me and you might get free shirts. Maybe she could work in the shirt factory and Dad could drive a bus, as long as there were no barricades, in which case being a bus driver would be dangerous.

Before I got into bed I said my prayers and looked out of the window. There was a heavy fog, the sort of thing a ship built in the Harland and Wolff yard might get lost in, its engine trembling, its siren calling for help. The ship drifting slowly, the dark waves lapping up against its sides, everything swaying.

The fog drifted in front of the street lights, all milky grey and white, like the whole world was a pint of Guinness that had been disturbed and was trying to settle down again so God might take a sip and smack his lips.

Danny looked at outer space and outer space looked back. The stardust twinkled. The spaceship rumbled like an old bus. Danny wished UNEXA had more money so they could have bought a bigger and better rocket.

He looked at the ship's instruments. Most of them were set dead straight in the middle of the dial, but one of them trembled a little. Danny wondered what it meant.

The lights flickered. Danny was frightened they would go out and he would be left in the darkness of outer space. He said a prayer.

Dad was working late on Saturday night. Maria was at a friend's house. Mum bought a bottle of pop, Tizer, and poured me a big glass to have after my dinner but I knocked it over on the carpet. She shouted and sent me to bed.

From the top of the stairs I could see the little outline of light from the living room. I crept down to see if she'd stopped being mad at me.

She had a deck of cards in front of her, on the coffee table. Some of them were face up. I saw an Ace of Hearts with the two, three and four layered neatly on top of it, so you could see all of them at once.

She knew I was there but didn't turn around. She pulled another card from the top of the deck and held it in mid-air.

'What are you doing, Mum?'

'Playing cards.'

'By yourself?'

'It's a game you play alone.'

'What's it called?'

'Patience. I'm no good at it.' She glanced at me.

I reached over and gently took the card from her hand. It was a queen. It was smooth to touch, like someone had polished it.

'Can I stay down here, Mum?'

'You can, Danny.' She put her arm around me. I stroked the card. It looked like the Queen was smiling.

Back at Mission Control, the Brigadier shouted at Danny, his voice all crackly and harsh through the radio.

'You're supposed to call in every day, Danny,' said the Brigadier, 'so we know you're safe and the mission can go ahead.'

'I'm sorry,' said Danny, 'But there's a needle trembling on my control panel.'

There was silence for a moment.

'Which needle?'

'The one in the middle.'

Danny could hear the Brigadier draw his breath and mutter to someone. Another voice whispered back. They had a secret, like grown-ups sometimes do.

'Be careful, Danny,' the Brigadier said. 'It might mean there's a meteor shower heading your way.'

The news today was all about bombs in pubs in Guildford. I asked Mum where Guildford was. She said, 'Somewhere near London. A long way from here.' The IRA did the bombings. Five people were killed and a lot more injured.

The television showed the first pub with its front blown off. It was like the pub wasn't made of bricks anymore but something you could crumple and fold. The pub was called The Horse and Groom. You could still see the name painted on the front, along with the name of the brewery: Courage. The second pub was called The Seven Stars. I liked that name more. It felt like something exciting might happen in there, something to do with space. I knew Northern Ireland was dangerous but I thought England was safe. But Guildford is a long way away, Mum said so.

The news said it was a soldiers' pub. I wondered who decided that and whether soldiers had to stick to one drink like the Irish and the West Indians.

Daily Mirror, Monday 7 October 1974

They were four teenagers who had been in the army for less than a month. Four rookies who had never seen a shot fired in anger, let alone fired one themselves. But they died horrifically violent deaths, victims of the vicious bombers who struck at two pubs in Guildford, Surrey, at the weekend, killing five people and injuring sixty-five…

Once again the terrorists will be congratulating themselves. They have killed people. They have maimed people. People having a quiet drink in a pub in a peaceful English town on a Saturday night. Some of them civilians. Some of them soldiers. Most of them young. **It was a brutal reminder**

that the IRA are still in business. Their own remorseless business. DEATH.

My parents had some people over a few nights ago. Maybe there was something to celebrate. They bought loads of drink – bottles of Guinness and whiskey and Campari. Me and Maria had to stay upstairs. I wanted to go down and see everyone but Maria said we weren't allowed. It was a shame. Maria was mad as anything because she wanted to be down there with them.

We heard the people arriving, my dad saying 'How about ye?' and the people replying 'Dead on,' or 'Sound enough,' followed by 'How's yourself?', or 'What's the craic?' We heard them talking below. Every now and then there was an explosion of laughs, and after the laughter faded away there'd be a few coughs, like people were settling themselves down again. I could smell the cigarette smoke and the beer, winding up the stairs.

As the night went on there was singing. One man started singing 'The Mountains of Mourne' and everyone listened quietly. It was Jamesie from the Irish Centre, the voice high-pitched for a man but it wasn't trembly like my dad's singing voice. It rang loud and pure, like Jamesie had been singing all his life and he was thinking about mountain streams or something like that. After he finished there was a silence, until a few deeper voices started 'The Broad Black Brimmer' but there was a lot of shushing and they stopped. I heard my mum say something about the neighbours.

Most of the talk was quiet but one man said, 'It's been coming,' and another one said, 'They need to know what it's like.'

I was still awake when the people started to go home. I went out onto the landing and peeped down. The man who was leaving looked like the man from the Irish Centre, the one who danced with my mum. She had her hands on his shoulders. He was whispering to her. I thought I heard her say, 'Darling.' My dad wasn't there.

Maybe she didn't say Darling. Maybe she said Dublin instead. Maybe that's where the man was from.

Mum spent the next day cleaning up. I was helping by emptying the ash trays, tipping them into a metal bin but doing it gently so I didn't send little clouds of grey and white ash into my face. Mum said, 'Mind your chest, Danny.'

I saw something on the floor behind the sofa. It was golden and shiny. I knew what it was. It was a bottle opener for beer.

I turned it over in my hand. The handle was a figure. The bit leading up to the jagged bit was arms. The figure had long hair and no clothes. I realised it must be Jesus. I asked Mum. She laughed and said no. She took it off me and put it in the kitchen drawer where we kept the knives and forks. She went back into the living room and switched on the vacuum cleaner.

I got the bottle opener out of the drawer and looked again. That's when I saw that the person had no mickey, and the chest was big, rising up from the surface. It was a naked lady with her long hair spread out and her arms raised up. She looked like the ones in *The Sun*. My mum was shifting the vacuum cleaner around, the noise moving up and down like it was trying to say something important.

Later, I got the bottle opener out of the drawer and had another look. She looked like the girls in the magazine that Andrew Cochrane had.

Danny opened the drawer. There was a tool in it, one he hadn't seen before. It was jagged at one end, little spikes of metal around a hole, and long at the other end like a runner bean.

'I found a tool,' Danny said to the Brigadier, over the radio.

'There's lots of tools on a spaceship,' replied the Brigadier.

'This one seems different. Do you want me to do anything with it?'

'Just put it back, Danny. There's other things to do right now, things you need to focus on. Do your best to keep the spaceship on course. Things might get difficult over the next few days. Your friends down here are thinking about you.'

November 1974

On Bonfire Night we all wanted the school day to end so we could get home to watch the fireworks. Miss Blake tried to keep us interested by telling us about witches and getting us to write a poem or draw a picture about them. I wrote one about how witches always wear black. I got away with having 'black' and 'cat' as rhyming words at the end of lines. Most people drew instead but I'm no good at drawing. They drew witches being drowned or burnt alive.

That night I looked out of the window, watching different parts of the sky get lit up by showers of brightly-coloured sparks. Dad was at work. Mum was looking at her old photographs. Maria was listening to music in her room. I opened the back door and caught the warm smoke of a bonfire. I thought of the Guy on top of it, a bundle of old clothes, newspaper and straw, shrivelling up in the flames. A banger went off and the sky shook.

My mum told me to shut the door because I was letting the cold in. The sound died but there were still bursts of colour and light in the sky, spreading out like bunches of flowers. When the fireworks stopped the darkness seemed deeper, like everything was black from one end of the world to the other.

The television said there'd been another IRA bomb in a pub. This time it was The King's Arms in Woolwich and there were two people dead. I asked Mum where Woolwich was. She said, 'London.' London sounded like it was as dangerous as Derry. And pubs sounded dangerous, too.

The television showed the pub after the explosion. There were piles of dust everywhere and all the furniture was smashed up. The reporter said the bomb was thrown through the window. It made me think it might be someone from Northern Ireland who did it, someone who was good at throwing because they might have thrown stones and petrol bombs before.

The camera looked around the area outside the pub. There were a lot of flats. It looked like the Green Hall estate. I thought about The Full Moon. I wondered what would happen if it was blown up. Would people blame us because we were Irish?

Daily Mirror, Friday November 8 1974

One man died last night when bombers struck at off-duty soldiers in London. At least twenty people were injured in the blast – some of them critically. The victims were all drinking in the packed lounge bar of the King's Arms pub at Woolwich – only a few hundred yards from Woolwich barracks... Soon after the blast an anonymous caller rang the Daily Mirror and said: 'The codeword is BASTARDS. We have planted bombs. The first one has gone off at Woolwich...'

A soldier who was in the pub said: 'One of my mates was standing by the dart board. He was blown through the window and is in hospital now.' Other soldiers told how on

Wednesday night a man with an Irish accent
walked into the pub and looked around.

The IRA are like an army but they do bad things, not like the British Army. They're the heroes in the film, *The Battle of Britain*. I said this to Maria and she said that wasn't the Army, it was the Royal Air Force, the RAF. She also told me we were not to like the British Army because we were Irish, and the words of 'The Men Behind The Wire' were about the bad things the British Army did in Ireland, especially internment. I only knew about internment from what Seamus told me, but the Royal Air Force still sounded great. I thought I might join them when I was older, before I became an astronaut. I could become a fighter pilot like Whiskers Greatrex in my science-fiction books.

There was a coupon you could cut out in *The Sun*, and if you gave them your name and address they'd send you stuff about how you could join the RAF. I tried filling it out but my writing was too big. It went over the line and onto the next story, which was about a collection *The Sun* was organising, to buy tellies for the brave soldiers in Northern Ireland.

I was in the living room. Mum and Dad were watching the news. It said there'd been a bomb in Coventry, near Birmingham. They said the bomber had blown himself up and they only identified him because he was carrying his National Insurance card. They said his name was James McDade.

'Jesus, Mary and Joseph,' said Mum. 'Jamesie.' She blessed herself.

'God have mercy on his soul,' said Dad.

Jesus looked out from his picture with blood running down his palms, his barbed wire wrapped heart in the centre of the frame.

The television showed the bomber's photo on the screen. He didn't look old like my mum and dad. He looked young like my cousin Seamus, but it wasn't Seamus. It was Jamesie. Definitely him. The same smile with the missing tooth, the top button of his shirt undone, his tie pulled down. I thought about the times I had seen him at the Irish Centre, singing 'The Wild Rover' or 'The Broad Black Brimmer.' I thought about him at the bar at the end of the night, drunk, and no one could stop him singing but no one wanted to because his voice was so beautiful. I thought about him that night at our house, his high, clear singing rising through the house like something pure and special, like someone in the choir at St Michael's, but not singing about God. Jamesie sang about the world instead of heaven. And now he was on television, but not for singing.

There were programmes like *Opportunity Knocks* where ordinary people got up and sang. That's what Jamesie would have been good at. *Opportunity Knocks* had a clapometer which showed you how many people in the audience liked what they saw and heard. Jamesie would have scored the most, the needle on the clapometer going up to one hundred as everyone clapped and cheered.

Dad left the house, jingling a few coins in his pocket. I didn't know where he was going. He didn't drink anymore so he wouldn't be going to the pub. There was a phone box at the bottom of our road but I couldn't think of anyone he'd be phoning. Maybe he was going to ring Northern Ireland to tell them about

Jamesie. The people back home would want to know. Jamesie's brother had been killed before. It was tough for them. It wasn't fair.

'People will be going to the funeral, Billy, lots of them. Should you go as well, pay your respects?'

'Sure, I'd never get the time off work. And I didn't know him well anyway.'

'He has two children, you know. I've met his wife. And you've told me you've spoken with him at Glebe Farm.'

'I know, I know. There'll be a collection. We'll give to it instead of going. I'll help with it at the Centre. They'll probably organise a benefit dance or something.'

'There'll be more than a collection and a dance, Billy. The boys will want revenge for Jamesie. He was from Ardoyne. You know what the Belfast fellers are like. Wild mad they are. They run everything over there. That lot are all Provos.'

'Annie, if any of the neighbours ask if we knew Jamesie, say we didn't. Let's keep our heads down. That's how we manage in this country, by keeping our heads down and doing what they want us to do. We co-operate. We do their work for them. That's what keeps us safe.'

'I don't feel safe, and what do you mean about doing their work for them?'

'I mean I drive my bus.'

'Billy, is there something you're not telling me?'

'No. No.'

In bed, I thought about Jamesie. He was always smiling, but you wouldn't smile if you were planting a bomb. I didn't know why a smiling man would do it. You'd think it was something only an angry man would do.

Mum said men from Belfast were Provos. I knew that meant IRA but I didn't know why. They didn't even sound the same, IRA and Provos. The only interesting thing about Provos was the rhyme. Pro-vo. She also said they'd want revenge. I knew what revenge was. Someone did something bad to you, so you did something bad to them. I'd got in trouble for that at school.

Mum and Dad said to tell a lie to the neighbours, to pretend they didn't know Jamesie. They'd always said to me and Maria to tell the truth. There was a story in the Bible about when St Peter pretended not to know Jesus when people asked about him. That was a bad thing and we were doing the same. Dad told Mum we needed to keep our heads down. Maybe that made it OK to pretend we didn't know Jamesie.

I said a prayer for him, my Matthew, Mark, Luke and John prayer.

The bombs had travelled from Guildford to Woolwich to Coventry, creeping their way towards us. They would be here soon. In Birmingham.

Mum and Dad were watching the telly downstairs. Someone must have told a good joke because I could hear laughter and a round of applause from the audience on the programme, but Mum and Dad weren't laughing.

The next day Mum took me by the hand. We walked to the bus stop, passing Barker's on the way. The headline in the paper said, 'Man Killed In Blast Riddle.'

We caught a bus to Sparkbrook.

'Where are we going, Mum?'

'To pay our respects.'

The house looked like ours except the curtains were drawn. It had a grey front. It was joined to another house on either side, like ours was. There was a long row of houses in the street all looking the same. They were huddled together like they were cold. Tiny gardens out the front. It could have been our own street.

A woman answered the door. 'How are you Annie?' she said. 'Long time no see.'

'I'm fine thank you, Mrs Callaghan.'

'Come in, come in. She's in the back room, God love her.' The lady hadn't said anything to me.

The front room looked like ours, too, with a glass case. There was no one in there, just a carefully folded tricolour on the window sill. There was also a black beret, a pair of sunglasses and a pair of black gloves, all nestled together behind the net curtain. I stood and looked at them, at the glasses looking back at me, the two black eyes like a big, hungry crow. I could see myself in them. It was like the sunglasses were asking me a question, asking me what I thought about the flag, the beret and the gloves.

All the women were crowded into the back room and the kitchen. A couple of them wore black armbands. There was one woman on the sofa with a small child on either side of her. The three of them looked embarrassed, like they didn't want the attention. They were holding hands, all of them linked together like a chain.

My mum went forward and bent down on one knee, leaving me a step behind. 'I'm so sorry,' she said. 'Sorry for your trouble.' The woman nodded and said, 'He just went out and never came back.' She whispered it as though it was a secret. She looked younger and thinner than the other women in the room. She had a small bruise under her right eye. The two little boys had freckles and round faces. The three of them together looked like a religious painting, with the most important one in the middle. She looked like the Virgin Mary but she wasn't smiling. She even had a shawl over her head, but hers was black, not blue.

A woman handed my mum a cup of tea. She tried to give one to me, too, but I shook my head. She went away and came back with a Jaffa Cake. She held it out with the spongy bit towards me. I smiled at her. I ate it slowly, taking the orange bit off first with my two front teeth. All the while I looked at the two little boys. One of them stared up at me. It wasn't because he wanted my Jaffa Cake. He just looked at me like he was a tiny, helpless thing, even littler than he was, and lost, a little chick without the big bird to look after it. It made me think of the day I was in the Infants and thought my mum had forgotten about me.

Mum stroked the back of my head. The whispers of the women were all around us, as though gas was hissing. It was like they were all murmuring 'I'm sorry for your trouble' at the same time. An old woman in black, sitting in a chair, rocked back and forwards, mumbling, praying, her finger and thumb worrying along a thread of rosary beads. There was no singing at Jamesie's house, just the sharp whistle of a kettle as it came to the boil, gushing a small cloud of steam. I thought of all the times Jamesie must have sung in the house, from room to room, and how alive it would have felt. Now it was not alive at all.

As we left the back room, I saw the rosary beads tying up the old woman's fingers, digging into her skin. I saw the two black gloves on the window sill in the front room. They overlapped, like they were holding hands too, trying to comfort each other.

Someone had laid a big wreath of flowers in the garden. They were white and in the shape of a harp.

A man on the other side of the road wore a big coat. He held a notepad and pen. He wore a camera around his neck.

I couldn't think of anything to say on the bus back home. Jamesie was sealed in his coffin. I imagined he was still singing, his voice echoing beyond the grave. All the Irish people in Birmingham hearing it and thinking about him, about how he had died, what he had done.

My mum wrapped her arm around me tightly. She was murmuring Hail Marys, doing the rosary without the beads, 'Hail-Maryfullofgrace…' The bus rattled. I looked out of the window. Birmingham was getting dark.

Mum went to take my hand as we got off. I said, 'You know Danny Boy, the song?'

'Yes.'

'What's it about?'

'It's about someone who knows they're going to die soon.'

The bus pulled up at our stop. As we walked down the road back to our house, Mrs Gow was walking up the other way. She walked quickly like she was trying to get away from something that annoyed her, her big handbag draped over her arm, banging against her hip. She didn't see me and Mum until we were right by her and she had to stop.

'Hello, Mrs Gow,' said my mum. 'How are you?'

'Not bad I suppose, but this country's going to the dogs,' she snapped. She sniffed, like there was a bad smell nearby and walked on, bustling up the road.

That night, the four of us went to the Irish Centre. Someone had handed out pieces of paper. They were on every table:

On November 21 at 3:30 the remains of our comrade, James McDade, will be escorted from Coventry to Birmingham and on to Belfast. We consider it the duty of all Irish people to be present at Coventry mortuary. The coffin will be draped in the tricolour that covered the coffin of Michael Gaughan who died on hunger strike. Transport will be available for mourners.

I picked it up and saw that Michael Gaughan was real after all. I asked my dad, 'Who was Michael Gaughan?'

'Can't you read? He died on hunger strike.'

'Was he in the IRA?'

He didn't answer.

'Are we going to Jamesie's funeral, Dad?'

'No.'

'Where will he be buried?'

'Belfast, I suppose. Milltown cemetery.'

'It says here it's our duty to go to Coventry.'

'No, we're not going.' He took the piece of paper from me. A minute later he said quietly, 'We keep our heads down.' He slid the paper into his pocket. 'I'm going to talk to that feller over there.' He went and joined some other men by the fire exit.

I now knew hunger strike was a real thing but still didn't understand how anyone could go through with it. You'd have to eat if you were hungry. You just couldn't bear it.

I looked around. Someone had left a copy of the *Daily Mirror*. The headline was, 'Uproar Over IRA Bomber Parade.' It was all about Jamesie. It said hundreds of Irishmen from all over Britain were expected to turn up in Coventry and they'd all be wearing the IRA uniform of black beret and dark glasses.

I didn't know about the dark glasses. I thought that was just a thing at Jamesie's house. I couldn't see why anyone would wear sunglasses in November. The *Daily Mirror* also interviewed an M.P. who said the people who turned up for Jamesie would be torn to pieces by an angry crowd.

The people around me at the Irish Centre were people who might go. I was always bored there but I was scared by the thought of the people being torn to pieces. I looked at the door. Anyone might come in. There might be an angry crowd waiting outside.

There was no ceilidh on the stage. Instead, there was just one man playing the Irish pipes. It was a really slow tune. I asked Mum about it. She said it was a lament. I listened again. The pipes wailed through the room like someone crying, like the person was in pain, their voice trembling. I thought about the *Daily Mirror*. Jamesie was famous, more famous than if he'd been on *Opportunity Knocks*.

Two old men were at the table next to us, with pints of Guinness in front of them. One of them took a long, slow sip from his glass. He said to the other man. 'Did you even know where the Coventry telephone exchange was, had you ever heard of it before?'

'I did,' said the other man. 'I worked near it once. It's in Salt Lane, in Greyfriars.'

'I never in my life heard of it anyway. What was the point of blowing it up?'

'To stop all the phone calls I suppose. Making a nuisance so the Brits would pull out.'

The first man laughed, but it wasn't a laugh like he'd found it funny. It was more like he thought Jamesie was stupid, but Jamesie was my friend. The first old man took another drink and spoke again.

'The last thing he said was, how many of you bastards have I taken with me?'

I was surprised to hear an old man swear. I thought it was something teenagers did. I guessed he was talking about Jamesie, but if he blew himself up, I didn't see how anyone would know what he had said, unless someone else had been with him.

On Sunday there was an Irishman interviewed on television. I could tell he was from the South because his accent wasn't like Mum's and Dad's. He spoke fast, the words tumbling from his mouth. He said the British had to realise they would suffer the consequences of the terror they waged in Ireland. He said there would be more bombs. I asked Mum who the man was. She didn't answer me and walked out into the kitchen.

Maria whispered, 'O'Connell. He's an IRA man.'

He didn't look like an IRA man. He looked more like a teacher or a priest, with a serious face and no smile, not like Jamesie.

Thursday 21 November 1974

The filing cabinet drawer sticks. Andy forces it, slams it with the heels of both hands and it crashes home. The bang makes others look up from their desks. A floor supervisor raises his eyebrows. Andy pulls his tie knot loose.

Wayne sees the clock above Andy's head: quarter to five.

'Beer after work?'

'Sure.'

'Tavern?'

'The beer's flat, mate. And too many underage drinkers.'

'You didn't complain about that one you were snogging the other night.'

Andy glances across to the new girl, Joanne. He thinks she's out of his league but hopes she's overheard and she'll turn up in The Tavern In The Town later.

He looks at the Christmas lights straddling Corporation Street. He wonders what he can get for his Mum this year. Rackhams stays open late on Thursday.

Through the door and down the stairs. Underground pub. No windows: no distractions. Concrete columns and a low, beamed ceiling. Crowded at weekends and after work. An old carpet. A furry glue on the soles of your shoes, willing you to stay put for the night. Low strip lighting. All squeezed together. An arm can graze a tit and no one says anything. Linda's already here, the one with the red hair, making her way to the bar. Kev says he's had her, that she's easy.

Pint glasses like chess pieces on a crowded table. One beer becomes two becomes three becomes a session. Packets of cheese and onion crisps deaden the hunger pangs. Wayne blows up an empty bag and pops it with his hand. A girl at the next table jumps. Wayne chortles.

'How many times have the Blues won the cup? None, isn't it? Villa have won it seven. Come on the Villa!'

'So fucking what? Shit on the Villa. We've got Trevor Francis.'

A roar from the other side of the room. A hand slaps a shoulder. A fat man wobbles on a stool.

An old, brown suitcase squats in a corner, to the right of the stairs, out of sight.

Someone puts a coin in the jukebox. The needle pierces the vinyl. Strings sweep up a scale and lyrics rise above the din in a high voice.

'What the fuck is this?' says Wayne.

Andy tilts his head and listens. 'I know it, it's called 'Sad Sweet Dreamer' or something like that.'

'It's shit, like something for old bastards.'

Andy's eyes scan the room. A girl in a cheesecloth blouse. He keeps looking, hoping their eyes might meet.

Joanne, wearing a black dress, walks in with another girl he doesn't know. Andy waves frantically. It looks like a warning. Joanne takes one small step towards him b-

A paraffin blue flash.

Just one scream, like someone has told an excellent joke.

142

A roar and rush of furnace heat.

The lights go out. One strip bulb flickers and dies, falls from the last threads of the ceiling, swings in a gentle arc. Groans.

The silence.

And the noise.

A helpless infant's scream howls from an adult's lungs.

Glass rammed in a cheek. Glass sickled in a wrist. Glass skewers an eye.

Collapsing concrete crushes skulls. Bones snap and jaws unship from faces.

A perfect arc of blood spouts from a neck. An arm straggles. A leg pines for a home.

Wayne inhales pulverised concrete and flesh.

Andy holds his arms up. His hands are on fire. Plaits of blood race down his wrists.

The stampede.

Feet trample on heads, on an abandoned half-leg, the shinbone pointing to the sky like a preacher.

A guffaw of leather-black smoke as The Tavern In The Town spews out its innards into a mystified New Street.

Joanne takes a last breath of smoke and ash, falling headlong into tarthick blood. Her soft, coral lungs clog and calcify.

Outside, it is a cold, late November night, not a cloud in the sky. New Street is motionless, beautifully peaceful in its own, unremarkable way.

Folded napkins grace tables in the closed Lyons café. Large cloths overhang in neat triangles. Menus, pert, stand to attention, inviting glances from passers-by. Fairy cakes and macaroons.

143

The bright bell of the first ambulance breaks the silence. Wayne, shivering on the pavement, marvels at the delicate stillness of it all until the first bell summons another and another. Police cars, ambulances and fire engines brick up the road. Wayne sees a parked bus and wonders why it has no windows and why there is so much broken glass under his feet, right up to his ankles.

The first policeman jogs up, the glass crunching beneath his feet like deep snow. Wayne cannot understand why the policeman isn't running faster because someone might be hurt in there. The policeman's lips move, his eyes seep wild fear but Wayne cannot hear a word he says, only a high-pitched whine behind his own eyes.

More people catapult into New Street from The Tavern. A young couple, their clothes seared from their bodies, reach for each other's hands. Bloodied youngsters pour through the gash where the door used to be like ants teeming from the nest. They vomit, or press hands to bloodied wounds, or just stare, like Wayne stares, at a moonlit sky and the blown-up pub coughing smoke and the swelling army of police cars, ambulances and fire engines.

Blue lights strafe the darkness. A siren like a weary complaint. Steam rises from a pool of blood.

A grey-faced fireman stumbles from the Tavern, sinks down on his haunches and covers his eyes. The steam drifts and weaves into the night sky, rising sinuously from fresh corpses.

In dozing suburbs door bells ring. Parents are told the news by whispering policemen shuffling from foot to foot. A fatherless child howls into the sky.

A dog sulks behind a front door, waiting for its owner to return, scratching at the worn carpet.

Firemen shovel blackened limbs into red canvas bags, hearing the raw, throaty rasp of steel against concrete.

At three in the morning the plate glass window of the Hasty Tasty café tumbles from its frame.

Wayne sits on a hard seat at the hospital. He wonders why Andy isn't here. He hasn't seen him since… since…. Wayne cannot understand why someone is making a roast dinner. The smell of cooked meat is everywhere.

The dust cloud from the Tavern boils up and creeps over Birmingham, over the Irish Centre, over the Catholic churches, over the small bedroom where Danny Cronin sleeps in a soundproofed sweet dream of astronauts in white spacesuits bobbing in zero gravity, the team on another mission, all working together. Their radios crackle. They gesture to one another through the dark glass of their helmets.

Danny in his dream can't hear what they're saying but knows they have a problem. He twitches under his blanket. The dust strokes his window.

The ice cold night,

a crescent moon,

a spectral cloud of breath.

A lone voice sings, 'When we've got all we want we're as quiet as can be, Where the Mountains of Mourne sweep down to the sea.' The word 'morn' echoes through Birmingham's dead streets.

Five Irishmen get the seven fifty-five train from Birmingham New Street to Heysham that night: Hill, Hunter, McIlkenny, Power and Walker. A sixth, Callaghan, waves them off. The Irishmen are catching the Belfast ferry to visit family and pay their respects to Jamesie McDade. McIlkenny and Walker carry mass cards for McDade, bought and signed at St Chad's.

The Irishmen change trains at Crewe. They play cards and smoke Park Drives and Sweet Aftons.

The Irishmen see a policeman with an Alsatian dog on the platform at Heysham. The dog tugs at its chain lead, lifts its two front paws off the ground and barks at the men, like a warning.

The passengers queue at the ticket barrier. Four of the Irishmen stand together: Hunter, McIlkenny, Power and Walker. Hill, some way ahead, is already on the ship.

The four Irishmen are asked to go to the British Transport Police offices. They are asked to turn out their pockets onto a table. Loose change, handkerchiefs, twills of tobacco: mass cards for McDade.

The policemen freeze.

'You need to come to Morecambe police station lads, for forensic testing. If you're clean you can go.'

'But what about our mate?'

Hill, sipping a Harp lager in the warmth of the ship's bar, feels a tap on the shoulder. It is the policeman with his dog. Hill walks back down the gangplank and into a waiting police car. The dog whines.

A call is made to Birmingham. Minutes later, three cars race up the M6, three police in each one.

They arrive in Morecambe at three fifteen on the morning of 22 November, itching to start.

In Morecambe police station, the forensic scientist washes his hands. He does it carefully, sweeping down the inside of each finger, digging out the dirt from under each nail. He holds his dripping hands to the strip light and smiles. His shirt hangs out at the front, his belly lapping over his belt.

The first Irishman is brought to him. The forensic scientist puts ether on a blob of cotton wool and cushions it into the Irishman's palm. He draws it back under the Irishman's nails. He squeezes the swabbed cotton wool into a bowl and adds more ether, caustic soda and a re-agent. He repeats the ritual with all five Irishmen. He notices that Hunter bites his nails and that Hill's hands are greasy. At the end of the process he says to each Irishman, 'That will be all.' His voice is self-satisfied and reassuring.

If nitroglycerine is present the mixture turns pink within ten seconds. Power's sample turns pink, as if suffused by rose petals. So does Hill's and Walker's. The forensic scientist clucks, sits back. He wheezes. He slaps his thighs.

A detective sergeant pokes his head around the door.

'Well?'

'I'm ninety-nine per cent certain,' says the scientist. 'Ninety-nine.'

The whisper scuttles around Morecambe police station. They have the bombers. The actual, fucking bombers.

The Irishmen are made to undress. They are given ill-fitting shirts, jackets and trousers. No underwear. No socks. Their bags are searched. The remaining mass cards for Jamesie McDade are found.

147

In Birmingham, the men's houses are raided at five in the morning. Nothing is discovered except at Walker's, where the police find receipts for teddy bears and alarm clocks.

The men's children, shaken roughly from the troughs of sleep, rub their eyes. Soft toys nestle in the crooks of their arms. A rabbit with a grin.

The walls of the press room at Morecambe station are bare except for one large piece of paper stuck to the wall with drawing pins. It says 'No Photography' in black marker pen.

The hacks blow cigarette smoke through puffed cheeks.

'Must be big.'

'Heysham's only four and a half miles away.'

'What, you reckon it's Irish?'

'Those bombs in Birmingham last night.'

'Morecambe coppers have caught those bastards? Morecambe plod couldn't run a bath, never mind run a mass murder investigation.'

'What else can it be? We never get called in at this time. And there's three coppers talking in Brummie accents in the car park.'

'Fuckin ell. Couldn't catch a cold but can catch terrorists. This'll shift some papers.'

'It's only a guess, like.'

The press room door opens. A hush falls. A portly Chief Inspector strides to the small podium. He holds one piece of paper. The peak of his cap is dead between his eyes. Hacks scramble for the few remaining chairs. The unlucky ones go down on one knee and rest their pads on their thighs. One licks the tip of his pencil.

'I have a brief statement. There will be no questions. Five men were detained at Heysham harbour at 10:40 last night. They are being interviewed by senior CID officers from the West Midlands in connection with last night's bombing incidents in Birmingham. They will be escorted to Birmingham later this afternoon.'

He turns sharply and marches from the room. A second of silence and an eruption of noise. 'Sir, can you confirm….' 'Are they Irish?' 'Is it the IRA, Chief Inspector?' 'Who made the arrest?' 'Got pictures of the terrorists?'

Chairs kicked to the floor as hacks flee the room like schoolkids at home time. Newsrooms hum. Editors stare at pictures of the dead and try to dream up captions.

Nothing feels adequate. Nothing feels right.

Daily Mail, Friday 22 November 1974

The IRA took its cruel revenge upon the city of Birmingham last night. It did so in the way it knows best – in a terrible slaughter of men and women and teenagers… A young girl, distressed and weeping, said she was drinking in the Tavern in the Town when the bomb went off. 'I went to the bar and suddenly there was an almighty bang. The ceiling came down and the lights went out… I saw a girl who lost her foot. It was terrible. You just can't say how you feel. I thought I was dead. I heard people shouting "Irish bastards."'… But today will not just be a day of grief and mourning. In some scruffy back parlours in the Ardoyne and Andersonstown Belfast, they have a new

victory to celebrate, new heroes to acclaim
- these Irish patriots who slew the innocent young. They will raise their glasses
to these brave boyos of the provisional
IRA.

Hunter sits alone in a cell, rubbing his hands. The sun rises. He hears screaming. It is Hill.

McIlkenny hears it, too, in his own cell. Hill shouts, 'Let go of my arm. You're breaking my arm.'

In Hill's cell, two officers have him pinned against the wall. One has Hill's arms twisted behind his back. He whispers to Hill, 'You're covered in gelignite from head to toe.'

A new scream is heard. It is Power.

Power is punched and kicked. 'You dirty murdering IRA bastard. You've got gelly on your hands. We're going to put you in handcuffs and drive you back to Birmingham. We're going to throw you out of the car. We'll say you were trying to escape. We'll probably get medals for it.

'I'll keep this simple for you Power. There's a mob outside your house. God only knows what they're going to do to your wife and kids. We've got coppers protecting the place but they won't stay for long. The only way to save your family is to tell us what we want to know.'

'I don't know anything.'

'The mob is chanting that your wife is an IRA whore. What do you think they're going to do to her? It's going to be worse than what you bastards do in Belfast. A lot worse than tarring and feathering.'

150

Power is dragged into a dark and windowless room. It is full of men. He is punched and kicked. When he falls he is dragged up again by the hair. He fouls himself. He is spread-eagled against a wall. Someone says, 'Stretch his balls.' A voice he has not heard before whispers in his ear, 'You'll never have sex with your wife again.'

Power falls. His whole body gives in. 'I'll tell you anything you want me to say.' He signs a confession at 12:55 on 22 November, sitting in his own excreta.

Walker stares at a gun. The gun stares back at him.

The police put a blanket over his head. They press the barrel to his temple.

Walker has a blister. They stub a cigarette out on it. Walker blacks out.

Walker wakes on the cold stone floor of his cell. He flushes the toilet, wipes his face with the water.

Power's confession is held aloft in the locker room. There is cheering. The drinks cabinet is opened, the Chief Super brandishing his special key to a hearty round of applause. Glasses are clinked. The warm, complacent smell of whiskey wafts through the room. Arms wrap around shoulders. Chins wobble.

'You did it, you fucking champ.'

'Who stopped them at Heysham?'

'A BT.'

'I could kiss the cunt.'

Cigarettes are lit. An officer leans back against the wall and puffs out a cloud of smoke. His sigh is blissful, post-coital.

The Irishmen are dragged barefoot to waiting police cars for the drive to Queen's Road station, Birmingham. The smell of drink is sour, palpable.

The Irishmen arrive at eight in the evening of 22 November. Power tries to sleep but his whole body aches from the beating. An officer barks at him to stand up. Twenty minutes later another officer barks at him to sit down. He can hear screams from another cell: 'Leave me alone, leave me alone.' It sounds like Hunter.

The handcuffs on Hunter dig tight into his skin. His feet are freezing. Deep scratches run diagonally from his shoulder to his navel.

He is taken for interview. A coat is thrown over his head. Looking down at the ground, he sees the feet of policemen and women kicking at his ankles. A dog barks and Hunter jumps.

In interview, an officer says, 'You don't like dogs, do you Gerry?'

'No.'

The door opens slowly. A constable has an Alsatian. The dog growls and barks at Hunter. The constable goes down on his haunches and whispers in the dog's ear: 'Get him. Get him.' He lets the lead out slowly, link by link of the chain. The dog is inches away from Hunter's face.

Back in his cell, a uniformed sergeant gives Hunter a glass of water and a pork pie. He allows Hunter to wash. He sees Hunter's body.

'What happened to you?'

'I fell.'

Hill is punched in the jaw. He falls to the floor and is kicked. An officer whispers in his ear, 'We haven't started on you yet.'

The same officer says, 'You can have it the easy way or the hard way. If you don't make a statement you are going round the walls again.'

Another officer enters the room. He puts a firm hand on Hill's shoulder. 'I made a promise to Billy Power, Hill. I told him I would take his wife and children to a safe house if he confessed, to save his family from the mob. I'll do the same for you.'

Hill shakes his head. Hill is punched. The officer, still with his hand on Hill's shoulder, whispers, 'We're going to get a statement out of you or kick you to death.' He squeezes hard.

The officer's voice sidles to the back of his throat.

'Your wife's an IRA whore, Hill. Your children are IRA bastards. Your daughters will grow up to be IRA whores. Go on, Hill, you're getting mad now. Take a dig at me.'

McIlkenny is punched in the face. His nose drips blood onto his white shirt.

Walker is asked where he was born. He replies, 'Derry.' His face is slapped. 'It is Londonderry.'

At 10:45 on the night of 22 November, Callaghan returns from the pub to his council house in Aston. He digs his hands deep into his coat pockets against the cold. He does not see the armed police hiding behind neighbours' hedges. He does feel the steel ring of a gun barrel against his head as he opens his front door.

I, William Power, wish to make a statement. I want you to write down what I say. I have been told I need not say anything unless I wish to and that whatever I say may be given in evidence.

I, Noel Richard McIlkenny, wish to make a statement. I want you to write down what I say. I have been told I need not say anything unless I wish to and that whatever I say may be given in evidence.

I, John Francis Walker, wish to make a statement. I want you to write down what I say. I have been told I need not say anything unless I wish to and that whatever I say may be given in evidence.

I, Hugh Daniel Callaghan, wish to make a statement. I want you to write down what I say. I have been told I need not say anything unless I wish to and that whatever I say may be given in evidence.

Neither Hill nor Hunter confess.

The funerals of the victims of The Mulberry Bush and The Tavern In The Town are conducted to the sound of shuffling feet and angry, tearless sobs. A six-year-old girl asks where her Daddy has gone.

Days after the bombings, tiny shards of vertebrae, teeth, rib cage and innards litter New Street. The tell-tale sign is a crow or magpie stabbing at the ground.

For weeks afterwards, passers-by see blood in the puddles whenever it rains.

Hospitals are crammed with the maimed.

An amputee stares at the space where her arm used to be. Sometimes she can still feel the missing fingers.

Birmingham distils its fear and anger, spitting it out onto Irish nurses, Irish bus and taxi drivers, Irish workers on the track at Longbridge. Irish bank cheques are refused in shops, shoved noiselessly back across the counter.

Irish mothers are refused service, dragging away their open-mouthed, disbelieving children, the words 'Bloody Irish' and 'IRA scum' hissing in their ears. Their English neighbours cross the road when they see them. Market traders in the Bull Ring refuse to handle Irish goods.

The families of the arrested men are followed on their way to mass. Nooses are hung on the gates of their houses.

The six arrested men are served meals with shards of glass buried in the mash. Their mouths bleed. Their cups of tea hold the sharp sting of urine.

Minds harden like the harshness of the winter ground shuttering and sealing the young dead. Bricks batter through windows in Catholic schools. A Union Jack whips fiercely, cracks in a furious wind.

'The fuckin' Irish. The fuckin' fuckin' Irish.

'One bloke told me his mate knew someone who was a fireman. He spent the night working at The Mulberry Bush dragging bits of bodies out of the rubble. The next day he looked in the mirror and saw his hair had turned white. Completely white. Not from the dust but from the shock.

'Another bloke he told me, he knew someone, a girl, and she was blinded in The Tavern In The Town. Blinded. Seventeen years old and now blinded for life.

'That's what they should do with those IRA bastards. Stick a red hot poker in each eye and blind the bastards for life. Only it's too good for 'em. Too good for 'em.

'What d'you mean, they're not all the same? They are. They fuckin' are. Oh yeah, there's the ones that plant the bombs but they need the ones that make the bombs and the ones that have the safe houses, and they need the ones that supply the gelignite, and they need the ones that give money. And they all need the ones in the Irish pubs and clubs, singing their fuckin' songs. Pissed out their fuckin' heads. You see the way they carry on. Can't have a drink without a fight. They're psychos. Fuckin' psychopaths. Every last one of them. Send 'em back. Their kids are going to grow up to be bombers. The longer we leave 'em here the more bombers they'll have, breeding like rabbits. Send 'em back. If anyone had any fuckin' sense they'd fuckin' send 'em back now.

'Theyneedfuckin'hangingstringupthebastrdsIsaystring'emup.'

November-December 1974

Two pubs in town have been blown up. It's on the telly all the time. I asked Mum if I could read about it in the paper. Mum said there are no papers. But we usually have one. Maybe there's no papers because of the bombs.

The pictures on television showed people being taken away with blood all over their faces. I recognised the Rotunda. None of the people being led away were crying. I would if I was hurt like that. Maybe they were braver because they were adults. I asked Mum if that was the reason they weren't crying. She said they were in shock. Mum was very quiet. Just staring at the television. She was slid down into her seat. She looked shorter. I said 'Mum,' but she didn't hear me. Maybe she was in shock, too, like the adults on the television.

I looked at the sign on one of the pubs. It had blown off the front and was lying in the middle of the road. The 'Mul' had vanished; all you could read was 'berry Bush.'

I wet the bed. Mum said nothing. She rubbed my legs down with a flannel. The water was cold. Maria went out without saying good-bye.

At school assembly we were told to pray for the killed and the injured. We sang 'All Things Bright And Beautiful.'

Later in the day, our class was sitting in the hall, getting ready to watch a programme. There had been rain and hail all morning and we hadn't had our playtime outside. Miss Blake wheeled the television in. It was on top of a big, iron stand, like one of the climbing frames in the playground at the Infants' end. It ran on castor wheels like the wheels on a supermarket trolley. The television was on a slope. One wheel was hanging half-off at the back.

We sat cross-legged on the floor. Miss Blake wheeled the television into place. The castor was hanging off further than usual. The television sloped from left to right.

We whispered to each other about what we were going to see. It might be *The Boy From Space*. He was found by two children, Helen and Dan. They called him Peep-Peep.

The Boy From Space wrote words backwards but when a mirror was held up to the words you could read them properly. I could always guess the word as he was writing it but some of the stupid kids couldn't. After the programme finished, we went back to the classroom and spelled the words the boy from space had written.

The Boy From Space was a good programme but you knew it was about spelling because the characters always kept repeating the words that were important. There was one episode where a man kept saying 'fantastic.' Miss Blake put 'fantastic' up on the board and asked us to make up as many words as we could from it. Straight away we all got 'fan,' and 'at,' but after that it got harder for some people. I was doing OK but Miss Blake was up at Neil Gordon's desk and telling him how good he was. Someone else told me Neil had come up with 'attic.' Miss Blake always went to Neil first for an answer, or Elizabeth Plunket or Eileen Lynch. The rest of us got used to just sitting there.

Miss Blake stood back from the television and looked at the castor. She left the room. We stared at the dark grey screen, waiting for something to happen. The castor snapped off, making a clean-sounding rip, like my mum tugging off the bone at the bottom of the roast leg of lamb. It rocked on the floor, ticking on the tiles like it was tutting. The television started to slip down slowly from left to right. It reminded me of another thing I'd seen in a programme, a big ship launched in Belfast, at the Harland and Wolff shipyard. We all sat there, doing nothing.

Miss Blake walked in, with Mother Assumpta behind her. The television fell into space. Mother Assumpta shrieked and ran to try and catch it. Her black robes stretched out behind her.

The television crashed down. Shards of glass flew through the air towards us or skittered across the floor. They bounced in front of us like hailstones or rice. Some of the children ran to the back and one girl cried, but the rest of us just kept on sitting there with our legs crossed, waiting to be told what to do.

One shard came to rest by my feet. It was a jagged little slither of glass like a bolt of lightning. I picked it up. It was shaped like the letter zed. I stared at it. The glass had caught the sunlight coming through the window. There were blues and reds inside the bit of glass, like the colours in the windows at St Chad's. I turned it around slowly and watched the light change and the little shadow shapes it made on the floor.

I heard Mother Assumpta scream, 'Out! Out!' Miss Blake clapped her hands. We ran back to our classroom. I stood on a small lump of glass. It crunched beneath my shoe. For the rest of the day we all wondered what the school was going to do, now there was no telly.

I walked home down Hurst Green Road and along Galton Road. I was near our house and looked in the window of Barkers. They had papers. The headline on the *Daily Mirror* said, 'Massacre in Pubs Blitz.' It said eighteen people were killed. The *Daily Express* had, 'It's Slaughter by IRA Bombs.' They said there were seventeen dead. The *Birmingham Evening Mail* was there, too. It said, 'Worse than Ulster, 19 Dead, 202 Hurt.' The picture was of two men carrying a body in a blanket. The blanket sagged, like the body was heavy. I was wondering which newspaper was right about the number of dead when two boys in Feldon Street uniforms walked towards me. I had never seen them before. As I tried to walk away one of them said, 'Hey, you!' I turned to look at him. He was right in my face.

'All Irish are thick,' he said to me, 'Thick and murdering bastards.' His friend laughed. I started to walk away. One of them must have swung his bag at me because the next thing I knew something hit me on the back of the head. It didn't hurt but I stumbled and turned around again. The boy's friend was swinging his bag around, back onto his shoulder. They were both laughing now. I ran.

I didn't say anything when I got home. Mum and Dad said I had to go to my room as soon as we had eaten because they needed to talk. We weren't allowed to turn the telly on.

The door of my bedroom was open. I could hear Mum and Dad whispering. It was a harsh sound like the hissing of snakes. I crept downstairs as far as the front room. Mum and Dad stopped talking.

There were a couple of mass cards on the table: 'Sacred Heart of Jesus have mercy on the Soul of Lieutenant James Patrick McDade, Birmingham Brigade, Killed in Action.'

I recognised his picture. He was grinning from ear to ear like a little boy, just like he always did at the Irish Centre.

I went back to my room. It began to rain, getting harder and harder. It drummed against my window, battering the glass, trying to get in.

Daily Mirror, Saturday 23 November 1974

A Birmingham pub managed by an Irish Catholic was blasted by a petrol bomb early today. The attack was seen as the most vicious reprisal yet following the IRA pub bomb outrages in the city… The wave of revulsion and anger which has swept Britain is fair warning of what the IRA can expect from now on. The public has the will. The government **MUST** give the lead. There must be no surrender. No refuge for slaughtering maniacs. No appeasement. If the IRA believe their case is helped by massacres they are deluding themselves. They have plunged into a bloodbath of which they will be the ultimate victims. **They have sown the wind, and they shall reap the whirlwind.**

Daily Express, Saturday November 23 1974

At Longbridge, fights and scuffles between English and Irish workers broke out

161

in the giant British Leyland plant. Then thousands walked out to a demonstration chanting 'IRA out'... In shops and pubs there were cases of people being refused service for having an Irish accent... Bring back the death penalty for terrorists... The burns are as bad, or worse, if possible, than those caused by napalm.

I went to Neil Gordon's house. It was bigger than ours, with a kitchen extension and a garage for their Ford Escort. His Mum had an aquarium in the living room and dropped little flakes of food into it, the orange and yellow fish drifting from spot to spot, a never-ending stream of bubbles rising to the surface. She stopped when she saw me and left the room. The pump hummed.

There was a copy of *The Times* on Neil's Dad's chair. A picture on the front page showed one of the people from the bombings in a hospital bed. The caption underneath said he was seventeen. The boy was lying on a bed with his head off to one side. There was a nurse standing over him. She was doing something with a tube stuck in the boy's arm. The caption underneath the photo said he was in The Tavern In The Town. I wondered if his Mum was mad at him for being in the pub.

I turned the page. There were more photos. They showed the other pub, The Mulberry Bush. It was all criss-cross lines and sharp shapes, like bolts of lightning in a comic. In the middle of all the lines were two bodies lying on their sides.

It said in *The Times* that the police had arrested some men. I wanted to read more but Neil's Mum came back and snatched the paper from me. She said something under her breath. I couldn't make out what it was but it sounded like one of the words was 'bloody.' I looked at the aquarium. The fish moped, open-mouthed. Neil was quiet all day and didn't want to play anything.

I walked home in the darkness. It was too cloudy to count the stars but you could see the soft, creamy light of the moon behind the clouds. If you asked people they said the moon was silver or white, but if you looked closely you could see marks on it. They had to be the craters, places an astronaut could explore. On winter mornings you could still see the stars when you left for school, so you knew the universe and all the planets were out there, waiting for you to visit them.

The clouds might make it more difficult for a moon landing if I was to try space travel on a night like this. I was sure Mission Control would check the weather before sending me up in a rocket. It would be better to travel on a clear night.

When you're in space the Earth is a lovely bluey-green colour beneath your feet. You have the whole thing to look at. Maybe you could make out the big countries like America, but you wouldn't be able to spot the gap between Britain and Ireland. Space travel would make you forget your troubles because you'd see the world is just a small place. And you'd be weightless, too, just floating above it all. No one to harm you.

There was a man in a brown suit sitting on a chair in our living room, all alone. He looked like he was my dad's age. He was bald on top but had sideburns. You could see his hair had been red before he lost it. His face was rosy, his eyes bright blue. He was holding a cup of tea. His hands were large. The cup and saucer in his hand looked like they belonged in a doll's house.

He smiled for a second and said, 'Hello.' I could tell from his voice that he was Irish. He sounded like my dad, but the man's voice was deeper and softer. My own voice caught in my throat as I tried to say hello back to him and we just stared at each other.

I heard footsteps running down the stairs and Mum came in the room. She stopped when she saw me.

'Hello, Danny. This is Eamonn,' she said. 'He's staying for a few days.'

'Are you over on holiday?' I asked him.

'Yes,' he said. 'Just a quick one.'

I turned to Mum. 'Where is he sleeping?'

'In the front room, on the sofa in there. It's just for a little while. A few days.'

The man nodded, like Mum had said something clever.

I looked back at Mum. 'Does Dad know?'

'Of course.'

They both looked at me. They were waiting for me to say something else. I left them and went into the front room.

There was a suitcase propped-up against the sofa. It looked old. It was brown but some of the colour had peeled away.

I walked over and had a closer look. I could hear Maria's music playing upstairs in her bedroom, something about love and needing help. There was a thick handle on the suitcase, shaped like the letter D. There were two metal clasps, one at each end.

I leant my hand against the case. Something jolted inside it. Maria's song finished. She lifted the needle back to the beginning. I heard the crackling sound like a bonfire. The song started again. Just the same words over and over.

My mum and the man were talking. Their voices got lower and lower until it seemed they were whispering and I couldn't make out a single word. It was softer whispers than when Mum and Dad were together.

I walked upstairs and stood outside Maria's room. I talked to her through the door, over the noise of the music.

'Who's that man?'

'He's from Derry, or maybe Belfast.'

'Is he an uncle?'

'No. He might be a cousin of Mum's or Dad's. I think he's going to find work over here.'

'Mum says he's on holiday.'

No answer.

'Maria, has he been in England a while or has he just come over?'

'Go away, Danny.'

She turned the music up. I went to my room and looked out of the window. The streetlights were a pale, foggy white, like ghosts. I ran my hand along the net curtains and poked my finger through one of the holes. Maria switched off her music. My mum and the man were speaking softly. They stopped. There was no sound at all, just silence, but it felt like the kind of silence that means something, like the kind you get after a jet plane has flown over, or after an ambulance has rushed by, when the air is still tingling.

Two boys had hit me. I could do nothing about it. Two pubs weren't there any more and people were lying in hospital beds with tubes in their arms. I thought about what the blown-up pubs must look like now, all sharp lines, darkness and dust. Jamesie

165

started to sing in my head: 'I'll be here, in sunshine or in shadow, Oh Danny Boy, Oh Danny Boy, I love you so.' I could feel Jamesie finish his song and smile like a happy little boy. There was a loud cheer and people banged their hands on the table.

It was getting harder to breathe. I counted as I inhaled: one, two, three, four, five six, seven. I counted again as I breathed out: one, two, three, four, five, six, seven, eight, nine, ten, eleven. I thought about doing the numbers backwards so it would sound like the countdown to a space rocket being launched. I tried it and it worked. It felt like I was doing proper astronaut training.

In the Hugh Walters books, part of the training is putting yourself into the centrifuge. It's like a fairground ride but it's more to do with science because they put you in a pod and whirl you round and round and you feel the G force. It starts with a shudder before pinning you down onto your seat and you can't get up. I wouldn't look forward to that bit, being spun round and round until you didn't know where you were and you couldn't move, but it was needed to prepare you for the tough parts of space travel. Your rocket also needed to burn a lot of fuel to escape the Earth's atmosphere. There'd be fire and heat everywhere but once you were through it you'd be free, free as a bird.

I took my story back from Mum's pile of books and thought about what I could write next.

The alien looked at Danny. It had a shiny head made of a hard metal.

'Do you come in peace?' asked Danny.

The alien whirred. Its motor hummed and tick-tick-ticked.

A different creature flew overhead. It looked like a little bird. It squawked, like a warning.

166

There was a rumble in the distance. The alien kept whirring. Danny didn't know what to do.

I hadn't added enough to show Mum yet, but at least something important was happening in my story because Danny had met an alien. I put it in my PG Tips sticker album for spaceships so the whole thing would look bigger and have pictures, and slotted it between two of Mum's books.

Dad got in from work and there was a lot more talking. Things got loud. The man was talking loudest of all. I crept downstairs. Dad had left his copy of *The Sun* on the table in the front room. The cartoon on page four showed Big Ben. There was a ladder going up to its face and a man at the top of the ladder wearing a black beret and sunglasses, like the ones at Jamesie's house. Frank Spencer wore a beret on the television programme, *Some Mothers Do 'Ave 'Em.* Maria said he was really funny but my dad said he was an eejit. The man in the cartoon in *The Sun* was carrying a stick of dynamite. I knew he was supposed to be Irish because the caption underneath had the word 'dat' for 'that.' He was saying, 'Sure, Oi'm just changin' the battery, or sumtin' like dat.' But my mum and dad didn't say 'dat.' Maybe it was what the people from the South of Ireland said, the ones who said 'tirteen' for 'thirteen.'

On page five there was a headline, 'The Sun Says.' It talked about the Irish. It said if the Irish didn't want to obey our laws they should all go home, get out of the country, go back where they came from.

The adults were still talking. I crept close to the living room door. My dad finished saying something. My mum said sharply, 'Never mind why. How did you do it?'

A soft, deep voice answered her. 'I left it where it wouldn't be noticed, then went to make the phone call but there was a problem. The phone had been vandalised. By the time I got through I knew it was too late. I heard them go off.'

I didn't know the man had been in town when the bombs exploded. He was lucky.

'God, Eamonn,' said my mum. 'What have you done?'

'It's a war, Annie. The sky above Belfast is alive with helicopters day and night. At least three of them in the sky all the time. The sound of them in your head, never stopping. We could be having a funeral, burying one of our own, but they're still hovering above us, like hawks getting ready to swoop down, their shadows right over us.

'The house keeps getting raided, my younger one dragged out of bed at three or four in the morning, the place full of soldiers swearing, the floorboards ripped up, the gas pipes torn out.

'They put a curfew on the whole Lower Falls. No one could get out to buy food and the Brits had stripped the shelves anyway. Little kids crying of hunger in the night.

'Do you know children get stopped in the morning on their way to school, made to empty out their satchels onto the street? If a man gets searched he's likely to take a punch in the balls, too, or else get a baton around his knees or his kidneys.

'The soldiers fire CS gas. You feel like you're going to throw up your own insides. They have an observation tower on top of Divis Flats so they watch us all the time, and the walls in the flats are so thin the bullets come through them. You're not even safe in your own home. The Brits round us up into hovels, like the Yanks put the Indians on reservations. I don't make phone calls home because everyone knows there's not a single phone in Belfast or Derry that's not tapped.' He stopped and panted, like he was gasping for breath.

I didn't understand all of what they were saying but I got the bit about the gas because of what Seamus told me. I'd be no good in Northern Ireland, with all the CS gas. It would give me an asthma attack. I'd be better looking down from space. I'd just be hoping the fighting would stop. Maybe the top of Divis Flats was safe if you were a soldier. Eamonn said the army looked down from helicopters, but looking down from space would be much better. From a helicopter you could see gas and bullets and people running away screaming, but in space you would hear nothing. Everything would be calm.

I knew it must be hard for the people over there, being watched all the time. It would be like when the nuns and teachers are mad so we all keep our heads down and just look at what's on our desks.

The man said there were no streetlights. It wouldn't be like the walk to Dr Burnett's where you watched your shadow. With no light the stars would be brighter than ever and you could see more of them. They'd light your way.

The man started talking again. 'Remember what we know: Ireland unfree shall never be at peace. You have to fight fire with fire, you have to fight an army with another army and the Brits were the ones who sent their army in. We've had five years of street fighting and raids over there and now we're bringing the war over here, right into the heart of their cities, the heart of their so-called empire. We have plenty of money, don't you worry, every American with Irish blood is queuing up to give us their dollars. They're shipping Armalite rifles over to us and we get free gelignite from the Republic. We're going to make it impossible for the Brits to stay in the North. We'll force them out.' He paused. A teacup clinked on a saucer. 'There's going to be more stuff coming in. We've got baggage handlers at the ports and airports. We're going to need safe houses. It's time for people like yourselves to step forward.'

Someone was crying. It sounded like my dad but I couldn't be sure because I had never heard him cry before. I knew the bit about Ireland unfree never being at peace because it was on the cover of Mum and Dad's record, but I didn't know what a safe house was. I hoped our house was a safe house. I didn't want it to be a dangerous one. I didn't want soldiers coming in and ripping up the floorboards. I was glad there was no CS gas in Birmingham. Maybe that was why Eamonn was over, to get away from the gas. Maybe he had asthma, too. He was talking about war but the war ended a long time ago. There wasn't war in Ireland, only The Troubles.

Astronauts have to cope with loneliness. Maybe the ground controllers in Houston and Cape Canaveral speak to them every day, to keep them company. Just voices in the icy darkness to remind them there's someone out there after all. In *Nearly Neptune*, the astronauts' radio is broken. Tony repairs it and they all cheer when the first message from Earth comes through.

When astronauts do a spacewalk they have a line connecting them to the capsule, and because of the radio communication in the spaceship it's like there's another line, too, connecting them to the Earth, only it's an invisible line, a radio line, stretching all the way from Texas or Florida to outer space.

I got hold of my story again.

'Danny?'

'Yes, Mission Control?'

'You're on your own in the capsule. The spaceship needs repairs. You must do a spacewalk. You'll need to be brave.'

'I will.'

'And Danny?'

'Yes, Mission Control?'

'Watch your chest. Watch your breathing.'

'I will.'

'We'll give you a countdown before we open the airlock, Danny.... Counting down from ten.'

Mr Lambert gave us a lift part of the way home from school the next day, as far as The Full Moon. There were his boys, Noel and Rory, and Neil Gordon and me, all squashed up in the back. As we were getting out I told the others about the cartoon in *The Sun*, with the IRA man climbing up the ladder to Big Ben. They laughed. Mr Lambert told us off. He said it wasn't funny.

There was a huge Union Jack hanging in the window of The Full Moon, all sharp lines and bold colours. At home, the news said they'd arrested the men that did the bombings. I was glad to hear it. We were safe.

On Wednesday I said to Neil, 'Do you want to come to my house next weekend?' He shook his head and walked off with David Hennessy. I had never seen him play with David before. That

171

afternoon, on the way home, the same two lads from Feldon Street threw stones at me, calling me an Irish bastard. There was another couple of boys with them. They'd been waiting for me. One of them came up behind me and punched me on the back of the head. They all laughed. I kept walking, praying to Holy God and Jesus and Holy Mary for the boys to leave me alone, hearing stones whistle either side of me. I raised a hand to protect my face. A sharp stone caught me in the palm. I licked the smear of blood off when I got home and stared at where the stone had hit me. I scrunched my hand and a bubble of blood came up in my palm.

ATV Today said the National Front had demanded that all Irish people be declared aliens. I didn't know why. There were aliens on *Doctor Who* and they were creatures from another planet. We were not from another planet, just another country. We came from just across the water.

The television people interviewed someone. I didn't know who the man was but he was wearing a suit. He looked a bit like Dr Burnett but his voice was sharper. He said it was a Catholic problem. 'Look at Ireland,' he said. 'That backward little country. Look at Latin America. Wherever they settle they're dirty. They live in slums. They have more children than they can afford. They breed like rabbits or rats. It's what they do. They're not like us. They're ignorant and superstitious. They're dirty drunkards.' The interviewer asked him if talks with the IRA would help. 'We don't negotiate with terrorists,' snapped the man. 'They're men of violence.'

ATV Today also showed a demonstration. They said there were four thousand people there. One man was carrying a sign saying 'Go Home Paddy.' Another held his sign up to the camera. It said

'Bring Back Hanging.' It looked like he had made it himself. It wasn't just those two, there were loads of men with banners saying 'Hang The IRA.' There were women, too. They looked like our neighbours. They looked like Mrs Gow across our road.

The reporter stopped one man and asked him what he would like to see happen. 'Send all the Irish back to Ireland,' the man said. 'Get them out of this country.'

You could see the demonstration was in the grounds of a big factory. I asked Mum where they were.

'Longbridge,' she said. 'They make cars there.'

'Didn't Dad work at Longbridge?'

She didn't answer.

I had a day off on Thursday because of my asthma. I wet the bed again, too. There was just me and my mum in the house. I followed her while she did the housework and the washing. My white sheet swelled up on the line. Mum wasn't singing.

'How do you know Eamonn?'

'I knew him back home.'

'Does he have a wife?'

'Yes.'

'And children?'

'Yes, two girls.'

'Why aren't they here?'

'He's just paying a quick visit.'

'I thought he was working. That's what Maria said.'

'Visiting and working. Go and get me the little watering can. The plants are wilting.'

'Maria says Eamonn is coming here to work but I think he's having a holiday. Who's right, me or her?'

'He's seeing a man about a job.'

'What kind of job.'

'Something to do with cars. Or maybe buildings.'

'Is he on the lump?'

'Go and get me that watering can, Danny.'

In one of my Hugh Walters books, life on Earth is under threat because of spores from Venus. There's stuff like fungus everywhere and nothing can stop it from smothering all the people. It's impossible to kill the spores. They're like a low smoke rolling and tumbling their way across the world. The different countries try flame-throwers and petrol but still the spores keep advancing, growing like moss. The fungus swells up at the top and explodes and spores get flung all over the place.

The problem starts in Africa but moves into Europe and eventually Great Britain. There are refugees everywhere. The book says Britain is swamped by them, that the refugees bring all their children. The astronauts are sent up to Venus to find an antidote. When they do, their leader Chris says, 'Thank God,' and Earth is saved.

All the other astronauts call him Chris, though his full name is Chris Godfrey. They don't call him Captain Godfrey. If I was in charge, I'd like it if the others called me Captain Cronin because it would mean I was the important one. That's what a title does for you, make you big and important. Captain Cronin. Lieutenant McDade.

I stayed off from school on Friday, too. Asthma makes me wheeze when I breathe, like a broken engine. My asthma wasn't as bad as I was making out but I wanted to steer clear of the

Feldon Street boys. Mum was cleaning upstairs and singing. Eamonn was upstairs, too. Maybe the man hadn't given him a job. Dad was at work. Eamonn's suitcase was shoved under the glass case in the front room. I pulled it out carefully, undid the metal clasps and looked inside. The singing stopped. I heard a door close.

Eamonn had clothes, a toothbrush, a razor and shaving foam in his case. The clothes had dust on them. He also had an alarm clock with Westclox printed on it. It was a bit like Maria's, but this clock looked like it was broken.

Upstairs, a mattress squeaked, and squeaked again. Maybe Mum was getting something off the top of her wardrobe. The silence everywhere else in the house made it sound louder. It felt like Peep-Peep, the boy from space, was trying to tell me something. I put the suitcase back. The mattress groaned.

I watched cartoons on Saturday morning. Nobody bothered me so I stayed in my pyjamas and ate my Frosties. Eamonn was out. Dad came home in the afternoon but he didn't change into his overalls and do things around the house and garden. Instead, he just sat in his bus driver's uniform in the kitchen while Mum stayed upstairs. Dad pulled his tie knot loose, making me think of Jamesie, but there was no singing, just the ticking of the clock. The house was as cold and quiet as outer space. Mum gave us fish fingers and peas for dinner.

On Sunday the television showed the men who had been arrested for the bombing. There were six of them. Their photos were all on the screen at once, in three rows of two. They looked like normal men, the kind of men you'd see at the Irish Centre. Mum and Eamonn were watching it with me.

175

I said to Mum, 'Do you know who they are?'

'No. Never seen them. No.'

Eamonn stood up. 'I'm away out for a while.'

I turned to him. 'Where are you going?'

'To see a man about a dog.'

'Be careful, Eamonn,' said my mum.

The men's faces were still on the screen. It was dark outside. I wondered where Eamonn was going. Maybe to a pub or to the Irish Centre. The men were staring straight out, their mouths closed.

There were lots of Irish people in the news over the next week. They had a report on it on *ATV Today*. Irish people were being arrested because of a new thing called the Prevention of Terrorism Act. It made the IRA illegal. The arrested ones were helping police with their enquiries. I thought it was good that they were being helpful.

Mum switched the television off and told me and Maria to go to our rooms. I hadn't got further than the bottom of the stairs when she called me back.

'Danny, you're awful quiet. Is anything wrong at school?'

'No, not at school.'

'Out of school?'

'No, nothing.'

Mum and Dad always say, 'Tell the truth.' Dad says there's a black mark on my tongue when I'm lying. He's lying and they're wrong. A lot of people tell lies. Adults, too. What you have to do is not get caught. I'd say that to Mum but she'd get angry. She'd also know I was right.

There was no point telling Mum and Dad about the Feldon Street boys. There was nothing they could do and Dad would tell me to stop being a baby.

I knew the boys would be waiting for me again. At least I had my asthma to keep me off school.

There's an episode of *The Boy From Space* where Helen and Dan find a meteorite. After we watched it we were all looking round the playground and the field to see if we could find one. Francis Byrne said he had picked one up and it burnt his hand. It would be great to find a meteorite because they're special but you'd need to be careful that you didn't get caught in a meteor shower. If you did you'd have to dodge all the rocks as they pelted down on you. Hot rocks from space aimed at your head. It would be different if you had an astronaut's helmet. That would make you safe.

In *Passage to Pluto* the astronauts are in trouble because one of the fuel tanks has been hit by a meteorite. They only just make it back to Earth safely. The last thing they do in the book is thank God. The captain, Chris, prays in *Journey to Jupiter*, too. Maybe the astronauts are Catholics, like us.

At school, Pat Stapleton told us his Dad didn't have a pub any more. It had been burnt down and so had another Irish pub in Kingstanding. David Hennessey looked at the ground and didn't say a word. Francis Byrne said there'd been a fire at St Gerard's school. I looked at him and knew that, just this once, he wasn't lying.

I looked around at our school. The Infants' end of the playground. The dinner hall.

They showed the six Irishmen again on the telly. Eamonn was out. The reporter said the men were in court. There was another demonstration outside. A woman was carrying a banner with the words 'Hang In Shame' written on it, above a picture of six stick men swinging from six nooses. The woman wasn't any good at drawing, not like the girl at school who could draw a star from two triangles.

Mum said to Dad: 'Where do those men live?'

'Over Aston and Nechells way. One of them lives in Erdington, I think.'

'Are any of them from Derry?'

'They're from Belfast, I've heard. New Lodge. Maybe one of them's from Derry.'

'Have we seen them?'

'Probably, at the Centre.'

'Have we spoken to any of them?'

'I've spoken with Walker. He does the raffles. I sold a few tickets, too, remember?'

'Does he know our names?'

'He knows our first names anyway.'

'Jesus.' Her voice got higher. 'None of them were here that night, were they Billy?'

'No.'

'Thank God. Thank God.'

My dad lit a cigarette. My mum asked for one. She didn't normally smoke at home. She leant forward. Her hand trembled as he lit the cigarette for her. She inhaled sharply.

At mass, Father Duggan told us to respect our neighbours' grief, not to cause a fuss. We went to the Irish Centre afterwards.

We didn't normally go on Sunday lunchtime. It was very quiet. Two of the windows were boarded up and there was scaffolding around the roof. My dad and a man I'd never seen before talked in a corner.

There was no ceilidh or dancing or songs about the IRA. The whole place was almost silent, just whispers and the shuffling of feet. Pints of Guinness sulked on the bar.

I leant against my mum's shoulder on the bus and closed my eyes. I'd thought the Irish Centre was a safe place for Irish people in Birmingham but it seemed as though nowhere was safe anymore. I heard my dad tell Mum that plain clothes policemen, Special Branch, were coming into the Irish Centre and listening to people talking, and that police and the army were turning up to Glebe Farm whenever there was Gaelic football or hurling. The police were also approaching people in the streets outside the Centre, asking them to be touts, and there were people taking photographs, too. People no one had seen before.

My dad also said the man in the Irish Centre told him that the McAnespie's house had been raided because the neighbours had heard them singing Irish rebel songs, and that people had been putting bricks through the windows of Sean O'Sullivan's vans and lorries. Mum sniffed and put her hand to her eyes. Maria looked out of the window.

Dad said, barely above a whisper: 'Jim Hegarty's been arrested.' My mum said 'Jesus,' and wrapped her arm around me tightly. Maria went to say something but stopped. I shut my eyes and kept them closed until we reached the stop for our house. I didn't know what a tout was but it didn't sound good. I knew what a raid was and I knew Jim Hegarty. He wasn't as good at singing as Jamesie. Mum was scared of him. As we turned the corner into our street I was worried I was going to see police cars outside our house, or maybe a crowd of angry people with stones, carrying banners saying they wanted to hang us, but there was nothing. Just the row of grey houses all looking the same. Mrs Gow swept her curtains closed.

My dad slept in the afternoon because he was starting a week of night shifts. Maria stayed in her room. Eamonn was out again.

I woke up in the middle of the night. It was pitch black.

I lay on my back. I could hear my mum moaning, like sobs without the tears. She was moving around in her bed. I didn't know what was upsetting her. It could be all the bad things that were happening to us. It could be something I'd done, like wetting the bed, or not telling her about the Feldon Street boys. It might have been her moaning that woke me.

I hoped she hadn't woken anyone else. I hoped she hadn't woken Eamonn downstairs. I wished my dad wasn't on a night shift. The moaning stopped. I turned over, faced the wall, shut my eyes.

In *Destination Mars*, the astronauts hear strange voices on the radio as they approach the planet. They describe the sounds and moans as a choir of the damned. Tony shouts at the others to turn it off because he can't stand it. The voices make him collapse in a faint. The Martians appear to the astronauts as glowing balls of light. They're aliens but they need a new home. The astronauts leave the Martians behind.

There were no glowing lights in my room, just darkness.

Mum got me ready for school the next morning. She was in a hurry about everything. I went upstairs to brush my teeth. Mum and Dad's bedroom door was wide open. The sheets were all crumpled and tangled like they'd been fighting.

I stopped outside the bathroom door. The taps were running and tumbling. Eamonn was quietly singing.

'She wore a bonnet
With ribbons on it
And around her shoulders
Was the Galway shawl.'

I turned round to go back downstairs. My mum was at the bottom. Her mouth was open. I tried to tell her I hadn't brushed my teeth, but she just handed me my school bag and bundled me out the door.

I don't want to be Irish, I want to be English. If I was English the boys from Feldon Street wouldn't pick on me. Each day after school I get called an Irish bastard on my way home. My backside gets kicked as I pass them. They throw stones and swing punches at me. One of them shouted, 'Go home, Paddy!' Another one spat at me. I wiped it off with a piece of toilet paper when I got home. It left a smear on the arm of my jumper. I sniffed it to see if it smelled bad.

Someone has chalked 'Irish Bastards' on the wall of the alley behind our house, as well as 'National Front.' They're written right above the bare, spiky branches of the berry bush. I licked my palm and smeared it down the writing to blur the words.

I think I must be English. I was English that time they showed the important football match between England and Poland on television. Maria drew me a picture of a little Union Jack with the word 'England' underneath it. England could only draw, which meant they didn't go to the World Cup Finals. Scotland went instead so I supported Scotland, but they were out after the first bit. Then I wanted Holland to win because they had Johann Cruyff, but Holland lost in the final to West Germany. There was an English referee in the final, Jack Taylor, and he was on the television. They showed him in his butcher's shop, swiping his big knife through a large slab of meat and laughing with his customers. There was an English bit in the World Cup after all and everyone felt proud. Jack Taylor looked a little bit like Fred. I wanted to go back to Fred's and hear my mum laughing, the way she used to.

When we play army at school we're always English. Me and David Hennessy marched across the playground together one day saying 'Rule Britannia.' We didn't know any more of the words so we just kept repeating 'Rule Britannia.'

I'm sick of being picked on by the Feldon Street boys. It's because I go to a different school to them. It's because I'm the only boy on the estate with an Irish Mum and Dad. It's Mum and Dad's fault and the IRA's fault. If I wasn't Irish and I was like them, they wouldn't hit me.

The four of us were sitting at our table in the kitchen, eating dinner. I had something to tell them. I said, 'I wouldn't be Irish for all the gold in the world.'

My dad said, 'You should be ashamed of yourself.' He shouted the 'shamed' bit really loudly. He drew it out into two syllables. He put his knife and fork down to say it. They clanged on his plate. No one else said anything.

I started walking a different way home to avoid the Feldon Street boys. Instead of going the quick way down Galton Road, I went along Overton Road and into Summerfield Avenue. I stayed out of the alley, too, in case they were there. I thought about the blackberry bushes on their own, any last berries rotting on their stalks, growing fur. Or maybe there were just bare branches, like thorns or spikes.

A boy in Feldon Street uniform stopped me on Overton Road. He said, 'There's a gang of lads out to get you.' I ran most of the rest of the way.

There were two, grown-up men outside Barker's, looking at the papers in the window. One of them said, 'They must be guilty. They were going to that funeral.' The other man nodded and said, 'They're all the same, all of that lot. They give money, you know, and they know full well where it's going. I've walked past Irish pubs and heard them singing. It's all about the IRA. They're all in it together.'

Dad was out at work. Mum and Eamonn were in the living room. She told me to go upstairs. I stopped in the front room instead, where I could hear them.

'It can't happen again, Eamonn. I mustn't do that to Billy again. You're a family man now. We had to leave Derry because of all the gossip. Maria –'

'But Annie, Bridget was pregnant. I had to marry her but I've never loved her. Derry and Belfast are like that, Annie. The Bogside's nothing but a village. Ardoyne's the same. Everywhere over there is like that. It's different here. We could go to London. No one would know us. We could both leave our pasts behind. I'll quit the movement and everything. This is more important. You can take off his wedding ring and wear a ring of mine. This is love, Annie.'

'They won't let you quit. They'll find you, wherever you are.'

'I'm not scared of them and I'm not scared of the Brits. I was in Derry on Bloody Sunday. A Para said to me, "Get your hands on your head, you Irish cunt." He shoved the barrel of his rifle in my mouth. I could taste the gun oil. After what I saw that day, I'll never be scared again.'

'I have Danny, Eamonn, as well as Maria.'

'A child should be conceived in love, Annie. You were my first love. The love of my heart. Remember Brighton? We should have stayed there. None of this would have happened if we'd stayed there. Just a quiet Irish couple, known to no one, bringing up our own children.'

'I didn't want another child, Eamonn, that's true. I thought I'd timed it right. But you're talking rubbish. You have to face the truth.'

'And what about Maria, doesn't she deserve to know the truth?'

Someone moved. The talking stopped. I went upstairs.

I'd only heard the word cunt once before. Andrew Cochrane said it. Eamonn told my mum she was the love of his heart. That was a line in the song, 'The Boys of the Old Brigade', but it was sung in Irish – A gra ma kree. Eamonn shouldn't have been saying any of those words to my mum. I didn't know if I should tell Dad because he should be the one saying things like that to her. Eamonn also said a child should be conceived in love. It sounded like a line from a poem, or like something Father Duggan would say. Mum said she didn't want another child, so I wouldn't get a brother or another sister. She'd talked about timing it right but I didn't understand that at all. And Eamonn wanted Mum to wear a ring for him. Maybe rings were like berets or beers. They said who you were and who you belonged to.

I didn't know what to do about what I'd heard. I thought it might make sense to hold on to what I knew, for a while at least. Sometimes it was better to keep a thing on the inside. You wouldn't get a black mark on your tongue. I wouldn't tell on someone.

Space is silent. All astronauts hear is the quiet bleeping of their instruments, like a heartbeat. If there is a problem the bleeps get louder until it sounds like a police car or an ambulance, and you know you must do something to solve it. That's why not everyone can be an astronaut. You have to be one of the clever ones. If you get a signal from your instruments you have to know what it means, or be able to figure it out. You have to time it right.

American astronauts wear NASA spacesuits. Russian cosmonauts have CCCP on their spacesuits. I wouldn't mind which suit I wore as long as it was safe and kept me breathing oxygen. Astronauts shouldn't be too worried about which spacesuit they wear as long as everything's OK. In the future we'll live in space. I want to live in the future, or anywhere that's not here.

I thought about adding more to my story but it was all too confusing. I didn't understand why adults would worry so much about which ring to wear. Saturn had rings but they were just beautiful and they didn't mean that Saturn belonged to anyone. Space was simpler than down here and it made more sense.

Eamonn & Billy

'What in God's name have you done, Eamonn? It's a mortal sin. It's murder. Thou shalt not kill. It's the sixth commandment.'

'I'm fighting for Ireland to be free, Billeen.'

'It's the Irish Army should be doing that.'

'You're joking of course. What's the Irish Army? A handful of illiterate farmers with World War Two guns. Those mean-minded feckers in the Republic are too busy robbing land off each other to worry about us. Do you know what the Irish Army did when the North blew up? Opened a couple of field hospitals and refugee centres over the border. Gave out cups of tea. Cups of fecking tea, Billeen! Forget about them. It's up to us to carry the fight.'

'And who is us, Eamonn? You get little kids to throw stones and petrol bombs. How many soldiers have the Brits got? How many RUC have the Prods got? You can't kill them all, they'll just send new ones in. And who is getting killed? Civilians, that's who. You're dreaming, Eamonn.'

'Our leaders say we have to bring the campaign over here. They say we're weakening the Brits' will to stay.'

'The leaders think about themselves, or else they're fighting amongst themselves. They line their own pockets. Don't tell me you know nothing about the armed robberies back home. And anyone who disagrees with them gets a bullet through the knee-caps. There's young ones will never walk again thanks to your leaders. They're not looking after me. A little old woman in a headscarf called me a bloody murderer as she got off my bus. And I'm getting a lot worse than that. My passengers used to give me sweets and now they spit at me. Your leaders don't give a damn about what this is doing to our lives over here. Your leaders hate the Brits but collect their British social security payments every week and live in council flats paid for by the Brits. Your leaders don't recognise British courts but they're quick enough to recognise a British dole cheque. When Annie went back for her sister's funeral she took a wallet full of English money for her family. And we've given her family and mine money besides that, sending a postal order every week for the first eighteen months we were here. England has done more for me than Ireland ever did. I'm keeping my head down, Eamonn, and hoping you lot will go away so we can go back to our lives. You don't live here. You just make our lives hell. You think The Tavern and The Mulberry Bush will weaken their will to stay? You think they'll give in? Not at all, not a cat in hell's chance. It will do the opposite. They'll just dig in. There's plenty of working class lads over here that will join the Army because it's the only thing on offer. This nonsense has got to stop, stop altogether. The whole lot of you should drop your guns and your bombs and get a, what do they call it, a negotiated settlement. Just talk to the Protestants.'

'Will you listen to yourself, Billeen? Talk to the Prods? The Prods' police beat us off the street when we marched peacefully. And what was the other thing? Oh yes, a "negotiated settlement." The Brits don't want it. Do you know they opened a laundrette to spy on us? The driver of the laundry van didn't last long before the lads shot him. The Brits even opened a whorehouse in Belfast.

There's no such thing as a negotiated settlement, Billeen. You don't talk about peace until you've won the war. They'll speak with us, no matter what they say. When you're weak you make sure you don't negotiate, and when you're strong you don't have to because they do what you want. And we're getting stronger now. The Brits attacked us, Billeen, not the other way around. They turned a blind eye when we were burnt out of our homes. Either that or they joined in. There's power in the barrel of a gun and there's power in a bomb and if some people are in the wrong place at the wrong time, so be it. It's a war. We'll be fighting in Ireland as long as the Brits are there and by God we'll outlast them. We've had eight hundred years of them and they've never beaten us yet. And a bomb in England is worth ten times more than a bomb in Belfast. The Brits couldn't care less what happens over there but if we bring it to their doorsteps that's a whole different story. They thought it was just mad Paddies, just peasants killing each other, but they're thinking differently now their boys are coming back in coffins and wheelchairs. They can ignore bombs in Belfast but not bombs in Birmingham. They brought the war to us and now we're bringing the war back to them. It's a revolution. You can lie down or run away, or you can stand and fight. It's time to pick a side. Time to be a man and not a frightened little boy, Billeen.'

'It's a revolution now, is it? What are yous, a bunch of communists? Then why are yous running protection rackets in Belfast and Derry and South Armagh? Just think about The Tavern and The Mulberry Bush. They were innocent people, Eamonn. You're not killing generals and politicians. You're killing girls and boys.

You're killing working people like yourselves. Whoever did the pubs deserves to go to prison. Someone should tell the police.'

A pause. Billy wipes his hand across his eyes. 'And Annie: what are you doing to her, Eamonn? Don't you know the seventh commandment?'

Eamonn's voice drops down low. 'You just remember whose side you're on. You're either with us or against us, and once you're against us there's nothing to stop you informing. We know there's touts everywhere, watching us like fecking birds of prey, and we all know what happens to touts, don't we? Did you hear about that one on Creggan, the one who lived near Central Drive? Dumped behind the shops he was, hooded and barefoot. Sometimes I think round the back of Creggan shops must be one of the most dangerous places in the world.

'There were three bullets in the back of the tout's head, Billeen. Bruises and cigarette burns all over him. Eyes taped shut. Hands tied behind his back. His body wrapped in black polythene, strapped up with masking tape. He looked like a bundle of rags. And the smell from him, like shit in a slaughterhouse. You know why they wrap the polythene tight at the neck don't you? To keep the blood in. You'd been at school with that lad, Billeen. You were his friend. So you know enough to keep your mouth shut about everything. Just remember the RUC at home and the police here, they're just extensions of the Army, another part of the Brits' rule. The police don't carry truncheons and handcuffs for the fun of it. The Brits' courts are the same. There's no justice for Irish people over here. You stay onside.'

'Just don't take Annie from me, Eamonn. Don't take her from me.'

'Sure, I wouldn't dream of it, Bill.' Eamonn says it slowly and fondly, like he is talking to a child. He pats Billy on the back. He leaves his hand there.

'The feller from Creggan, Billeen, he made a taped confession. I heard it. He started by saying he was making his confession of his own free will.' Eamonn stifles a laugh. 'Never heard anything so funny in my life. And we all know the penance he got for his confession, don't we? And I've heard another rumour that one in every twenty of us is a tout. Can you believe that, Billeen, or do you think it could be even worse? Do you think it might be one in ten?'

'I wouldn't know, Eamonn.'

'You might know more than you're letting on, Billeen. Bus drivers meet a lot of people. They know where people go. There was one in Derry who was in the UDR on the quiet. Dragged from his bus, he was, with the schoolkids on the bus screaming and howling. The boys threw him in a car and he was found a few hours later round the back of Creggan shops again, shot in the back of the head, and his blood as thick as tar.'

Eamonn explodes with laughter. 'Sure I'm only pulling your leg, Billeen! You're sound as a pound, aren't you?'

My dad and Eamonn were in the living room, talking quietly. Maybe they were scared. There had been bombs in Guildford, London, Coventry, Birmingham. Someone was behind it all. And the police were arresting Irish people.

And kids were called Irish bastards and got kicked and punched.

And Irish families ran barefoot up the streets, carrying bits of furniture while their houses went up in flames.

Eamonn was out the whole of the next day. In the evening the doorbell rang. I ran to get it. I thought it would be Eamonn but it was Jim Hegarty. There were bruises all over his face, black and blue splodges. His eyes were bloodshot. His top lip was swollen. Maybe he had got into a fight on the buses again, like the time the police came to our house to take a statement from my dad. We looked at each other, neither of us knowing what to say.

My mum trotted down the stairs. 'Jesus, Mary and Joseph!'

Jim stepped in. He walked awkwardly, dragging one of his legs behind him. Mum pulled him into the living room and called for my dad. 'Billy, come here!'

My dad ran down the stairs. He stopped dead when he saw Jim. 'Danny,' he said. 'Go upstairs. Annie, put the kettle on.' His voice was firmer than usual. I went into the front room and stood very still. Jim started talking.

'They took me in. Came at five in the morning. Raided the house. Took the bloody door off its hinges, so they did. Loads of them. Alsatian dogs and everything. Said they'd been keeping an eye on me for months, that someone had informed against me, a bloody tout. Marched the wife and kids into the kitchen, the boy just wearing his underpants. They took his Boy's Brigade uniform. Thought it was something to do with the IRA. They asked the wife and kids if I was an IRA member. Asked my wife for her name. When she told them it was Theresa they said the only name for her was IRA whore. Took all the leaflets and newspapers, the money for the families, all the copies of *Republican News*.'

'Did they do that to you? Just look at your face. Your mouth.' It was my mum's voice. There was silence for a minute.

'Did they say who the tout – What did they want from you?' asked my dad.

'Names. Names and addresses of everyone I knew in the IRA or Sinn Fein. The names of sympathisers. Everything.'

'Did you give them our names?'

'I had – no, no I didn't. But I told them all the Birmingham IRA people I knew. What choice did I have? They had photos of me singing at the Irish Centre, doing the raffles, talking with people outside, even a photo of me at the Irish Parade. They kneed me in the bollocks, told me there was a mob outside my house, that my kids were in danger if I didn't cooperate. Told me they would crucify me and dump my body.'

Mum whispered, 'Jesus Christ. Photos at the Irish Centre. We could be in them.'

Jim spoke again. 'They also wanted to know how well I knew the six lads they've charged.'

'Do you know them?'

'A couple of them, just to say hello to. And of course I knew Jamesie, like we all did. But those six fellers they've got won't know anything about the bombings. The police have got the wrong men. I think some of the police know it. But there's no stopping it now. If they can't lay their hands on one Irishman they'll grab another. Any of us will do.'

Jim paused and his voice lowered. 'Get rid of anything you've got. Keep your heads down. Don't speak to anyone.'

'But we have a visitor.'

'Who?'

'Eamonn from back home. From Creggan.'

There was a pause. Someone breathed out loudly.

'Feckin hell,' said Jim. 'Has anyone seen him? Any of your neighbours?'

'I don't know,' said my mum. 'I don't think so. He's lying low.'

'Not low enough, knowing him. Do you think he knows who planted – Or maybe he – Just tell him to go. Tell him to go at night-time. When he won't be seen. Make it tonight.'

'No one can tell him anything.' It was my dad's voice. The kettle came to the boil and screamed. I walked backwards to the bottom of the stairs, tiptoed up and hid under my bed, grabbing hold of my P.I. gun.

I asked Maria what a tout was. She said a tout was a tell-tale, the lowest of the low, because they took money for telling on people. Touts were always willing and able to lie. Touts got shot dead in Northern Ireland because they talked to the police and the RUC.

No one liked a tell-tale at school. If someone hit or kicked you in the playground you knew not to tell on them. Either you got them back or you put up with it. But Maria said a tout was much worse because they told tales to the police. I couldn't work out why that was so bad because the police were there to help you. If someone burgled your house you would tell the police so they could catch him.

One of the good things about a space mission is that everyone works together and helps each other. You wouldn't get a tout there. In *Nearly Neptune*, Tony tried to sacrifice himself to save the rest of the crew but they wouldn't let him. Chris did the same in *Journey to Jupiter*. All the astronauts stuck together and no one was a tout.

You had to have money. That's why people did jobs. If your job didn't pay you enough money, you had to get more. But you shouldn't have to tout for it. And to be a tout you had to be willing and able to lie, that's what Maria said. Being able to do it was one thing, you'd get away with it sometimes, but there'd have to be something wrong with you to lie to your family and friends, to tell on them to the police. And if the place where you lived was dangerous, like Northern Ireland, there might be more than one tout around and you'd have a world where loads of people spied on each other. One tout might tell on another tout just to keep himself out of trouble.

You could tout in England, too, then you wouldn't feel safe anywhere. England would become like Northern Ireland. You'd have people watching you all the time, using binoculars or the periscope-type thing my cousin Gerard owned. You'd have soldiers pointing their rifles at council flats and houses like ours, like they did to Divis Flats. The Army went into Northern Ireland because the police couldn't handle the situation. They could do the same here. I'd always thought the police and the Army were there to protect us, but what if they weren't?

People wouldn't just volunteer to be a tout. Maybe they could be forced to do it by someone stronger than them. In that case they shouldn't be punished for it if they had no choice. Or maybe they would do it just for the money, even though it wouldn't be worth it. Or maybe they'd do it for revenge. Maybe, if someone did something really bad to you, you'd get them back by telling someone, maybe your teacher or something like that. Like if you

194

were a man and someone stole your wife or something like that, you'd tell on them, you'd tout, to get your revenge.

Eamonn was by himself in the living room. There was a bottle of whiskey in front of him. I could see the label, Jameson's. More than half was gone. He held a glass in his hand and turned it around slowly. I saw the smudge of his fingerprints against the gold.

'Hello Danny,' he said, smiling.

'Hello.'

'My name's Eamonn, by the way. Call me by my name.'

'OK.'

'Do you like school, Danny?'

'No, not really.'

He smiled. 'I didn't care for it much either, to tell you the truth. Nuns are a vicious breed. And ceilidh? Do you love ceilidh, Danny?'

'No.'

'But you're Irish. You should. It's the music of your people.' He paused, took another gulp. 'It's all changed, I suppose. Pop music and that. I have one daughter mad for Donny Osmond and another mad for Marc Bolan. No sign of them growing out of it. And you, what do you want to be when you're grown up, Danny?'

'I don't know. An astronaut, maybe.'

Eamonn laughed. 'Sounds grand. Aim high, I suppose. Just be careful you don't end up like me.'

'Did the man not give you a job?'

'What man? Never you mind about a man, young feller.'

He downed the whiskey in his glass in one gulp and poured another.

'It couldn't have gone much worse, Danny,' he said. 'We couldn't phone the warning through in time. I had the password ready, Double X, so they'd know it was genuine. But, but, vandalised phone boxes, Danny. You have a fierce problem with vandalism in this country. No respect for property at all. All we needed was to speak to someone, to warn them what was coming their way. And once a timer's started there's nothing much you can do to stop it.

'But those civilians, the boys and girls in the pubs, my God.' He rubbed his hand over his forehead. 'All we aim for is... But never mind. It's too late now. They have six Irish lads lined up to take the punishment and I'm sure they're taking it already. Never mind, never mind. But those young people... just having a drink... like I would... the innocent... the girl with the red hair... Jesus. All that blood. They'll never clean it up.'

He took a drink again. 'I had a dog once, Danny, when I was a boy, about your age. It got hit by the coalmen's lorry. It took about half an hour to die, lying in the middle of the street and all it could do was howl and the sound's never left me. It got fainter and fainter until he was just bleating like a goat or a lamb. I never meant to harm anyone in my life, Danny. Not until...' He drank some more. 'There's a saying, Danny, Ireland unfree shall never be at peace. Do you know who said that?'

'Padraig Pearce, Eamonn.'

'Clever boy. You're dead on. Maybe you can say that on the moon when you're an astronaut, make it your first words when you walk on the surface of a planet. That kind of knowledge would get you a long way in my line of work, but I'd advise you to steer clear of it. An astronaut doesn't need to know that sort of thing. The stuff I know is best suited for a man with his feet stuck fast in the place where he came from. When I joined up I knew all I would get was a cell or a coffin. That's the shadow hanging over every Volunteer, Danny, they told me so in training. It's one or the other. You can't escape it forever. They also told me the Irish people would support us like the tide. It might be in or it might be out, but it would always be there. It's out now, anyway.' He sighed. 'Will you look down and wave at me when you're in space?'

'I will. Where will you be?'

'I think I'll be in the same place for a long time. Maybe somewhere cold, maybe somewhere really hot. You'll be fine though and so will Maria. You have a lovely sister, Danny. Lovely red hair. She's my weakness, Danny. She's my own special girl. An educated young man like you might call her my Achilles heel.' He lifted his drink to the light to inspect it, as if he expected it to tell him something important, or as if he might find something there, something he had lost.

As I walked away I could hear Eamonn singing softly. 'Better to die 'neath an Irish sky.' He sang it slowly. His voice slurred. He hiccupped and mumbled. It was like he was remembering something that made him happy, something from a long time ago.

I climbed the stairs and heard a big bump coming from the living room. Maybe Eamonn had fallen over. I left him alone.

I stopped outside Maria's room. It looked different somehow, as though the door and the walls were more solid than before, like there was a barricade between us.

I told the lads at school that a tout was the worst thing you could be. Pat Stapleton said he knew already and his big brother had told him what the IRA do to touts. 'They put a hood over you,' he said, 'make you kneel down, hold a gun to the back of your head and bang! Your brains are all over the place. They don't give the body back either, so you don't get a funeral and you don't go to heaven. They just dump your body in an empty road near the border.'

Being a tout would be a lonely kind of life, having secrets you could share with no one. Being scared all the time of what might happen to you, saying things about the people you knew, just for some money. It was like the thing Judas did to Jesus, betraying those closest to you for a few coins. And once you'd got used to the money you'd keep coming back, telling more and more. You'd mix lies up with the truth and everything. You'd end up telling on people who'd done nothing wrong, just to keep the money coming in. You might have a house and a new suit on your back, but you'd be worried all the time. And you'd see the people around you all upset because they'd know something bad was happening but wouldn't know who was doing all the telling. And you'd end up like Judas who hanged himself, or you'd be dumped in an alley or rain-ditch somewhere, just a lonely, dead body with nobody to mind it, picked at by magpies and crows.

Touting was terrible but it wasn't the same as lying. A lie was something you might have to do now and then. A priest would make a good tout because he'd know everybody's secrets. And the people who killed the touts, they'd have to be pure, just like the priests.

The alien spoke in a strange way. It was like it was trying to speak English but kept drifting off into its own language.

'Whirr-whirr – Danger.'

'Clang-clang – Earth in danger.'

The clang-clang got louder, like an emergency was happening. And the clang-clang kept happening. Clang-clang-clang-clang-clang, like the banging of dustbin lids.

The sound stopped suddenly and the alien spoke in perfect English.

'Tick-tick-tick – Earth in danger Danny. You have to do something. Phone a warning.'

December 1974

It looked like Mum and Dad were going to have another party because they were tidying up a lot, as though something important was happening. I asked Mum and she said there would be no more parties, but I knew something was going on.

It was pitch black when the door rang. My dad answered it. Jim Hegarty stood there.

'Is he in?' asked Jim.

My dad nodded.

'Right. Let's get this sorted out.'

Eamonn walked out of the living room towards them. Dad shut and bolted the door.

'Hello, Jim, how are you keeping?'

'Not bad, Eamonn.'

'It's been a long time.'

'It has, Eamonn.'

'Your mother was still going strong, the last I heard.'

'Her legs give her trouble, Eamonn, but she still gets about. Says the rosary every night.'

'They make them of strong stuff in the Bogside, Jim. Just like Ardoyne.' He paused. 'I hear you had a bit of trouble.'

'I did, Eamonn, I did. They gave me a right going over. Cuts and bruises from head to toe. Day after day of it. Told me they could keep me there for seven days.'

'It's a war, Jim. Everyone plays by big boys' rules.'

'I know what it is, Eamonn. I was in one of their cells taking a beating. But I've been thinking about it since. There was one funny thing. After they'd beaten me they left the cell and this other copper came in and gave me a pork pie. I think it was his own lunch. It was the first thing I'd eaten in thirty-six hours.'

'He was just trying to soften you up so you'd talk. You know the golden rule: whatever you say, say nothing.'

'I don't think so. He said he didn't agree with all the violence.'

'You fell for that one, Jim? You'll be turning tout next. And what did you tell them, by the way?'

'Honest to God I'm no tout. I didn't tell them anything they didn't already know. But there was one decent man amongst them, Eamonn.'

'Will you cop yourself on, Jim Hegarty. They're Brits. Violence is the only thing they listen to. It was stones, guns and bombs that drove them out of Cyprus, Aden and Kenya. They lost their other colonial wars and they'll lose this one. The British Empire never left anywhere because people asked nicely. Those bastards invaded us eight hundred years ago. Cromwell's men massacred women and children, kicked us out into reservations and renamed the towns on our own soil. Bloody British Army. I've no idea what the fuck they teach their officers at Sandringham, but they put us under curfew in Belfast and Derry and fired CS gas at us, and told us we'd be shot if we went outside.' He stopped for a second and wiped spit from his lower lip. 'And by the way, Jim, there's a tout somewhere. A Judas amongst us. Someone will have given them your name and I think you might just have given them a few more crumbs. If they raid here I'll know who to thank.'

201

My dad knocked an ashtray over, the grey and white ash and the black, dead matchsticks sprawling over the carpet. The matchsticks looked like little men.

Jim stared at Eamonn. 'I told you I'm no tout, Eamonn, and I don't believe there's one amongst us. There's no newcomers. We've all known each other too long. Yes I gave them names, Eamonn, because I was having the shit kicked out of me, but I only know the names everyone knows and I didn't know you were over here. I'm not so deep in. Listen to me, Eamonn, I'm not a tout.'

'They have touts right in amongst us, Jim. A good one is a pearl to them. They only need one feller in a high enough place to bring us all tumbling down. They pay the bastards. Money talks and it gets people talking. OK, you're not one, but keep your eye out for anyone with a lot of money all of a sudden. And don't turn your back on the armed struggle, Jim. That's the only thing that will force the Brits out.'

'And where is the armed struggle getting us, Eamonn? Poor Jamesie blown to smithereens. A young man with a wife and children.'

'Jamesie was a hero. They'll be singing songs about him for years to come. He died for his country, Jim, and we gave it back to them with interest in the pubs. Are you man enough to do the same?'

My dad suddenly noticed I was there. 'Go up to your room, Danny.'

Eamonn said they'd be singing songs about Jamesie. I'd heard the people at the Irish Centre sing about James Connolly and they sang other songs with people's names in them, too: Sean South and Kevin Barry. Maybe there would be songs about Jamesie McDade. It wouldn't be a hard word to rhyme: made – paid – betrayed. Maybe his wife and children would be happy to hear the songs about him. But I thought about the little boy who watched me while I ate a Jaffa Cake. He didn't want to hear a song. He wanted his Dad back. There would be no songs about Jamesie's wife and his little boys.

I didn't have a library book so I reached under my bed and pulled out one I had when I was little. It was stories about Brer Rabbit. He was small but he was clever and that was how he beat his enemies. There was one story where a fox caught him and Brer Rabbit said to the fox, 'Do what you like but don't throw me into those bushes.' So that's what the fox did, but the fox didn't know Brer Rabbit had been born in the bushes and was safe there. Maybe that's what you had to do to be in a safe house, stay in the place you were born or go back there. But we'd come to Birmingham because we weren't safe in Derry and now we weren't safe in Birmingham. The McAnespies had been raided. Jim Hegarty had been raided, taken in and beaten up. All I wanted was a safe house. I was small and clever like Brer Rabbit. The stories showed how a small creature could beat a big one by outsmarting him and knowing more about the land. I tried reading more of the stories but I knew them all, and anyway I was too old.

Maria had some books in her room, from school. I'd taken one when she wasn't in. It was told by a young girl. She lived in America and everyone was tough on black people. The young girl, Scout, couldn't see why they were so bad to them. Her Dad was quiet but you knew he was good. He shot a mad dog one time and killed it stone dead, but apart from that he didn't use a gun. That's the Dad I wanted to have. A strong and clever Dad and a safe house the police wouldn't raid.

The shouting woke me up. I peeped down from the top of the stairs. It was like the time Mum and Dad had a party, only this time my mum was shouting at Jim Hegarty. Dad and Eamonn were there, too.

'I don't care if they talk about me. They'll find someone else to talk about soon enough.'

'No one will talk about you,' said Jim, pressing his hands down.

'Get the fuck out!'

I had never heard my mum swear before. My dad put his arm on her shoulder and tried to pull her back. Jim Hegarty opened the front door and limped out. He turned back.

'They called my wife an IRA whore, but I only know one IRA whore round here. You know what they do to women like that at home, don't you? Hey, Billeen, ever wondered why you have dark hair while your daughter's is red?'

My mum sprang forward. My dad pulled her back by the arms. Jim Hegarty headed into the dark, slamming the door behind him.

There was silence. Eamonn turned away and ran his hand over the top of his bald head. My dad let go of my mum's arms and said quietly, 'You've all been making a fool of me.'

The Space Para crouched down, took aim at Danny and fired. Danny ducked but he heard someone go 'Yeoww! Clang!' behind him. He turned around and saw the alien on its back, its little arms and legs waving in the air. Danny took aim with his own gun and fired a ray of laser light at the Space Para. The Space Para threw his arms back and crumbled into dust.

There was the sound of the heavy clump of spacesuit boots. More Space Paras were coming, lumbering up to the nearest crater.

Danny turned and ran back into a cave and waited. His breath was heavy inside his space helmet but he did not get asthma. He had been lucky this time, he would have to be cleverer next time. He would set a couple of space bombs, one on the path where the Space Paras ran and another off to the side, in the direction they would run when the first bomb went off. The Space Paras had done lots of really terrible things but Danny would make sure they would pay for them. The Space Paras would have to get out, get the something out.

Then he wondered, how many Space Paras would they send to attack him? Could he take on all of them? He was just one astronaut. But he wasn't afraid of them. Beneath their space suits they were just like any other living thing. A ray of laser light would kill a Space Para just as easily as it would kill a dog or cat, even though it would be wrong to kill a dog or cat.

There were broken cups on the floor in the morning. There was tea and ash on the carpet, and an empty Guinness bottle. A drop of the black stout hung at the rim.

Mum was on her hands and knees, scrubbing at the stains. She was whispering to herself, 'I must wash my hands when all this is done, when all this is done, wash my hands.'

'What happened Mum?'

'A little accident.'

'Where's Dad?'

'Out working.'

'Where's Eamonn?'

'Out too, I think. I don't know.'

'Why is there all this mess?'

'There just is and now I can't get rid of it.'

'Mum – '

'Danny, leave me alone.'

As I headed to my bedroom I could hear her talking to herself: 'Nothing will get it clean. Nothing will get rid of it. Jesus.'

I walked past Mum and Dad's room. Some of my mum's clothes lay on the bed, folded up. One of her drawers was open. Knickers and bras spilled out of it. I pressed them down and pushed the drawer shut. It juddered.

Mum had put her books in a big box next to her side of the bed. They looked lonely. I got my science-fiction books and laid them next to hers, so that all the books would have some company. They nestled up against each other.

My mum's pillow had ripped open. Feathers smothered the spot where her head normally lay. I wanted to rest my own head there but the feathers were bad for my asthma.

Mum's statue of the Virgin Mary had fallen from her dressing table. It lay on the floor, facing the ceiling. One of her arms had broken off.

My dad worked that night. Mum knelt by her bed alone and prayed: 'HolyMaryMotherofGodprayforussinnersnow…' There were no lights on in her room but the landing light was on. It made the back of her head glow a little, like the last flicker of flame on a match before it went out.

In *Mission to Mercury*, radiation shooting out from sunspots was destroying the astronauts' brain cells because the shielding on their spaceship had failed, but they didn't know it and they were all arguing. The same thing was happening to the people around me – my mum, my dad, Eamonn, Jim Hegarty. Bit by bit they were all turning on each other and none of them knew the real reason why. It was something outside of them, poisoning them.

In the same book the astronauts had to change course suddenly to avoid colliding with a satellite. I couldn't see anyone in my family changing course.

Maria moved into the nurses' home at the hospital. She packed one suitcase and left. All her eyeshadow and mascara and lipsticks went with her.

She must have gone in a hurry because she left her record player behind, and a hairbrush. The brush had lots of her hair on it, bright threads spilling out all over her window sill. It looked like a huge red spider.

She'd got a magazine, *Fabulous 208*. There was a girl on the front cover with dark hair parted in the middle. She was smiling a big, toothy grin with her head tilted to one side. She wore a tight necklace. The front cover said there was a free choker inside. I picked the magazine up and shook it to make the choker fall out but there was nothing there. I didn't know what a choker was anyway. Maybe it was the thing round the girl's neck. It looked like it was choking her. I didn't know why anyone would want to wear a tight thing like that.

There is no air in space. You breathe compressed air from a tank. Breathing might be hard inside a space helmet, like wearing a choker. Perhaps that's why astronauts sound like they've got asthma.

When I go for the job I can tell them I'll make a good astronaut because I already find it hard to breathe. I'll keep an eye on *The Sun* to see if they have a coupon to fill in about being an astronaut, like the ones they have for joining the British Army or the RAF.

The Hugh Walters books talked about G force in space travel. That's why the astronauts went in the centrifuge as part of their training. G force was the only bad thing about travelling into space. As you pulled away from the Earth it tried to pull you back. There was pain and the flesh on your face tugged backwards, like it didn't want you to leave. Your grip was tight and there was pressure on your head and your face and your teeth clenched and your tongue couldn't move in your mouth and it felt like there was a massive weight on top of you, but once you'd broken free of Earth's atmosphere there was a sudden release and everything was quiet and peaceful and you floated in space without ever falling to the floor or hurting yourself.

It looked like you had to have a bit of pain to get to the good place. It was like heaven – you went to purgatory first to pay off your sins. I hoped purgatory was just a boring place where you sat and waited, like Dr Burnett's surgery. I hoped there was no pain. No demons to torment or torture you, or punch you or throw stones at you or call you names.

When I am an astronaut I will check my instruments. They will be on a panel above my head. I will reach up and press anything needing attention. I will tell Mission Control that everything is

OK. Mission Control will say 'Mind your breathing, Danny.' I will look into space and it will be black as a pint of Guinness. I will see a bright light on the surface of the planet. I will head towards the light.

It's someone, a boy, all alone. He's the boy from space.

Danny looked out of the round window into outer space. It was black as a pint of Guinness. The other astronauts were on a spacewalk. Danny had to stay and mind the ship. He wondered what would happen if they didn't come back and he was left all alone.

A red light flashed on his instrument panel. An alarm sounded, echoing through the spaceship.

There was only Danny. He was alone after all.

Christmas 1974

Mum's gone. Eamonn's gone too. There's twelve days to Christmas. That's what my advent calendar says. It's like a countdown.

Eamonn's suitcase wasn't in the front room anymore. I looked under Mum and Dad's bed, behind their record player, and another suitcase was missing.

In the afternoon I was sitting on the floor in the living room. I was watching cartoons but could see through into the kitchen. My dad was sitting at the table by himself. The back door opened and Uncle Pat came in. He shook my dad's hand. Neither of them said anything. They never normally shook hands.

I love the Corona drinks at Christmas. We get four of them. Maria chooses two and I choose two. She always picks cherryade which is red, and I get limeade which is green. We mix the drinks. Maria calls it cocktails. Mum buys a block of Wall's ice cream and cuts a slice and puts it in our drinks. The drink fizzes up over the top. The inside of the glass gets coated with ice cream. I stick my tongue down the glass and lick around the sides. It's like when Mum makes a cake and gives me the spoon at the end and I eat the mixture raw. It's better than the cake itself.

Mum calls Corona 'minerals,' but she's not here. Someone else will have to buy the ice cream this year and make a cake, and someone else will have to flick Holy Water on my head when I go back to school. Maybe Maria will be here for Christmas Day, unless she's working at the hospital.

The Christmas lights are up in town, but they don't seem as bright as last year. There's mist and a soft rain. The clouds look like they're covered in bruises. The lights blur until there's just a red and orange glow, like the end of a fire. Everyone's keeping their heads down, lugging bags of shopping, shoulders slumped.

There's an old man dressed in a Father Christmas costume in Rackhams but there's no queue of little children waiting to meet him. He just sits there and drinks from a flask. Tinny carols squawk from a speaker, singing about a little donkey, or the stable in Bethlehem.

I took the paper with my story on it from Mum's pile of books and added some new bits.

'It's no use,' said the Brigadier. 'We will have to abandon the mission.'

'No,' said Danny. 'It's much too important.'

'But now we know what it's like, Danny. There's people from different planets fighting each other. They're blowing up each other's spaceships. The Space-Paras are raiding everywhere. People are getting killed!'

'It doesn't matter, Brigadier. I'm going to see this through, myself alone,' said Danny. 'If we don't free outer space it will never be at peace.'

I tried writing it a different way.

'Look Danny,' said the Brigadier. 'Chances are this problem will all settle down in the end. The aliens will go back to their world and we'll have our world. I know they're causing problems now but we're better off just waiting and being patient.' He nodded to his secretary, pretty Miss Annie. She nodded back. The quick clack-clack-clack of

211

her typewriter sounded like a round of applause. She had a straw-berry-coloured drink in front of her.

'Are you sure, Sir?' said Danny. 'I don't think we can wait. Some-one needs to step forward, come up with a plan to beat them.'

'It will take a brave astronaut, Danny,' said the Brigadier, rub-bing his moustache thoughtfully.

'I am that astronaut,' said Danny. Miss Annie stopped typing and looked up, her head on one side. The room was suddenly as silent as a graveyard.

Pretty Miss Annie had given Danny a framed photo of herself, pulling the same face. Danny kept it with his spare oxygen tank.

It was on the news that the police raided the home of an Irish family in London, the Maguires. At least it wasn't Birmingham. But the bombs started in London before coming to Birmingham. Maybe Mum and Eamonn went because they were scared of the raids and the touts, but Mum wouldn't go and leave me behind.

Maybe the rest of us will be leaving soon, before we get raided. I had better pack something. Maybe we'll be like the families in Belfast and Derry, running up the road carrying our sofa between us, or carrying our glass case. We're not liked around here any-more. No one is sorry for our trouble. We're Irish bastards.

Maybe Mum left because of me, something I did, like asthma or wetting the bed. I remembered what my dad said to me: 'You should be ashamed.' Maybe I did the thing that made her go.

I missed the last day of school before the holidays. We were going to have carols at St Michael's and Miss Blake said she'd bring in a Christmas cake, but after Mum went I had an asthma attack and I wasn't pretending. Dad told me to keep the windows open for fresh air, but after he went to work I shut them because of the cold. Lots of our neighbours already had their decorations up. Our house looked bare.

Maria came home to put our stuff up. She said I could help. I said OK because she didn't normally talk to me at all and we hardly saw her anymore. When she did come she chatted non-stop to my dad, like she didn't want him to get a word into the conversation.

We had two paper chain things. Maria had them going from corner to corner of the front room. They didn't meet exactly in the middle. They were purple and shiny like the wrappers on one of the Quality Street sweets. We had Christmas lights for the tree, too. We needed to be sure each bulb was screwed in tightly. If only one wasn't screwed in, the lights wouldn't work. We had to be quiet and concentrate.

The silence in the room felt wrong. I said to Maria, 'Why don't you come round much anymore?'

She said, 'Because this isn't my family anymore.'

'You're still my sister though, aren't you?'

'I'm only your half-sister.'

'Is that because you live in the nurses' home now?'

She stopped what she was doing and looked at me. 'Yes. Mainly.' She tossed her head. Her hair rippled. We turned on the Christmas lights. They shone on Maria's red hair.

Maria also took me to confession. She and my dad talked and I got called downstairs. My dad said it was important, that I had to go to confession because of Christmas. I thought Maria would come too, but on our way to St. Michael's she used the phone box on the Green Hall estate. Someone had drawn a pair of tits on the front of it. She bundled me outside so I couldn't hear what she was saying. I only caught snippets. 'Yeah, just outside… Yeah, sure I will.' She took a bottle of perfume from her pocket and sprayed it on her wrists and neck.

There was a Ford Capri parked outside St Michael's. The engine was running. Smoke puffed from the exhaust. The passenger door swung open. I could hear a Marc Bolan song playing loudly.

Maria said, 'You'll make your own way home, won't you?' I nodded as she hurried away, clumping in her platform shoes. I called out to her, 'Don't you listen to Donny Osmond anymore?'

'No one listens to him.' She stepped into the car and it roared away like a rocket, leaving a cloud of grey-white smoke and the smell of petrol hanging in the air.

There was only one person waiting for confession before me, and no one after me.

'Bless me father for I have sinned. It has been two months since my last confession.'

'And what sins have you committed, my child?' Father Duggan purred.

'I made my m –' The words stopped. I was about to tell. I would confess but it would be like touting because I was going to tell about the big thing that happened and name someone else.

My breathing started to get heavy. All the dust and darkness in the box was sucked into my chest and lungs, clogging me up. 'I made my m–.' It happened again. I was a tout, a Judas. I was going to name my mother to the priest.

Touting and confession were the same after all. No one forgave a tout. Did that mean confession was useless, that God had nothing to do with it? There was no air to breathe, only the dry and heavy dust. The confessional box felt darker, the walls felt closer and the priest breathed deeply. I felt like I was kneeling on nails.

I ran out of the box, down the echoing aisle and out of the church. I gasped into the cold December air, clouds of mist over my head. I did my counts of seven and eleven like a prayer, but at least the counting was useful.

I was worried Father Duggan would call at our house and tell my dad what had happened. But the priest hadn't known it was me. I kept doing my breathing exercise, counting to seven on the way in, eleven on the way out.

Confession was stupid. You didn't say what you had done. You told the priest what he wanted to hear. Any kind of confession was useless because you would say anything they wanted you to say, thinking it would get you out of trouble when it got you into more of it. I could see why Maria didn't go. She looked after her own life, getting rides in Ford Capris, roaring down the road. All I could do was count the long days until I could leave home and get my own car, drive along the motorway with the windows open, feel the wind in my hair.

Maybe I wouldn't go to confession when I was grown up and maybe I wouldn't go to mass either. There was no devil. There were no divine mysteries. God and Jesus with his bloodied palms and Mary and all the saints weren't doing anything for me. Holy Water was not keeping me safe. Holy God was not looking at me. He couldn't care less.

My dad gave me a comic annual for Christmas. It was called *Teddy Bear*. It wasn't wrapped. Maria got an annual as well even though she was a teenager, an adult, and had left home.

At mass on Christmas day, Father Duggan said Christmas was a time for healing, a time for families to be together. Everyone said Amen. There was a huge holly wreath nailed to the church's front door. All the streets were empty.

I watched the Queen make her speech on television. She talked about families, too, and about the Mother of Parliaments. I didn't know what that meant. Near the end she talked about the first Christmas, how it had happened at a dark and threatening time but, she said, 'from it came the light of the world.' I looked outside. It was already getting dark.

Maria came home to cook Christmas dinner. We had turkey with potatoes and cabbage. I was going to say we could make it more special by using our best cups and plates, but when I looked in the glass case a lot of the stuff had gone. I remembered seeing my mum clearing up broken cups on the floor. She said there had been an accident. The plastic doll was still in the glass case but her outstretched arm had broken off. There was just a stump in its place. I turned her key. She danced and twirled, the clockwork motor whirring like it was thinking about something, the grin fixed to her face, the little doll rocking from side to side.

The telly was on all evening. We watched Bruce Forsyth, *Some Mothers do 'Ave 'Em* and Mike Yarwood. Dad fell asleep. I watched the news on my own. They talked about Christmas in Northern Ireland. They showed a young lad in Andersonstown carrying a gun. He had a handkerchief covering the bottom part of his face. The handkerchief was snow-white and folded into a neat triangle. You could see a British Army fort at the back of the picture.

The television people showed another family from East Belfast eating their Christmas dinner round the table, joining their hands together first and thanking God. I went to bed.

There was a heavy shower. It sounded like a roll of drums against my bedroom window, or like someone was trying to get in.

I also got my first pair of long trousers for Christmas. I think Dad got Maria to buy them. They were in a plastic bag with Foster's written on it, waiting for me when I woke up. I could feel the inside of the cloth against my knees and shins. They felt a bit rough but I didn't mind. I think people looked at them at mass, but in a good way. I threw away a pair of my short trousers. I checked the pockets and found a roll of caps. I put it under my bed.

I got a deck of cards for Christmas, too. It came with a booklet with the rules of different games. I taught myself to play stud and draw poker, Gin Rummy, Forty-Five, and Don. I liked the smooth feel of the backs of the cards. I played Patience all the time. I got good at it.

My dad didn't talk to me much over Christmas. Uncle Pat was round a lot and the two of them talked in the kitchen. Aunty Kate didn't come. When Uncle Pat was leaving on Boxing Day he came into the living room to say goodbye to me. He stroked the top of my head.

Maria gave me a photo album. It had 'Ireland' written on it and a map of the country in bright green and gold. There were lines along it, marking off the four provinces: Leinster, Munster,

Connaught and Ulster. I filled the album with photographs of myself, my dad and Maria. I could only find one with Mum in it. It was of me, Mum and Maria in a field. My dad must have taken it. Maria was wearing a pale blue dress with no sleeves. My mum was wearing pink. She was looking down at me so you couldn't see her face, only her black hair. I had a stripy tee-shirt with the collar tight at my neck. I was looking off to the left and towards the sky. I couldn't tell if my mouth was about to break into a smile or a howl. Maria was looking at me, too. They were waiting for me to do something.

There were a lot less photos in the box than before. The photo of my mum on Brighton beach had gone.

Something else had gone. The record by Hughie Maguire. There was no one to sing ah gra ma kree, love of my heart.

My dad worked the night shift on New Year's Eve and Maria went back to work. I watched telly and saw people linking arms and singing Auld Lang Syne. There were fireworks, bright lights and loud bangs. The people on the telly stared up and grinned. A rocket exploded and arcs of light peeled away from it, like an angel's wings. The bangs got louder and louder. When it ended there was a split second of silence, then a long round of applause and cheering.

January 1975

On our first day back at school we had Art in the afternoon. We were sitting around our tables, painting. We had to protect our uniforms. Most of us were wearing our Dads' old shirts. Eileen Lynch dipped her brush in the jar to clean it and said the IRA were Catholics, like us. A whirlpool of red clouded the water. Neil Gordon said that couldn't be true. Miss Blake passed by. Neil said, 'Miss, are the IRA Catholics?'

'Yes,' said Miss Blake. She walked off before we could ask anything else.

I did a painting of a television on a stand. Eileen asked why there was no one watching it.

I got myself up for school that morning. Just before I left I saw my hair was sticking up. I ran upstairs to the bathroom and used some of my mum's hairspray. It was quicker and easier than dragging a brush through it. The hairspray had a clean smell, like a posh soap. It hung in the air like a mist. It dried on my fingertips but still felt sticky.

I ran downstairs. I still had the can of hairspray in my hand. I put it in the pantry on the middle shelf, where we kept tins of food piled up. I slid it in behind them. I didn't want Dad shouting at me for using it. I knew it would be there if it was needed again.

Dad went shopping once a week. Each time he bought tea and sugar. I didn't drink tea and Maria had gone, like Mum. I asked him to buy Camp coffee but he forgot.

The tea and sugar weren't kept in the pantry, either. There was too much so it was all in a cupboard in the front room. He was storing bags of tea and sugar where all the photos used to be. It looked like one of the trenches in the First World War, like pictures Miss Blake showed us at school, soldiers living behind stuffed bags and smoking cigarettes in the rain. I wanted to say something to him but I couldn't say anything. Any word at all got me shouted at, so I stayed quiet. The bags of tea and sugar mounted up like our own First World War bunker or a barricade.

As well as the tea and the sugar there were bottles of Guinness. I saw the empty ones in the living room when I came down in the morning. They lay criss-crossed on the floor, pointing at each other.

I looked in the bin and my dad's Pioneer badge was in it. The small red heart stared up at me like a little worried animal. I thought of the time I stamped on the ants with Neil Gordon.

There was a piece of paper, too, torn from a pad. It was in my dad's handwriting. There was a different name on each line: Hegarty, McAnespie, McDade. There was another word, too, but it was scribbled over, like my dad was angry when he wrote it.

The picture of Jesus was still in the living room. The glass frame had a heavy coating of dust. I didn't pay any attention to it. It was just a picture, a badly painted picture. The plastic holy water well by the front door was empty and dry. The Virgin Mary's halo had chipped. A cobweb clung onto her robes.

I kept expecting to hear the key turn in the door. She would come back, like the time she came back after my aunt's funeral, or the time I thought she'd forgotten about me at school. Maybe she would have photos of herself from the place she had been to, wherever it was.

There might be another one from Brighton beach. We could keep them in the photo box, look at them together when Dad was out.

I came down for a glass of water just as my dad was taking the top off another Guinness with the naked lady bottle opener. His eyes were watery, his face pale and blank.

'Why don't you go to the pub, Dad?'

'They don't serve Irish.'

'Do you buy the bottles from Barker's?'

'I go to the supermarket. Nobody hears my accent there.'

'Could you try to sound a bit more English?'

'An Irishman will never be an Englishman.'

The next night I heard a crash of glass. I came down. Dad was in the kitchen with his back to me. The tap was running.

'What happened, Dad?'

'An accident, a wee accident.' His voice slurred. 'A bottle fell. Fell down, so it did. Go back to bed.'

I crept closer. There was a deep cut on his arm. The blood ran with the water and spiralled down the plughole.

'Do you want any help?'

'No. It's nothing. Just an accident. There's plenty more blood where that came from. Go back to bed.'

In one of my books the four astronauts were on a mission to Neptune. I was sitting in my bed, reading it. The four of them had lost contact with Mission Control. Chris was telling them to stay calm. That was his job as the captain, to set an example, because the crew was abandoned in the cold outer reaches of the Solar System. I couldn't see how they would make their way back to Earth safely. They were done for.

I started to feel my breathing get harder. It was happening bit by bit, almost as I moved from page to page. It was like a tractor rumbling up a hill and you knew it would never get to the top. My lungs pushed and pushed but nothing happened. It felt like someone was holding a pillow over my face, smothering me. I was clutching at the air, in and in and in, but I couldn't press any of it out. My lungs swelled up. There was no room left, nowhere for the dusty air to go.

I jumped off the bed and stood up. Everything was perfectly still. No sound, no movement. No traffic, no birdsong. A fluttering of eyelids. I swayed like a dancer. A sound like the crackles between radio stations. A topple to my right. A crash.

An astronaut's helmet was really important. You had to be able to see through it but it also had to be strong enough so your air supply was protected. You didn't want to die because you couldn't breathe. That would just be awful.

I read in a book that the see-through bit in an astronaut's helmet was made of the same stuff as a riot shield. An astronaut had to be able to see what was on strange planets, and the police and the Army had to know who was throwing stones and petrol bombs at them.

Dr Burnett listened to my chest, his stethoscope cold against my skin. He shone lights into my eyes and shoved something else cold into my ears. He told my dad he could find nothing. He said it might by psychological.

Dad and I walked home. I asked him what Dr Burnett meant by psychological. He said, 'Nothing. Nerves.' My shadow crept forward until it was right underneath me.

March 1975

The Christmas tree was still up. Dad hadn't taken it down and he hadn't gone into the garden either to turn the soil over, even though Spring was coming. Maria had got herself a steady boyfriend and wasn't bothered about us.

I asked Dad about the Irish Parade. He said there weren't going to be parades anymore. I didn't mind. It was boring anyway. All those flags and drums and pipes, walking around town for no reason at all, singing a national anthem in a foreign language and ending the day with a long mass.

I took the tree down while he was at work. It was hard to bend the branches back into place. They kept tugging back to where they had been before. I put the ornaments back in their box. I put the crib away, being careful not to break the baby Jesus. I blew the dust off him. I taped the box shut. I wrapped the tree in black polythene and shoved it under my dad's bed, behind the record player, where the suitcase used to be. It looked like a dead body.

Some little, green, shiny strands came off the tree. I hoovered them up. The tree had been there in the front room all that time, where anyone looking in from the outside could see it. I was sure people had been laughing at us.

The room looked suddenly bare, like something had been lost, like the space was bigger. A few threads of tinsel remained on the carpet. I tried to get rid of them again, but when I finished one or two threads still looked up at me. I switched off the hoover. Its loud moan fell away into silence. I got down on my hands and knees and looked closely at the carpet. It didn't seem to matter what I did; one or two bits of the tree were still there.

I didn't know where my mum was. I didn't know where Eamonn was. I walked home from school the long way to be safe. I stayed in my bedroom, reading. My uniform needed washing. There were tidemarks on my collar. My socks had holes. Everyone at school talked about the new schools they were going to in September.

I sat the exam paper for St Thomas's but couldn't answer many of the questions. I ended up drawing a spaceship in the margin. I tried to draw Saturn but couldn't get the rings right.

September 1975

It was my birthday in July. I got more long trousers. I put the last pair of short ones in the bin.

There weren't any cards. The one from my mum might have got lost in the post, or maybe she'd got other things on her mind.

I failed the eleven plus. St Thomas's wouldn't have me.

I go to Moat Hill comprehensive. I catch the bus, sitting on the top deck towards the back. The lads from the fourth and fifth years smoke. One of them has a marker pen and writes swear-words on the backs of the seats.

I'm crap at most subjects except English and History. Maybe I've turned out to be English after all. Andrew Cochrane is here but ignores me.

The big kids hit the little kids at Moat Hill and the teachers do the most hitting of all, but they only hit the boys, not the girls.

I tried to get out of rugby in my first week by showing the P.E. teacher a blister on my foot but he made me do it anyway. The field is full of molehills. We kick the soil at each other when the teacher's not looking.

Neil Gordon got into St Thomas's. I don't see him anymore. David Hennessy is at Moat Hill with me. He's different already. He's grown his hair and spends every day saying school is fucking shit and the teachers are fucking crazy. I think he's right but the swear words don't sound as good when I say them and my hair isn't growing quickly enough.

David never mentions my mum. He told me he still sees Pat Stapleton who's living in a rented flat above a shop in Aston, now his Dad doesn't have a pub.

Everyone at Moat Hill supports Blues or Villa. There are fights. You either line up with the Blues fans or the Villa fans. If a group of lads asks you who you support you try to figure out which side they're on before you answer.

Moat Hill is the opposite side of town to my old school so I don't run into the Feldon Street boys. I don't tell anyone my mum and dad are Irish. I call myself Daniel instead of Danny. Two of the bigger kids said to me, 'Are you Irish?' I said no. They said, 'Are your Mum or Dad Irish?' I was going to say I didn't have a Mum, but just said, 'No.'

A few of the fifth form lads play poker behind the Maths class-room at dinner time. You know something's going on because of the clouds of cigarette smoke. They told me to go away. I said I was only watching. I knew the rules anyway and could work out what was happening. I saw you didn't need a good hand to win. You just had to play it well. Eventually they let me join in, making sure I had cash on me and telling me I'd get a kicking if I grassed them up. I doubled my dinner money yesterday. It turns out I'm good at lying. I don't know where I learned that.

One of the lads tried to cheat me the first time, taking a card from the bottom of the deck and using it to say his hand was stronger than mine. He said, 'I swear on my mother's life' and that's when I knew he was lying. I stood my ground and his mates called him a wanker. His fag fell from the corner of his mouth and they all laughed. I realised what I'd done. I'd set him apart from his mates and from then on I had him. If it had been a full-

227

on row I would have lost because he would have started hitting me, but I found a way to beat someone strong.

When it died down one of the other lads watching the game called me Cool Hand Luke. He was right on the edge of the group, as though he wasn't really interested. He was reading a paper, the *New Musical Express*. It had a picture of a man with sunglasses on the front cover, playing an electric guitar. I could see the headline: 'With one resounding B flat chord, Eddie and the Hotrods save Rock and Roll.'

The lad blew a smoke ring. He had spiky black hair and wore a badge with a picture of a man wearing a beret and looking upwards, raising a fist. The lad saw me looking, 'Che Guevara,' he said, tapping at the badge with his forefinger. 'Read what he says.'

'Don't you like Bowie?' I asked.

He smiled, like I was a little child who'd said something stupid. 'Che's not a musician, he's a revolutionary and a writer, and by the way Bowie's a fascist,' the lad said. 'Read what Bowie says, too.' He turned back to his paper.

I was walking across the playground the next day when some older girls shouted 'Lukey.' I ignored them. One of them stepped in front of me and held out an apple.

'Take this,' she said.

'What?'

'It's a Cox's.'

The girls behind her giggled.

'Cox's,' she repeated. 'They're the best of British.'

I took it from her and threw it to someone else when I got back to my classroom. Fuck the best of British.

David Hennessey grabbed me by the shoulder. 'I saw what happened,' he said. 'Why didn't you talk to her? She's bloody gorgeous.'

'She was taking the piss out of me.'

'She can take whatever she wants out of me.' He walked away, shaking his head.

On the way home I went into the hippie bookshop round the back of Marks and Spencer. There was a tramp outside, sitting on the floor and playing a tin whistle.

A string of bells rang as I pushed the door. There were handwritten signs sellotaped to different bookshelves: Economics, History, Politics, Feminism. There were no science-fiction books or ones about sport. I used my poker winnings to buy a book by Che Guevara called *Guerrilla Warfare*, because of what the lad with spiky hair said. I stepped over the tramp as I left. The tune he was playing sounded Irish.

I didn't think much of the book at first, or understand it. It said revolutionaries had to win power, which was obvious, but it also talked about guerrillas having the support of the people. It made me think of Creggan in Derry and Ardoyne in Belfast. The book said the regular army existed to work for the powerful, but when they fought the people on the people's own ground they lost their power. It seemed to me that the army was always going to be a target because you could see it, because they had uniforms, but a guerrilla army was invisible because it looked like everyone else and just blended in.

The book said it was OK to use violence, you just had to use it at the right time. It was like school. You wouldn't fight one of the bigger lads because you'd get a kicking. You wouldn't fight unless you were sure you were going to win.

The book got weird towards the end. It said guerrilla units had to be mobile, and they had no alternative but death or victory, and death was much more likely. It sounded like the sort of thing Eamonn said to me that time he was drunk, but Eamonn wasn't a revolutionary. He was a sad old man singing boring songs about the past, and he was also the bastard who stole my mother. He was as bad as the army he was fighting against. He was in Britain where he had no support, except from the singing drunkards at the Irish Centre. That was the opposite of what the book said. Eamonn and his pissed-up friends sang about the sons of Ireland, but he'd taken my mum.

Eamonn's songs, like most of the Irish songs, were about failing. I couldn't see the point. Failing was failing. But I could see how you had to be mobile so they wouldn't catch you – a moving target was harder to hit. Your enemy could do nothing to you if he couldn't find you. It would be like being the Tomorrow People. You could just disappear, be invisible.

If soldiers attacked you, you could run away. If they had bases you could attack them. You could dig in for a long war and tire them out, and if they retreated you would end up being the one doing the chasing. But you had to be constantly learning, too, and you wouldn't be learning if you were just churning out the same old songs and the same old words, looking at the picture of the hills on the stage of the Irish Centre when there were no hills like that in Birmingham and no stupid little cottages either. You'd be singing crap about the countryside when you lived in a city full of cars and buses. Going on about dead heroes, 'They fought for auld

Ireland.' They're all dead – rest in fucking peace. Eamonn was too stupid and drunk to learn. I don't know what my mum saw in him.

The six men who did the pub bombings were sentenced to life in prison in August for murdering twenty-one people at The Mulberry Bush and The Tavern In The Town. The football season started the next day. Birmingham are down near the bottom of the league but Trevor Francis is still there. The football scores and the killings in Northern Ireland are reported the same way. Birmingham lost two-nil: two British soldiers were killed in Belfast.

They interviewed a British officer on television about a gun battle in South Armagh. His accent was the same as the Queen's. He said, 'People should come forward and say "I have information."' Why would they do that? All they would do is give the Brits what they want. It wouldn't solve people's problems. The interviewer said something about eye witnesses swearing the army shot first. The officer said, 'I hesitate to call people liars...' and called the people liars anyway.

I saw pictures of the six bombers in the *Daily Mirror*, in the window at Barker's. The paper said they did the bombings in revenge for Jamesie, but the paper didn't call him Jamesie. It called him their 'fallen comrade, James McDade.' Five of the six are from Belfast and one from Derry, but the *Daily Mirror* called it Londonderry. It was strange to think of Jamesie being the cause of all this, strange to think that Jamesie was the reason I got hit and spat at on the way home. He was funny and happy. People came to listen to him sing. He wouldn't hurt anyone.

The Birmingham massacre victims were doomed from the moment IRA 'Lieutenant' James McDaid blew himself up with his own bomb. McDaid – drunkard, braggart, wife beater – was acclaimed by his IRA pals as a hero... The evening's rendezvous was at Birmingham's New Street station. Like Power, the other five went by bus. It was not the first time the hard-up Provos had had to use public transport for a bombing mission. On at least one previous occasion an IRA man travelled to his target – and made his getaway – on a Birmingham corporation bus.

The bombers were the classic material of terrorism. They were men who travelled the whole road from Republican sympathy to active violence. All six had lives in Birmingham for many years after quitting the Catholic ghettoes of Ulster in search of 'the better life.' At first their IRA activities were limited to rattling collecting tins in Birmingham's Irish pubs. Then James McDaid loomed large in all their lives... The extrovert McDaid would clamber on stage and sing rebel songs. He became the first to turn to terrorism – and that made him a hero to his pals. Slowly the brotherhood of blood ceased to be simple fund raisers for 'the cause.' The ancient hatreds of Northern Ireland began to poison their minds.

Daily Telegraph, Saturday 16 August 1975

The 21 victims of the Birmingham pub bombings on November 21st last year are now thought to have lost their lives because of a vandalised telephone kiosk. The IRA man deputed to make the coded warning call after bombs were planted in two city centre bars was apparently prevented from doing so in time because he could not find a kiosk in working order… The six convicted yesterday of the greatest mass murder in British history, were part of an IRA 'sleeper' cell of Irishmen long resident in Birmingham… retaliation on Irish targets began with a petrol bomb attack on a Catholic church… the atmosphere in the Irish community just a year ago, at which several hundred people in Birmingham alone could be counted on as enthusiastic supporters of the Republican movement, many of the Provisional IRA itself. While shop-floor collections were openly being held in some Coventry factories, IRA fundraisers were hard at work in the demi-monde of card schools, raffles, dances and whip-rounds for the families of internees, or simply for the cause. It was in this climate, mainly through public-house contacts or friendships struck up at work, that the IRA in Birmingham was built up.

Daily Express, Saturday 16 August 1975

Police have no doubt that sheltering within the Irish communities in Britain is a small minority ready to activate their Republican dedication. Said a senior officer last night: '… We have a massive bank of intelligence on their associates.'

Daily Mail, Saturday 16 August 1975

I am living in a never-ending whirlpool of eyes and doctors. I can't sleep at night without tablets because I get the horrors, and I doze off at odd times and drop things. The strain on my mind is hard to bear. I really don't know if I will ever get better. I've never had anything against the Irish. I don't even know what it's all about.

In July, an American Apollo rocket and a Russian Soyuz rocket joined up in space. Their captains shook hands in the middle. The people on the telly said things would get better now but I don't think they will. Things like that, ending all the arguments, are only possible in space, where we can start again.

The trial for the Guildford pub bombs is on at the moment. There's four of them up for it. Their pictures are on television. They look like hippies, like they belong in the shop at the back of Marks and Spencer, like they all need a wash. One of them's a seventeen-year-old girl and she's English. But apparently they're all IRA bombers, too, because the headline in the paper says, 'Snipers guard the Old Bailey as Bombers go on Trial.'

Whenever they talk about the Irish on the news, politicians say they're not after 'decent, law-abiding people' or 'decent and responsible men and women.' When they use those words what they're really talking about is the people who just roll over and let them do what they want to them.

Bombs are still going off in London. The Queen should have spent more time looking out of her window before she made her speech on the telly at Christmas. There might have been a new light in the world but it wasn't what she thought.

Summer was OK because there was no school, but I got bored. One day in August I had the idea of riding on my dad's bus, so at least I could see town and maybe get some sweets if passengers gave him any.

I walked to the terminus to wait for him. As I got closer I could see he was already there. He was smoking a Woodbine and talking to a taller man. The man was writing in a notebook.

My dad glanced up and saw me. He threw his Woodbine down and said something to the man, who snapped his book shut.

The man walked away. He lifted his hands to his face and made a gesture to my dad, like he was taking a photograph with an invisible camera. The man smiled, as though my dad and him shared a secret.

'Is he a policeman, Dad?'

Dad looked startled. 'Yes, Danny, he is.'

'Why were you talking to him Dad?'

'Just passing the time of day.'

'Why wasn't he wearing a policeman's uniform?'

'I don't know.'

'Why did he do that thing like he was taking a picture?'

'I don't know.'

'I thought there was trouble again.'

'What kind of trouble?'

'Jim Hegarty trouble.'

'What do you mean? You saw nothing.'

'The time the policeman came to take a statement from you because of Jim Hegarty arguing with two lads on the bus. Remember? It was a Sunday.'

'Oh yes. Oh God yes. That's what it was. I was talking to the policeman about that time.'

He struck a match on the brick wall behind him and lit another cigarette. His hands shook.

'Anyway, Danny, what are you doing here?'

'I thought I'd ride on your bus for a bit.'

'Good idea. Get a seat to yourself on the top deck, right at the front. The one you like. If anyone gives me a sweet I'll make sure you get it.'

I started to climb the stairs.

'Danny?'

'Yes, Dad?'

'Don't say anything about the policeman. It's not worth talking about.'

'Yes, Dad.'

The engine revved. We lurched into the road. The brakes whined.

Birmingham looked the same as ever. People were working or shopping and it was busy at the bottom of New Street. The Tavern In The Town was still boarded up.

Mum said if someone hit me I was to hit them back. I did and got into trouble. I hit David Hennessey and wasn't allowed to watch the moon landing. At Moat Hill the teachers hit us hard, but we know we can't hit them back because the Headmaster, Mr Wells, would give us the cane.

At assembly Mr Wells talks about us being a community but we're not. A community is where people look after each other. The teachers hit us at Moat Hill and the bigger kids hit us, and all I can do is wait until I'm old enough and strong enough to do something about it.

The doorbell rang. There was a man standing there, his hands clasped in front of him. He was short, wore glasses and had a beard. His hair was greying and needed a comb. His jacket had elbow patches. He looked like a teacher. He smiled.

'Hello, Sonny. Is your Da in?'

I could tell straight away he was from Northern Ireland.

'No, he's at work.'

'Maybe I'd better come in then.' He stepped forward. I stood in his way. Across the road, Mrs Gow opened her door and stared out like she was sniffing the air. The man saw me looking and turned around. He took his foot off the doorstep and moved back.

'Well,' he said. 'That's a shame. Another time maybe. Listen Danny: it is Danny, isn't it?'

I nodded.

'Well, Danny, I believe you had a visitor before Christmas. A gentleman by the name of Eamonn.'

I stared back at him.

'I see you can keep your own counsel, Danny. That's a good sign. Now you listen to me. If Eamonn returns, you give him a message. You tell him the boys from back home are just dying to see him.' He rubbed his hand over his mouth. 'No, actually, just keep it simple. Tell him he needs to call Patsy. Can you give that message for me, Danny?'

I nodded.

'Good boy. We all have to take responsibility for our own actions, don't we, Danny?' I looked at him. He turned to go away. There was a car parked across the road, with a man in the driver's seat staring straight ahead.

The visitor turned back. 'Just one more thing, Danny. Have you ever heard of the phrase, "Loose lips sink ships"?'

'The Americans used it as a slogan in the Second World War, so people would keep their mouths shut.'

'I'd been told you were a sharp one, Danny. You're dead-on, absolutely right. You just pass that message on to your Da.'

'He won't understand it.'

His voice rose. 'Then allow me to be plainer. People talk and people die. He shouldn't fall for an old trick. The system uses fellers and spits them out. A man can be an asset one day and a liability the next. Is that too much for you to remember, Danny? A word like liability?'

'What's your name?'

'Smith.'

He trotted across the road and into the car. I heard him say, 'Let's go.' The car sped away.

I didn't tell my dad about the visitor. There was no point saying anything to him. He's got one thing he keeps repeating at me: 'The older you're getting the stupider you're getting. Do you know that?' That's another thing he's wrong about.

Not telling my dad about the visitor wasn't a lie. It was holding back what you know. The visitor knew something. He knew about Eamonn. I was beginning to know things about Eamonn, too, even though he had gone. I remembered the time he spoke to me when he was drunk. One thing Dad was right about was that people talk too much when they've had a drink.

Holding on to what you know is like playing poker. It's about not giving anything away with your expression, like you're wearing a visor slid down over the whole of your face, like the army or the RUC or an astronaut. No one can get at you.

Poker also taught you that if you staked everything you'd got you could win, even if you didn't have a good hand. You could get under your opponent's skin so he'd back down. Whatever the situation, the important thing was to hold something back and not let anyone get under your skin. Maybe the man would call again, my dad would answer the door and they could deal with it themselves. A nice chat with Mr Smith.

I like it best when I'm at home and the house is empty. I watch what I want on television. There's a new Doctor Who but he's not as good as the old one, and anyway it's for little kids.

I've started to buy my own records. I'm not so interested in the sweets in my dad's pocket but I take a little money from his wallet. He keeps a lot of cash in there these days. I bought the latest Sensational Alex Harvey Band single. I used the record player Maria left behind. I let the needle drop and waited for the music to come in. It sounded better than the Gallowglass Ceilidh Band, anyway. There's David Bowie, too, and 'Space Oddity.' It's a good song despite what the lad at school said. I asked the woman behind the counter if they had anything by Eddie and the Hot Rods but she'd never heard of them. I'm going to ask Dad if I can have a music centre next Christmas, it's a radio and a cassette deck and a record player all in one.

The lads who listen to Bowie and Alex Harvey have different haircuts to the others. They talk about tuning in to John Peel on the radio. They wear badges – Che Guevara, or Solidarity With Chile. I want a badge, too. Politics has nothing to do with me but I want to look like them.

A couple of them have guitars in soft cases, slung over their shoulders. They swagger around with them like they've been playing guitar for ever. It would be good to have one. Learn to play. Be the main man in a band. I'd call us The Unknowns, or maybe The Space Oddities.

Dad bought a car, a red Ford Cortina. I never knew we had that kind of money. I asked him how much it cost. He told me to mind my own business. I asked if we could get our own phone, too. He mumbled under his breath. I couldn't make out all of the words, but there was some swearing. I said, 'Are you alright, Dad?'

'A phone can be tapped. You know nothing.'

'Why would anyone tap a phone belonging to us, Dad?'

'You never know. I'm sticking to the phone box at the bottom of the road, so I am.'

'Couldn't that be tapped?'

We sat in silence. He tugged at his face. I moved closer to him. He needed a wash. I spoke more quietly.

'How can anyone listen to a phone call anyway, Dad?'

'I'm sure they do it at the telephone exchange.'

'Jamesie was trying to blow up a telephone exchange, wasn't he?'

'I wish I'd never heard that name, and there are other names I wish I'd never heard.'

He stood up suddenly, nearly losing his balance. He looked at me like he was seeing me for the first time: 'One by one they all go, Danny. I could be next.' He stumbled upstairs. He went into the bathroom. I heard a crash. 'It's OK, Danny,' he called down. 'Just a wee accident. Another tiny accident.'

The next morning I went to brush my teeth. The mirror in the bathroom had a crack running from the top to the bottom. There was more than one of me.

Dad bought a camera. It came in its own case. There's another case in the drawer. It's got an extra lens in it, a long one. There's a couple of cannisters of film as well. Maybe we're going on holiday this year.

When he comes in and asks about homework I tell him it's all done. Sometimes he doesn't believe me and asks to see my copy books. They're not called copy books, they're called exercise books. He used to be quiet and leave me alone, but since Mum went he's just an eejit who shouts most of the time and sits there silently the rest of the time, staring at the wall, drinking bottles of

Guinness every night. He hangs his bus driver's jacket on the back of the chair. There's dandruff on the shoulders.

I know what Dad means when he says copy books but I tell him I don't know what copy books are. He gets angry but he's angry anyway.

Last week he said, 'Does anyone ever call for me, Danny?'

'No.'

I stay away from school when I can, about a day a week. If Dad's working I don't tell him anything, and if I've wet the bed I can get the sheets washed and dried. If he comes in I tell him I had an asthma attack, leave the sheets on the mattress and hope they will be dry enough by the time I go back to bed. I open the window to get rid of the smell. Dad tuts about me missing school but that's all, and school is so big that no one cares. If you keep your head down no one even knows you exist.

I walk around the house if I'm alone. My dad's room stinks of stale air, sour Guinness and sweat. There's no smell of perfume in the air anymore.

He still takes me to mass on Sundays when he's not working. Father Duggan licks his lips: 'Blessed are those who hunger and thirst for righteousness, for they shall be satisfied.' When Dad's working on Sunday I stay at home and tell him I went to mass. He asks me who I saw there. I say 'no one.'

I only ever get noticed at school in History and English. In History we've been learning about the Spanish Civil War. The most important thing I figured out was that Father Duggan was a fascist. If the soul was a room I wondered what his was like? We also learned about the decline of the British Empire after World

War Two. It got smaller and smaller because the people in the occupied countries rose up against it.

In another History class, Mr Jenkins talked about military dictatorships in Latin America. They were Catholic countries. Some of the bishops and priests helped the poor, but most of them were on the dictators' payrolls. He told us we were lucky to live in a country like Britain and we were very lucky not to be in East Germany because of the Berlin Wall. It marked the barrier between East and West. It was only built at the beginning of the sixties but it was already permanent because there was no way the East Germans would ever take it down and their population was watched all the time by the secret police.

Mr Jenkins taught us about Vietnam, too. The Vietnamese didn't win because they could inflict more pain than the Americans. They won because they could take more suffering. The Americans had all the money and equipment but the North Vietnamese army, the Viet Cong, were fighting on their own soil and, bit by bit, they squeezed the Americans into a smaller and smaller part of the country until they were forced out altogether.

Mr Jenkins said he remembered watching the news about Vietnam on television and it showed the final few helicopters leaving the roof of the American Embassy in Saigon. I thought about the powerful helicopters fading to a tiny speck, buzzing like a little fly. From far away a huge helicopter would look like a tadpole. Vietnam showed you could win a long war against opponents who were a lot stronger than you. You just had to know more than them and endure more than them. If they threw everything they'd got at you and you were still there, what could they do? If you had roots deep enough in the soil you could recover from all kinds of setbacks because the roots would always be there.

The Viet Cong launched an attack on the Americans, the Tet Offensive, against military bases right across the country. It was the holiday to mark their lunar new year so the Americans were not expecting anything. The Viet Cong lost loads of fighters but it didn't matter because it showed they could take on the Americans and it made more Americans at home want to pull out. The Viet Cong didn't have to win. They just had to weaken the will to stay.

When the people back in America saw what was going on they didn't want it to continue. They saw pictures of little children being napalmed. Mister Jenkins said when napalm landed there was a flash, then a rush of heat followed by a smell of roast dinners because napalm burned flesh instantly.

I was surprised the American government hadn't stopped the reports getting out, about what napalm did. If you had control of communication you had something special. Even in the battlefield, if you took out your enemy's radio operator they'd be screwed. You could spread panic amongst them. If an army patrol in Derry or Belfast lost its ability to contact its base, it would panic. Just a handful of soldiers lost at night in Belfast or Derry streets.

Mr Jenkins said the Americans used CS gas to break up Vietnam demonstrations. I put my hand up and said CS gas didn't do lasting harm. He told me I was wrong. CS gas could cause permanent damage to the lungs, stomach and eyes. A kid behind me whispered, 'Div.' He was right. I was a div not to have realised it before.

All the countries we looked at had different people inside them. There were the people who were fighting but didn't think about ideas, because it wasn't as though anyone would listen to them anyway. There were other people, good talkers, who thought parliaments and all that bollocks would help them. And then there were the revolutionaries who understood ideas and thought about how to make them happen. You needed to make an impact and it had to be unpredictable like the Tet Offensive so people would take notice of you, but unless you had a bigger idea as well it was useless.

The other problem was if the British Empire had owned your country for long enough, when you finally got your freedom you'd just do what they did because it was all you knew. You could take down actual barricades, but the barricades in your mind were another thing altogether. If you were clever you would imagine another life before you tried to make it happen.

History teaches good lessons, like the fact that you can win, and everyone can have a part to play. For every one person that rises up there might be fifty who give shelter or food or money, people who march or bang a bin lid.

You didn't need an army of thousands, even two or three people could be enough to make a difference, they could make the spark that lit the fire, but those two or three would need to believe in something and have enough hate inside them to take on the world.

Not everyone could do it. You'd be alone. If you were from a big family like my dad you might need other people around you because it was what you were used to, but if you spent a lot of time by yourself you could take that first small step alone, like being the first to set foot on another planet.

The few also needed to be able to get weapons, or to make weapons from things around them: cars; people. If you pissed on a soldier's foot you were using your piss as a weapon. When Seamus said he wouldn't give blood to a soldier bleeding to death, he was saying the same thing. Your piss, your blood, your shit: you could use them all and create a battlefield anywhere. Anything would do: a wedding; a funeral. A riot was a battlefield, so were prisons, so were elections, and so were words.

You had to accept war was a bloody mess. Stupid bloody mistakes would get made because you'd have thick drunkards like Eamonn fighting on your side, and if your enemy was more powerful than you he would be watching you. But a weapon could travel though time as well as space. There was power in something as simple as the strike of a match. There was power in petrol fumes. Even if the first few volunteers had to sacrifice themselves, it would be enough if it inspired the people around them.

There were so many ways you could make yourself heard. Dancers banging their feet on a bare, wooden floor. The crunch of thousands of people marching. Dustbin lids clattering on Derry streets.

You could use a funeral to get your point across because everyone would be paying attention to you, like the people who turned up at Jamesie's house when he died, all crammed in together, murmuring the same prayers. All I cared about at Jamesie's house was my Jaffa Cake, but the little boy who was looking at me was thinking about something deeper. I just didn't know what it was.

Our Religion teacher at Moat Hill talked about Gandhi, a smiling little man with a blanket wrapped around him going on about non-violence, but that was going back to Father Christmas and Superman. The teacher talked about having an open mind. It made me think of an open trap with jaws like teeth, ready to bite the leg off any little animal that stepped into it. I'd rather be a detonator for an explosion.

You didn't need a huge number of people to change things. You just needed a small group with the support of the people. You'd find their support in places where people had it the hardest, like Belfast. Eamonn said the tide would come in and it would go out but it would always be there. Eamonn was too stupid to see that you could draw the tide in if you knew how to get your argument across, and if some English King Cnut thought you could hold the tide back he'd get swept away. If you just put one fist-sized stone in a stream you could change its direction.

In English I'm in the top set. We wrote a poem about third world famine. The teacher told us what famine was like, that after a while you didn't feel hunger pains because the stomach shrank down. It made me think of the famine in Ireland and it made me think of hunger strikes. You could do it after all because your body would prepare you for it and manage it, and no amount of food could keep death away forever anyway.

Your body would feed from you in a hunger strike, taking your fat tissue, your eyesight, your muscle, all the time keeping the brain alive. A hunger strike could turn a weakness into a strength because you'd be showing people they didn't have power over you. A government couldn't keep you in prison if there was no you anymore. You wouldn't be committing violence on anyone but yourself, and people would pay more attention to you because of how far you were prepared to go, dying inch by inch. The Catholic Church would say it was a sin but they talked a load of old bollocks anyway. You could do anything at all if it meant enough to you. You could put up with any level of pain. No one could break your spirit if your spirit refused to be broken. I wrote my poem while all those thoughts were still in my head but made sure it was about Africa so they wouldn't know I was Irish. The teacher read it out to the class. In the last line I said the starving were 'entombed in pain.' The teacher said it was a very mature choice of verb. I got called a poof by the lads at the back, but nothing else happened.

The teacher also told us he'd been to see a play at the theatre and the whisper of 'poof' scuttled round the room again. He said it was by Sophocles and it was about a king. He said you always knew what was going on in the play because there was a chorus at the front, between the cast and the audience. The chorus wore cloaks or blankets and they explained everything. The audience relied on them.

You'd never hear of an Irish man being called a poof because they work on the sites, get in fights, sign up for the IRA. I'm no good with a shovel and I don't have a gun. Maybe I'm not stupid or useless when I hold a pen, never mind what my dad says. I was thinking about it in a Geography lesson. No one was listening to the teacher, some old fart with a beard. I'd written a poem, but it wasn't enough because the people over there had other problems, like being murdered by the police and the army in South Africa and Rhodesia. Governments could kill and get away with it, but some of the people would just keep coming back and fighting back. I used the point of my compass to scratch an I on the desk, then an R. The teacher threw his book down. It thudded on the desk like a big fat drum. He shouted at everyone. We all stopped what we were doing for a minute before going back to talking. I put the compass away.

We're sitting a test on *To Kill A Mockingbird*. I've been reading it again at home. It seems to me you can learn more through living than you can through your lessons at school. You can get your message across by writing a book, like the woman who wrote *To Kill A Mockingbird*, but you can also get it across by scratching on a desk or painting on a wall. Free Derry. Irish bastards.

As well as *To Kill A Mockingbird*, I've been reading a history book about Ireland. It talked about things I hadn't heard of before, like the Curragh Mutiny in 1914, as Ireland was getting ready for Home Rule. The Protestant Loyalists in the North said they would fight against it, the British government asked the Army for help but the army told them they wouldn't fight against the Protestant Loyalists. Like Mr Jenkins said, we're lucky to be living in a country like Britain, not like Latin America at all.

In the autumn evenings people on the estate burned leaves and other rubbish from their gardens. I didn't expect there to be a bonfire at our house. Dad had lost interest. Any time I looked out of the kitchen window the garden was just full of bindweed and dandelions.

I got in late because there'd been a poker game after school, behind the prefabs. I won a quid. It would have been more but one of the older lads had a full house in the final hand. Jammy bastard.

I could smell it before I saw it. Dad was having a bonfire. It was huge. He had his back to me. Beyond him the orange and red flames were as high as his head.

He was swaying. He held a bottle in his right hand, the light from the flames catching the glass, making it look like he was holding fire or a petrol bomb, the clear spirits glowing in the darkness.

I stepped towards him and the wave of heat hit me. There was a yellow-white brightness in the heart of the fire. It glowed up into my dad's face. His skin shone.

The smell was rich, richer than leaves, more like wood. Whatever he was burning, it wasn't rubbish from the garden.

The fire cackled as I came up right behind him. My eyes stung. Tears trickled down my cheeks.

Dad glanced over his shoulder. 'Hello, Danny,' he slurred.

'Do you want to step back, Dad? You're close to the fire and you're swaying.'

'I'm OK.' He nodded to the fire. 'Do you like it?'

'What are you burning?'

'Your mother's books. All they ever did was turn her head. She'd be down on her knees praying to Holy God and the Virgin Mary one minute, reading about bad women the next. She should have done more praying and less reading.'

He raised the bottle to his lips. He pulled on it, as needy as a baby. 'I always said books were a waste of time and money,' he said. 'Like everything else.'

'Where did you get the books, Dad?'

'Next to her side of the bed.'

I stood alongside him, watching my own books go up in flames along with Mum's. My astronauts were finally heading into space. The story I'd written was there, too. I felt no G force but I did feel the heat, as fierce as any rocket. The chuckling fire ate my story and my books. Mine and Mum's.

My dad sang to himself: 'I'll tell my Ma, when I get home, the boys won't leave the girls alone.' He looked at me. 'There were rumours, Danny, back home, about your Mum and Eamonn. And my own Mother, may she rest in peace, told me Annie was no good. Flighty. Wanted to be treated like a princess. Annie used to watch myself and the lads play Gaelic Football when we were young, her skirt pulled high up her legs. She threw the ball at me and, fool that I was, I caught it.' He flicked his bottle at the flames. A mouthful of spirits hit the fire and it roared its approval, like he had blessed it.

He swayed forward towards the flames. I took hold of his jumper and yanked him back.

He turned round, staggered into the house and up the stairs. It was just me and the fire and the smoke and the smell of things that had gone from me and wouldn't be coming back.

The next morning was cold. My dad snored loudly. Before leaving for school I went into the back garden. It had rained in the night and the ash was flat and sodden. The ground looked scarred. I trod on the deepest part of the embers. They gave way beneath my foot like a sponge. I took one of Dad's bamboo canes and prodded it into the ash. A small, grey-white cloud puffed up for a second.

I bent down, stuck my thumb in the ashes and rubbed them across the back of my other hand. They left a black smear. I could make out the front cover of my PG Tips sticker album in the heart of the fire, and part of the spine of one of my books. I could see a word. Venus.

Maybe my mum has forgotten me, like she forgot about Brighton. But, like Brighton, I will live on in photos and I will lurk at the edge of the scenery in her dreams. I must be there. A murmur or pain in her heart, a sudden jolt in the rhythm of her day. I'm going to write another poem or story about it. Or a song. Not at school: just for me.

I know better than to ask Dad where Mum might be. I asked Uncle Pat and he said he thought she was in London. I asked Maria when she came around. She said she thought Mum was in Dublin. She was waiting to get a letter from her to know for sure.

I think she must be in New York. There's loads of Irish there. My mum will have a photo of herself in front of the Statue of Liberty, like the photo she had of herself on Brighton Beach, and she'll have visited the Empire State Building, the tallest building in the world. Her hair will have grown long again.

When the ceilidh screeches and the dancers whirl and skirl in Brooklyn and Long Island, does my mum think of what I might be hearing, Birmingham's traffic backed up along New Street and the buses grumbling? Or does she forget it all, knock back another Campari and soda and take her place with the dancers for The Siege of Ennis, twirling like a clockwork doll?

One day there'll be a letter in a blue envelope with the wavy lines and the air mail sticker. It will be from America and it will be from her, addressed to me. I'll open it and she'll have written that she's sorry and she loves me, things like that. I'll be OK about it and from then on we'll write to each other in secret. When I leave school, I'll join her in New York. Eamonn will have gone back to his wife and children in Derry. My mum and I will find a café and have a chat and I'll get my own room in her big American house and I'll drive a big American car. She'll have a library, too, with books for her and books for me all mixed together. I won't even mind if she listens to Doris Day and Shirley Bassey. Maybe they'll sound better in New York.

If I ever return to Birmingham it will just be to visit and I'll be amazed at how Birmingham has changed because it will be a place where kids don't get hit and kicked just for being Irish.

I'll keep an eye on our post. My mum will come for me.

Poem for my mum
You left
And I might as well be deaf
Or blind
Because you left me behind
Or in space
Because you preferred his face.
I'll go hungry
And get angry.
I'll take aim
And take the blame.
My chest will wheeze
But I'll never be at peace
Until I'm free
And you're here with me.

There was a letter. It was for my dad. It came while he was at work. There was something inside the envelope. It was small and hard with a pointed bit at the end. I couldn't open it because it was addressed to him, though I thought about doing it. If you opened a person's post you could find out a lot about them.

That night, he got more drunk than usual and mumbled about taking us back to Derry to face the music. I could see the opened envelope in his trouser pocket. I didn't understand him and I don't think he remembered any of it in the morning.

He's started going to Irish pubs in town. Most nights when he's at home he goes to the phone box at the bottom of the road. Maybe he's feeling better or he's got himself a girlfriend. I don't mind. It means I can watch telly on my own. I saw a man from *The Guinness Book of Records* on the news, saying he would beat the bombers and that all Irish should be made to register with the police. Maybe Dad was registered already.

I walked down to the phone box to see if there was any sign of Dad spending so much time there, like maybe he'd written a number down, one he was calling a lot.

The door was hard to pull open. There was a little creak from it, like it was telling me I was somewhere I wasn't supposed to be. Inside it smelled of piss.

I lifted the phone and listened to the purr of the dialling tone. There was a little crackle on the line. It was static, but it felt like someone far away was trying to tell me something, like a whisper from a ghost.

I had no one to call. I rested the phone back on its cradle. I put my shoulder to the door and forced it open. There were a couple of flecks of red paint on my arm. I took hold of my sleeve and shook them off. The door sealed shut behind me.

Even though he has money he's no better than before. It seems to me you can't just put a price on anything. There are some things you can't buy and sell. Maybe Dad has more money because there's only two people to look after, not four.

Our Religion teacher said money doesn't make you happy. We all laughed because we want to be rich. But my dad has money and is in a terrible way. He's pale and nervous-looking. The drink gives him the shakes. I worry about the passengers on his bus. One time last week the doorbell rang at night and he said, 'Don't answer it.' We sat there in silence. Whoever it was rang again then knocked, hard and sharp, like they were using their knuckles. Neither of us said a word or moved for five minutes, until he stood up and said, 'I'm away out.'

Later that night I put an empty crisp packet in the bin. There was a piece of paper in it. I didn't recognise the handwriting. It said, 'The next one won't be delivered in an envelope.'

I suppose it's all about what you get money for. I have no problem winning money at cards from older gobshites at school, but the money Judas got didn't make him happy, if any of that's true.

I picked up the can of hairspray in the pantry and looked at it closely. It was long and slim, with Elnett written on it. There was other stuff in the pantry that made me think of her, things she must have bought. Pineapple chunks. Cocktail sticks. A half-empty bottle of tonic water. I twisted the top hoping to hear a fizz but it was flat. I put the bottle to my mouth. The taste was bad. Bitter. I let the door close behind me and the darkness fell.

I remembered hiding in the pantry one day when I was very small, when everyone else was at mass. I sat down on the cold floor, like I had done back then. I pressed the top of the hairspray. It shushed. I felt the cool touch of the mist. I smelled flowers. If a smile had a smell it would be flowers.

It was OK to sit there as the hairspray went sticky on my face, shut away from the world, smiling back at the flowery smile-smell. I sprayed again. She was there in the flowery mist. Tears flowed down my face. A small boy in a field of flowers, crying.

The darkness got less dark and I could see the outlines of everything, getting a tiny bit clearer and sharper, minute by minute.

I heard the postman deliver our mail. I ran to the front door. There was a letter addressed to me, 'D. Cronin'. It was typewritten but it had the Airmail sticker on it and an American stamp. I was right after all. I tore it open.

Dear D. Cronin.

Thank you for your interest in the NASA space program. We thought you would like this picture of Neil Armstrong.

Best wishes.

There was a squiggle at the bottom. Someone's signature.

Neil was wearing his astronaut's uniform in the picture. His helmet was on a big black box by his side. He was smiling, but just a little bit, like he was proud but not showing off. There was a picture of the moon behind him and you could see craters, little blotches with lines running from them like veins. It reminded me of Eamonn's face, little blood lines on his cheeks.

Neil Armstrong's autograph ran diagonally across the photo. His writing was a bit scruffy but you could tell his name. I wondered if he had met my mum in America? Maybe she cleaned his house now, like she used to clean Sean O'Sullivan's.

He'd say, 'Good morning, Annie.'

She'd say, 'Good morning, Mr. Armstrong,' but he'd reply, 'Call me Neil.'

He might buy her a special polish she could use in his home. He might make her a drink but it would have to be coffee because that's what Americans drink. Maybe Neil has a bottle of Camp coffee in his kitchen, asking Mum if she takes sugar, Mum saying, 'No thank you, Neil.'

I kept looking at the picture, hoping Neil would say something instead of just smiling like he knew something, and I kept looking at the letter and turning it over hoping there were more words, but there was nothing more. Nothing else in the envelope. Neil Armstrong wished me well and that was all.

Maybe she'll die without me ever seeing her again and she'll be buried in a cemetery in New York, or London, or Derry, or Belfast. There'll be mourners slowly walking along beside the coffin, and the murmur of the rosary, and maybe someone playing the pipes. Her coffin will have a cross on it and maybe the Irish flag. There'll be people saying 'Sorry for your trouble' but not to me because I'll be here in Birmingham and I won't be able to put flowers on her grave, not even the white ones from bindweed.

I went into the front room today and sat on my knees in the chair by the window. I looked through the net curtains. They felt dry and brittle in my hand. I wanted to take them down so I could see more.

On a foggy night when the moon's all blurred, someone might be walking down your street and you wouldn't see them until they were right outside your door. So I can look, and even though I can't see anyone it doesn't mean no one's there. Someone might be there, a man or a woman just waiting to step out from the moony mist. A woman.

I found one of Mum's toenails on the stairs. It was small and thin like a crescent moon. I knew it was hers because it was polished and smooth to touch. It glinted in the light, like it was ready to start dancing under the lights at the Irish Centre. I won't show it to anyone because they might say it's my sister's, but I know whose it is.

I also put my hand down the back of our sofa, looking for coins. Instead, I found a small gold ring. I ran my finger around it, knowing I would never come to the end.

I clenched it in my fist.

I know what it is.

I'm keeping it.

I realised I had never finished my story for her. She never got to see the ending, what really happened to Danny. I grabbed a pen and paper.

The rocket was never going to make it home safely. Sirens were screaming. It was getting hotter and hotter. The insides of the spaceship banged and banged and banged.

Danny was as mad as anything because he knew now. He knew he wasn't thick, he wasn't stupid and he wasn't frightened anymore.

He knew he could stand up to the Space Paras. He knew he could beat them because he was cleverer than them.

But it was too late. It was all too late.

A flash of blue light. Danny's rocket exploded, with him inside it. The end.

But that ending was wrong. Things did not have to end that way. Danny could still come through.

The rocket was never going to make it home safely. Sirens were screaming. It was getting hotter and hotter. The insides of the space-ship banged and banged and banged.

But Danny hadn't just read the spaceship manual, he had studied it closely. And he had thought about it. And he had done really well on all the tests and had outscored the other astronauts. The trainer had read his work out loud in class. And he knew the Brigadier wasn't able to do it anymore because he could smell drink on the Brigadier's breath the last time he was with him at Mission Control.

It was time for a new leader.

Danny would have to disobey orders. He would be disobedient because it was necessary, because clever people knew you had to break the rules sometimes if you seriously wanted to get anything done.

He grabbed the accelerator and pushed the spaceship into over-drive. It howled in protest.

'What are you up to Danny?' screamed the Brigadier over the radio. 'You're doing it all wrong.'

But behind the Brigadier's voice he heard another voice, Miss Annie's voice. 'On you go, on you go you gurrier, you scut! On ye go Danny Cronin! You're out in front now!'

And Danny whizzed out of the solar system into outer space, ready for new adventures. He would leave this world behind and find the one where he belonged. He would take on the powerful because he knew they could be beaten. All you needed was a little craftiness and to just keep going, keep going.

Danny forgot about small steps and took a giant leap to where things could change and he could finally be at peace. Free Danny.

Afterword

William Power, Hugh Callaghan, Patrick Joseph Hill, Robert Gerald Hunter, Noel Richard McIlkenny and John Walker, you stand convicted on each of the twenty-one counts, on the clearest and most overwhelming evidence I have ever heard, of the crime of murder. The sentence for that crime is not determined by me. It is determined by the law of England. Accordingly, in respect of each count each one of you is now sentenced to imprisonment for life. Let them be taken down.

Mr Justice Bridge, 15 August 1975

The convictions of the Birmingham Six were quashed on 14 March 1991.

The people who bombed Birmingham on 21 November 1974 have never been brought to justice.

Ireland was ceded by the Pope to Henry II of England in the 1150s; he himself came to Ireland in 1171. From that time on an amazingly persistent cultural attitude existed toward Ireland as a place whose inhabitants were a barbarian and degenerate race.

E. Said, *Culture and Imperialism* (1993)

Acknowledgements

Thanks to the readers who gave feedback on early drafts: Geraldine Knights, Robbie Jones, Vivien Parry, John F. Macdonald, Geraldine Beattie and Sarah Heatley (sorry if I've missed anyone out).

Thanks are also due to Enda Kenneally, John O'Donoghue and Gavin Clarke.

A number of sources were used for this book, most notably the following: Collins, E. & McGovern, M. (1998) *Killing Rage*, London, Granta; Conway, K. (2014) *Southside Provisional: From Freedom Fighter to the Four Courts*, Blackrock, Orpen Press; McKay, S. (2008) *Bear In Mind These Dead*, London, Faber and Faber; Moloney, E. (2010) *Voices from the Grave: Two men's war in Ireland*, New York, Public Affairs; Mullin, C. (1986, this edn 1990) *Error of Judgement*, Dublin, Poolbeg; Robertson, G. (1976) *Reluctant Judas: the life and death of the Special Branch informer, Kenneth Lennon*, London, Temple Smith; Toolis, K. (2000) *Rebel Hearts: Journeys within the IRA's Soul*, 2nd edn, Basingstoke and Oxford, Picador.

The account of the arrest and interrogation of the Birmingham Six in the novel draws substantially from Mullin (1990).

The science-fiction novels of Hugh Walters are, disappointingly, out of print, but may occasionally be found in second-hand bookshops and online.

Michael Flavin teaches at King's College London. He holds a degree, three master's degrees and two doctorates. He is the author of two books on nineteenth-century literature and two on technology enhanced learning. *One Small Step* is his début novel. He grew up in an Irish family in Birmingham. The Birmingham pub bombings and their aftermath form part of his early memories.

Printed in Great Britain
by Amazon

39089202R00151